DECEIT

DECEIT

ROBERT WANGARD

AMP&RSAND, INC.

Chicago • New Orleans

ISBN 978-1-4675-4523-5

Design
David Robson, Robson Design

Published by
AMPERSAND, INC.
1050 North State Street
Chicago, Illinois 60610

203 Finland Place
New Orleans, Louisiana 70131

www.ampersandworks.com

———

www.rwangard.com

Printed in U.S.A.

For Esther,
a woman ahead of her time
in so many ways

ACKNOWLEDGEMENTS

An author receives input from many people while writing a novel and I wish to thank everyone who contributed in some way to *Deceit*. In particular, I'd like to thank Christy Olsen Field, the former Managing Editor of the *Norwegian American Weekly*, for her input on Seattle's neighborhoods and for coming up with the name of her counterpart at the fictional newspaper, *The Fjord Herald*. Suzie Isaacs has my thanks for her stellar editing of the manuscript, as does David Robson for his great design work and endless patience with my comments. Lastly, Hailey and Caitlin, to whom my first book was dedicated, inspired me throughout the countless solitary hours at the keyboard with their curiosity and pride in what Papa was doing. I love you both.

ONE

Pete Thorsen didn't pretend to be a seer, but as he gazed out at the forlorn landscape, he somehow knew that it wasn't going to be a good day. Three hours later, the sheriff called and asked Pete to meet him at the morgue to identify a body that could be his former lover.

The request made no sense to him, but he listened intently as the sheriff described the one-car accident. Then he said, "It can't be Lynn Hawke. She's in Seattle. Who's the other woman you mentioned?"

"Laura Mati."

"It must be her."

"It could be," the sheriff said. "Do you know Mati?"

Pete thought for a long moment. "No, I'm sure I don't."

"But you do know Lynn Hawke."

"Yes."

The sheriff was silent for a moment so Pete asked the obvious. "Since you called me, you must have a reason to think I might know one or both of these women."

"We found your business card in the vic's purse and no other contact information."

Pete thought about what the sheriff had said. He knew Lynn Hawke had his business card at one time, but Laura Mati? How would a woman he didn't even know get one of his cards?

He then asked a logical follow-up question. "If you have the victim's purse, you must have her driver's license and credit cards. Why do you need eyewitness identification in addition?"

"Normally we wouldn't, but there are extenuating circumstances in this case. I realize it's an imposition given the weather and everything, but would you mind meeting me at the morgue so we can get the ID we need?"

"You're not telling me something, Sheriff. This makes no sense."

"If you not willing to come," the sheriff said, his tone suddenly different, "could you give me the name of someone else who might know either or both of these women?"

Pete immediately thought of Harry McTigue or his girlfriend, Rona Martin. They had known Lynn Hawke longer than he did and in fact were the ones who'd introduced him to her two years earlier. Then he remembered that they were in Cincinnati for a newspaper publishers' conference and wouldn't be back until the weekend. There were other possibilities, but none he felt comfortable naming. When the sheriff continued to press him, he reluctantly agreed to meet him at the morgue at 2:00 p.m. that afternoon.

After he hung up, emotions he thought were firmly in his rearview mirror began to return. His relationship with Lynn Hawke had lasted exactly two months, but they were intense and stirred feelings in him he hadn't experienced since his late wife died. Then she called out of the blue one day and said she was on her way to the airport to go to Seattle to be with her suicidal daughter and wasn't sure when she'd be back. Even more disappointing, she didn't seem interested in talking to him when he called and repeatedly put off his proposals to come to Seattle.

Pete checked the time. It was 8:30 a.m. on the West Coast. If Lynn were still in Seattle, it couldn't be her in the morgue and he'd spare himself a very unpleasant experience that he'd already begun to dread.

He punched in Lynn's cell phone number, the only telephone number he had for her, but got no answer. *Same old Lynn,* he thought. He called again a half-hour later. After a third try, he banged the table with his fist and screamed, "God damn it, Lynn, answer your phone!" His research cards that were spread out on the table went flying and some of them landed on the floor.

Pete ignored the cards and walked to the window and looked out. The weather hadn't improved since early that morning. Angry waves rolled across the lake and exploded against the beach in cascades of gray and white spray. The dark clouds that hung low over the water churned and heaved and tossed in the wind. On shore, everything looked like it had been brushed with a thick coat of molten pewter. Pete pursed his lips. It reminded him of a morning after scene from a nuclear disaster film.

He slipped on a heavy coat and went outside and picked his way across the ice to his Range Rover. The stinging wind nipped at his face. Like everything else in sight, the vehicle was embalmed in ice. He chipped away at the coating on the windshield and on the other windows for a half-hour and then banged the driver's side door to break the seal so he could get in. The engine sputtered and came to life. He hoped that running it for a half-hour would melt enough of the ice so he could see to drive.

■ ■ ■

The traffic on U.S. 31 was a mess even at mid-day. He was sandwiched into a train of vehicles that moved at less than forty miles an hour because of the road conditions. As he slowly made his way east, he tried to remember someone named Laura Mati he might have known at some stage of his life. In his law practice maybe, or going back further, in college or law school. It certainly wasn't a woman he'd dated; that he'd remember. He tried to remember the maiden names of wives of friends and came up with nothing. Nada.

Distracted by his thoughts, he barely braked in time to avoid rear-ending the rust-pocked Malibu in front of him as tail lights flashed red like a string of progressively-timed holiday lights. He breathed out, and when the traffic began to move again, stayed an additional half-car length behind the sedan out of an abundance of caution.

He glanced out his side window. If anything, the storm had been more intense to the east of where he lived. The houses, the out buildings, the vehicles that hadn't yet moved that day, the tractors and other farm implements parked in side yards for the winter, the trees, the shrubs. Everything was covered by an inch of ice. Only the highway was clear and it was dotted with pools of water where the ice had been melted by salt spread by the county trucks that morning. Nothing dried in the gloomy weather and the temperature hovered just below freezing.

As the traffic resumed its slow pace, Pete thought about the good times with Lynn. Low stakes gambling at the casino, shopping and dinner afterward, the first time they practiced archery together. And the first time they made love. It had been good. Better than good even. But it was over and it wasn't in his DNA to continue to mope about a relationship that didn't work out in spite of what he'd hoped. He'd put it behind him and moved on.

Until now. Ringing down the curtain on a failed romance was one thing; the prospect of seeing her dead body stretched out on a slab in the morgue was another. Particularly since deep within him, where secrets lurked that he didn't share with even close friends, he harbored a faint hope that one day Lynn would move back to the area and they'd resume their former relationship.

The traffic continued to be stop-and-go, but the slow pace didn't bother him because he wasn't in a hurry to get to the morgue. Other drivers with more pleasant missions were less patient. The white SUV behind him swerved into the opposite lane, accelerated past Pete, and cut sharply in front of him to avoid an oncoming vehicle. Pete hit his brakes and muttered an obscenity at the idiot who'd just gained a single car length by his reckless driving.

Pete dropped back to a comfortable distance behind his new pace car and pulled the collar of his L.L.Bean storm coat tighter around his neck.

He could feel the damp chill worming its way through his clothing and into his bones. Two weeks earlier, the heater in his Range Rover had stopped working and he'd put off getting it repaired, telling himself that warm weather was just around the corner and he wouldn't need it for months. That was delusional, he now realized, because while the calendar might trumpet the arrival of spring, the ice storm demonstrated all too clearly that March weather in northern Michigan could alternate between splendid and downright brutal.

He saw the sign for the hospital and followed the access road until he came to the sprawling medical complex that was dominated by a multi-floor central building flanked by several smaller buildings. He parked in the underground lot and killed his engine. He sat there for a minute and then forced himself to get out and walk toward the door that was marked with a sign that said "Elevator."

Pete looked around the first floor waiting room, but didn't see any uniforms. He approached the receptionist, gave his name, and asked if Sheriff Emory Bond had arrived yet.

"Sir, Sheriff Bond called and said to tell you he'd be late. He had to make an unexpected stop."

"Did he say when he'd be here?"

"No, sir. He just said to give you his apologies and that he'd get here as soon as he could."

Pete's angst elevated a notch. Now that he was at the hospital, he was anxious to identify the body, hopefully as someone other than Lynn Hawke, and get out of there as soon as possible. Hanging around waiting for the sheriff would only add to the uneasiness he already felt.

To kill time, he picked up one of the health-related magazines from the table next to him — a typical medical rag found in every hospital or doctor's waiting room. Article after article chronicled the foods a person should avoid, the desirability of monitoring one's blood pressure six times a day, and the risk of contracting some dread disease if your great-grandmother once had or might have been exposed to it. He sighed. If you weren't feeling a little bit off when you entered these places, chances were good that would change.

He tried not to think about the morgue, but stories he'd heard over the years kept popping up in his mind like unwelcome relatives. The chemical odor was the one constant, and none of the stories topped Harry's for graphic detail. As a cub reporter, he had to go to a Chicago morgue to cover the aftermath of a grisly crime and said he was haunted for weeks by the odor that clogged his pores and filled his nasal passages and clung to his clothes in spite of countless washings. Twice-a-day showers did nothing to expunge the odor. Pete winced at the thought.

He checked his watch again. He'd been twenty minutes late himself because of the road conditions, and more time had passed since he arrived. He went to the men's room, more out of nervous energy than anything, and checked his cell phone for messages when he returned. Then he leafed through a six-month old copy of *Sports Illustrated*.

He was about to go to the reception desk again when a tall man in tan gabardine slacks and a chocolate brown corduroy jacket walked into the reception area with a hurried stride. He doffed his trooper hat and looked around. Pete waved to attract his attention. The sheriff saw him and came over.

"Emory Bond," he said. "Pete Thorsen, right?"

Pete nodded and accepted the sheriff's outstretched hand.

"Sorry I'm late," Bond said. "I had to stop at the scene of another accident on the way. No fatalities with this one, thank God."

Pete had no interest in engaging in social pleasantries or talking about Bond's other cases. He just wanted to do what he'd come for and then get out of there.

"I appreciate your coming," Bond said. "Again, I'm sorry to have to drag you over here on a day like this."

Pete took another stab at getting an answer to the question that had nagged him since their telephone conversation that morning. "Sheriff, explain to me again why you feel you need eye-witness identification if you have the woman's driver's license."

"I'd like to explain after you identify the body if you don't mind."

Pete shot Bond a look that said he wasn't satisfied with his latest evasive response. *Don't share too much information with civilians*, Pete thought. It must be something they taught at the police academy.

"Are you ready?" Bond asked. "The Medical Examiner is waiting for us and he has to leave for another appointment."

"Fine," Pete muttered.

Pete followed the sheriff down the hall and they took the elevator to the lower level. They stood shoulder to shoulder and stared straight ahead the way people seem to do in elevators. Pete's eyes flicked toward Bond. He was Pete's height, an inch or two over six feet, but looked a dozen pounds lighter. Sheriffs must have more time to work out than lawyers.

The elevator door slid open and Bond stepped out and headed down the narrow hall. He said over his shoulder, "I'm having the body brought to the viewing room so you don't have to go into the cooler."

Pete was grateful for the courtesy, but said nothing. An icy knot formed in his stomach when they reached the door marked "Morgue." He followed Bond into the viewing room. The lights were more muted than he imagined they'd be, but the surroundings were stark and the faint odor of chemicals wafted through the air. He remembered Harry's story and imagined the odor beginning to penetrate his clothes.

Bond handed him a surgical mask. "I suggest you put this on."

Pete slipped the elastic cord around his head. It eliminated most of the chemical odor when he breathed in.

Bond went to a box on the wall and pushed a button. "Yes?" a voice responded.

"Ethan, it's Emory Bond. We're here."

"Okay."

Pete stood next to Sheriff Bond alone with his thoughts. Disjointed images flashed through his mind and his stomach felt empty. *Is this the way it ends,* he thought, *with people waiting around a stinking viewing room to identify your body?* He also thought of Cara Lane and the sweltering

August day when they hauled her water-ravaged body from the lake. The EMTs had passed with ten feet of him with her body and he'd never forgotten how vacant her eyes looked.

A door opened and a man in green scrubs and a white surgical mask pushed a stainless steel gurney into the viewing room. A white cloth covered the hulking shape on the gurney. Pete recognized the man as Ethan Pennington, the Medical Examiner for the three-county area including Leelanau County where the accident had occurred. He'd met Pennington when he was investigating whether Cara Lane's death was really a swimming accident and liked him well enough, although he had a feeling that covering his ass was priority number one with him.

"Mr. Thorsen," Pennington said.

"Doctor."

"Okay," Bond said, "let's get this over with." He looked at Pete who was staring at the floor and added, "You ready?"

Pete nodded slightly and closed his eyes.

He heard a rustling sound as Pennington peeled back the cover. He opened his eyes and stared at the waxy face of the dead woman.

TWO

Lynn Hawke's eyes were cloudy and opaque. Just like Cara Lane's had been. The long honey-brown hair Lynn always kept immaculately brushed was in disarray and her head and neck showed a mass of contusions on one side. Pete had been to open-casket funerals before, but there was something unsettling about seeing a dead body in its most primitive form without the undertaker's artistic work to make it look like death had never occurred. Lynn looked the way Cara Lane had, without the ravaging effects of the water. But just as dead.

"Can you identify the victim, Mr. Thorsen?" Sheriff Bond asked.

Pete had prepared himself for the possibility that the body might be Lynn's, but felt a lump build in his throat and didn't respond immediately. The sheriff waited a moment and repeated his question.

"Lynn Hawke," Pete said softly, turning his head away.

"You're positive?" Bond asked.

"I'm positive, okay?" Pete snapped.

"I'm sorry," Bond said, "we need to be sure."

"You have your identification," Pete said in an edgy voice. He yanked off his surgical mask, flipped it toward a chair, and pulled the exit door open. He left the viewing room without waiting for Bond.

Bond caught up with him by the elevator seconds later. Neither spoke as the lift creaked and ground its way to the first floor. When the door opened, Pete stepped out first and headed down the hall with a long stride. The sheriff hurried to catch up again and said, "Can we talk for a minute before you go, Mr. Thorsen?"

"What's there to talk about? She's dead and I've told you who she is."

"I understand. But as I said earlier, I'd like to explain why we felt we needed eyewitness identification of the body. Since you're already here, I think it would be best to clear up everything now rather than have you come back."

Pete stared at Bond irritably for a few moments and asked, "How long?"

"Fifteen minutes?"

"Fine," Pete muttered. "Fifteen minutes, then I'm leaving."

They got coffee and found a corner of the cafeteria where they could talk in private. "Okay," Bond said, "let me tell you about the accident first. I don't know how the ice storm was around Frankfort last night, but it was terrible on the Leelanau Peninsula. We had well over two inches of rain and the wind was howling and the temperature was dropping fast. Driving conditions were horrible. We had reports of seven pileups.

"About 10:30 p.m., we got a report of a car going off M-22 near Suttons Bay. We investigated and found that the car — headed north, we're pretty certain — skidded off the pavement and piled into the rocks along West Traverse Bay. We're not sure what happened — maybe the driver dozed off or maybe the icy conditions caused her to spin out of control. We checked for skid marks this morning, but didn't find any. Remember, though, it was raining cats and dogs and any skid marks might have been washed away. Or maybe there weren't skid marks. Everything was turning to ice at the time."

Pete interrupted and said, "Was she dead when you arrived?"

"Unconscious. She died on the way to the hospital."

"I don't understand," Pete said. "Didn't her air bags inflate? What the hell good are air bags if they don't inflate and protect a person when something like this happens?"

"The bags were partially inflated when we found the vehicle. I don't know why they didn't fully inflate, or whether they would have saved her if they had. The impact had to have been brutal when the car hit the rocks. The car probably stopped instantly and then flipped on its side. The status of the seat belt is unclear. It wasn't fastened when the EMTs removed her body from the vehicle. Maybe it came loose on impact, we really don't know. We're going to have the vehicle examined to try to find answers to those questions."

Pete thought back to when he was dating Lynn and muttered, "Maybe she didn't have her seat belt on."

Bond raised his eyebrows and said, "Why do you say that?"

"She didn't always fasten her seat belt. I don't know why. When she rode with me, I sometimes had to needle her to get her to put her belt on. Other times, she buckled up as soon as she got in. I don't know what it was."

Bond took notes of what Pete said. He closed his small spiral notebook and cradled his paper coffee cup in both hands and gazed at Pete and said, "Earlier, you said you didn't know Ms. Hawke was back in this area. Were you in regular contact with her?"

"No. But I do know she was supposed to be in Seattle with her suicidal daughter. As far as I know, no one she was close to knew she was back."

"Who were her friends in Michigan?"

"I don't know all of them, but she was close to Rona Martin, who owns Rona's Bay Grille in Frankfort, and Harry McTigue, who owns *The Northern Sentinel* there. There are others, I'm sure, but those two stick out in my mind."

"Plus you?"

"Yeah, plus me."

"What was your relationship with her? Were you her lawyer?"

"We dated at one time. Two summers ago."

"Seriously?"

"I thought so at the time."

"When's the last time you saw her?"

"Last July. She had problems with some clients of her accounting practice and came back for two days on short notice to repair relations. She called and invited me to dinner. Harry and Rona were there, too."

"She had a house near Beulah, right?"

"On the lake," Pete said. "She's been renting it out."

"If you didn't know she was back, I suppose you don't know why she would have been over on the Leelanau Peninsula on a night when no one would be on the roads if they didn't have to be."

"I don't," Pete said impatiently. "Sheriff, all of this is very interesting, but I don't see what it has to do with your need for eyewitness identification of the body."

"Okay, let's get to that. I didn't want to mention this earlier because I didn't want to influence the identification process, but I'd like to show you something." He pulled a plastic bag from his pocket and handed it to Pete. "We found this in the vic's purse."

Pete took the bag and flattened it so he could see the card inside. He looked up at Bond and said, "So? You have her driver's license. That's my point. It says right there that her name is Lynn Hawke"

"That would be fine in the normal situation," Bond said, "but we also found this in her purse." He handed Pete a second plastic bag.

Pete went through the same routine so he could see the card. It was a Washington State driver's license issued in the name Laura Mati, but Lynn Hawke's photograph was on the license. The physical description was the same as Lynn's as well. Pete stared at the Mati license some more, and then looked up at Bond. "I don't understand."

"Neither do we," Bond replied. "That's the same woman on both licenses, right?"

Pete compared the licenses again. "No question. But why would Lynn have a second license in a different name?"

Sheriff Bond tossed his empty coffee cup in a receptacle. "We were hoping you could answer that. You obviously knew the woman as Lynn Hawke."

"Yes." Pete compared the two licenses side-by-side again.

"And according to what you said on the phone," Bond said, "you've never heard the name Laura Mati before."

"Never."

"Pardon me for asking again, but you have absolutely no doubt that the woman in the morgue is Lynn Hawke?"

"Sheriff, how many times do I have to say it? That's Lynn Hawke. I've known her for going on two years. I had no idea she was using another name. I'll bet Harry McTigue and Rona Martin would say the same thing and they've known her longer than I have."

"Okay," Bond said, rising from his chair. "Thanks for coming to identify the body. We'll take it from here."

The two driver's licenses raised new questions in Pete's mind and he remained seated. "What do you plan to do?" he asked. "You can't just drop this thing knowing what you do."

"We don't intend to drop it. We'll do what we do in any case like this. We'll examine the vehicle for malfunctions and defects and signs of tampering. Unfortunately, unless we find something, we'll have to write it up as an accident."

"Don't you think you should look into why she had the two licenses under different names? Doesn't that raise questions in your mind?"

Bond sat down again. "It does," he said, "but what do you think we should do beyond what I just said?"

"I don't know," Pete snapped. "I'm a lawyer, not a cop."

"Look, Mr. Thorsen, I understand your point, but thousands of people have fake driver's licenses for one reason or another. Maybe they lost their license or their real license was suspended or revoked. Or maybe they use the second license for some other purpose, like to buy alcohol."

"Lynn Hawke was in her forties. She didn't need a phony license to buy alcohol."

"The reasons I gave were illustrative," Bond said defensively. "There may be a dozen others."

"Did you check to see if there's a problem with Lynn's Michigan license?"

"We did. It's clean and doesn't come up for renewal for more than a year."

"That proves my point. This whole thing stinks."

Bond shrugged. "I'm open to suggestions."

Pete just sat silently.

"I'll tell you what we'll do," Bond said. "We'll examine the vehicle, like I said, and we'll look into the two-license issue. See if the Washington State license was validly issued, that sort of thing. We'll reassess the situation once we know the answers to those questions."

"Okay," Pete said slowly. "I'd appreciate it if you'd let me know what you conclude."

"We owe you that for making you come over here to do something very unpleasant on a nasty day."

Pete was glad to get out of the hospital. He didn't regard himself as unduly squeamish, but his experience in the morgue had unsettled him. It was another reminder of why he never considered going into medicine. Death might be part of life, but it was a reality he hadn't yet come to grips with.

THREE

Darkness was gathering when Pete pulled into his driveway. In the dim light, the icy landscape looked more dismal than it had when he left for the morgue. The wind had died down, but that was offset by the drop in temperature.

He checked his telephone messages and e-mail, and finding nothing urgent, he rummaged around in a closet and found the wool stocking cap Harry had given him a year earlier together with a preachy sermon, the essence of which was that much of the heat loss a person experiences in the winter occurs through the head. Pete liked to needle Harry about what a wuss he was for always wearing a stocking cap and continued to go bare-headed himself most of the time. Now, without Harry around to jump on his inconsistency, he pulled the cap over his thick sandy-brown hair and glanced at his reflection in the window. Just like Harry, he thought, except he had hair. He wrapped a wool scarf around his neck and substituted a pair of lined mittens for his gloves. Clothed for the average polar expedition, he grabbed his canvas log carrier and went outside to get fuel for the fireplace.

He banged the ice off an old axe handle that was leaning against the woodpile. He had deliberately left the handle there as a reminder of the hazards of splitting his own firewood. When he was a boy growing up in the wilds of Wisconsin, he used to split wood for the family stove all the time. One night he got careless and the axe glanced off a chunk of wood and carved an ugly gash in his instep. Blood filled his boot and the injury ended his high school baseball season before it even began. That taught him a valuable lesson. There are people who are good with their hands and others who make a living with their brains. He preferred the brain option.

He banged the ice from some low-hanging tree branches as he thought about his afternoon at the morgue and Lynn's two driver's licenses. The ice shattered into a hundred pieces and clattered to the ground. He whacked at other branches and more ice came cascading down. He continued his one-man mission of liberating the trees of their icy burden and felt good as branches sprang upward to their normal position.

Using the axe handle as a walking stick, he made his way down the icy slope to the water's edge and gazed out at the half-frozen lake. The remaining ice floe had blown to his end of the lake and formed a crazy quilt pattern of trapezoids and triangles and irregular rectangles along the shore. The fishing shanties that had dotted the ice in January and February were gone for the season. He'd watched the owners take them down ahead of the warm spell earlier in the month. A lot of hardcore fishermen marked the advent of spring according to when they removed their shanties. Pete found the ritual fascinating even though he never understood the appeal of dangling a line in a hole in the ice and freezing your butt off while you waited for something to nibble at it fifty feet below the surface.

He couldn't think of ice fishing without recalling his old army buddy's visit the previous winter. Jimmy Ray Evans called him one day after nearly thirty years without contact of any kind and invited himself for a weekend visit. Just to catch up and relive the old days, he said. Jimmy Ray, who'd never been north of the Mason-Dixon Line, exhibited endless fascination with the ways of the Yankees and nothing intrigued him more than the fishing shanties. He peppered Pete with questions and bemoaned the fact that Pete didn't have one so he could try his luck. Then he spotted a rectangular opening where some local ice sculptors had removed blocks of ice to create their wintry art. He was convinced that the opening was really a grave site and kept asking questions about how long it would take a body to rise to the surface if it were buried in the hole.

That wasn't the only manifestation of Jimmy Ray's fascination with death that strange weekend. He was a disc jockey at a backwater radio station in Wilson, North Carolina, a come-down from what he once hoped for, and lived and breathed "oldies" music from the fifties, sixties and seventies. In fact, he was the one who got Pete hooked on the genre during their army days. He brimmed with stories about the stars of yesteryear. He told of playing back-up guitar for the great Roy Orbison at a time when Roy was already dead, and of shooting Fats Domino in a New Orleans restaurant over a disagreement about the dinner bill even though the music icon was very much alive at the time he told the story.

Lynn Hawke crowded out memories of Jimmy Ray as he stood on the shore of the frigid lake. Why had the woman he'd once loved become such a shadowy figure? He thought about the two driver's licenses again. Something had to be going on in her life that he wasn't aware of.

He hacked away at the ice on the beach and suddenly felt drained and lonely. All of the lake houses surrounding his were dark and shuttered for the winter. Normally, he enjoyed the solitude, but tonight he'd prefer the company of an old friend like Harry McTigue. But he couldn't dine with someone who was hundreds of miles away.

Pete walked back to the woodpile and filled his log carrier. He placed the logs next to the fireplace and used crumpled newspaper and a few pieces of kindling to start the blaze. As the flames rose, the light glinted off the soft blue and rosy red and muted yellow minerals in the newly-cleaned fieldstones. Of all the restoration work that had been done when the cottage was rebuilt the previous year following the fire, he admired the craftsmanship that had gone into the fireplace the most.

He alternately stared at the stones and at the photographs of his late wife and stepdaughter on the mantle.

He felt restless and depressed as he looked through his music collection. His fingers lingered over the CD Lynn had sent him. It had arrived in late January although it was obviously intended to be a Christmas gift, and was the last contact he'd had with her. The note read, "I realize these songs aren't fifty years old, but I thought you might enjoy this CD anyway. Lynn." That was it. No inquiry about how he was, no holiday greetings, no hope to see you soon, no return address, nothing. He tried to call her several times to thank her for the CD and each time got her voice mail. She never returned his calls.

The CD, titled simply *19*, was by the British pop sensation Adele who depended on her voice to entertain rather than on sleazy costumes or shock routines. He poured a glass of Pinot Grigio and slipped the CD into his player. The melancholy lyrics of "Someone Like You" filled the room. It was easy to understand the entertainer's popularity; she sang love songs tinged with pain. Like a Patsy Cline or a Tammy Wynette from an earlier era, Pete thought with satisfaction.

Maybe he was overthinking it, but he wondered whether Lynn was sending him a message with her choice of the CD. His hopes had flickered briefly after it arrived, but faded again when he couldn't reach her to thank her.

Adele's poignant love songs made him feel more morose than he already was and he needed something upbeat to lift his spirits. The other woman in his life, sixteen year-old stepdaughter Julie, had also given him a CD for Christmas. Or more properly, had given him the CD two days *before* Christmas because she had to spend the holiday with her biological father, Wayne Sable, who'd regained legal custody of her after Pete's wife, Doris, died. The CD was *Songs of the Decades* by Straight No Chaser, an *a cappella* group with roots at Indiana University. Their repertoire included old favorites as well as new tunes. The CD was part of Julie's relentless push to bring his musical tastes into the twenty-first century as she liked to say.

He turned up the volume and listened as the group worked through the songs he loved so much. Songs etched in music history by Smokey Robinson and Elvis Presley and The Four Seasons and the Bee Gees. He refilled his glass, ignoring his personally imposed two-glass limit, and hit the "stop" button when the CD reached the nineties tunes. Then he replayed the great old music a second time and smiled. Julie obviously hadn't taken into account his prowess with the stop and replay buttons when she schemed to fast-forward his music tastes.

Maybe he should reopen the custody case. He liked the fact Julie called him Dad and the other guy Wayne, but whenever a holiday rolled around, he always had to play second fiddle to that drunk. He weighed, as he had countless times in the past, his chances of prevailing over a biological father. He always concluded those chances weren't good regardless of Sable's personal habits and Julie's obvious preference. Maybe it was best to wait things out until she turned eighteen. That was only fifteen months away. In the meantime, he took comfort in the fact he'd out-maneuvered Sable by getting Julie enrolled in a boarding school near Detroit where he could see her more often without going to war with Sable each time.

He eyed the wine bottle. It was still a quarter full, but he resisted the temptation to finish it. It was past his bedtime. He turned off the CD player, locked the front door, and clicked off the lights.

He stood in the dark living room for a long time. The embers glowed in the fireplace and the solitude closed in on him. After awhile, he wound his way back to his bedroom hoping he could sleep. If it wasn't over before, he thought, it was certainly over now.

FOUR

Pete was straightening up the living room from the night before when Harry returned his call. Harry hadn't heard the news and Pete told him about going to the morgue to identify Lynn Hawke's body. Pete could tell Harry was shocked from the way the telephone went silent for a long moment. Harry carried on a side conversation with someone Pete assumed was Rona Martin and said he'd call back in ten minutes.

Harry beat his promise by half and Rona was on an extension so she could hear the conversation firsthand. Pete had to repeat what he'd already told Harry about the accident and his visit to the morgue. Then they took turns peppering him with questions for which he had no answers. When there was a lull in the conversation, Pete asked, "How long have the two of you known Lynn?"

They exchanged recollections and Harry replied, "Almost five years. We met her shortly after she moved to Frankfort. She started calling on the small businesses in the area, including Rona's restaurant. Rona and Lynn bonded right away and the three of us became good friends. Then we introduced the two of you … "

Pete cut him off. "I remember when you introduced us," he said dryly. "But backing up, what do you know about Lynn's background?"

"Quite a lot," Harry said. "But why is that important?"

Pete parried the question with one of his own. "Did anything she told you ever leave questions in your mind?"

"I don't think so," Harry said. "Why would it? She was a friend and a solid woman. She told us stuff and we told her stuff. That's what friends do."

Pete said, "I have a feeling something was going on in her life that none of us knew about."

"Like what?"

"I don't know," Pete said.

"What's your point?" Harry asked. "You knew her as well as we did, or maybe better since you were in a relationship with her."

"I'll explain in a minute, but first tell me what she told you about her past."

Rona said, "I suppose I knew her best so I'll tell you what I remember. A warning, though. Even if you know a person fairly well, you don't recall every detail of every conversation. You might hear something, but at the time it might not strike you as important. Or you might not remember some things at all."

"I understand," Pete said. "Do the best you can."

"Well, Lynn went to DePauw University, I know that, and then she was with a big accounting firm in Chicago for about ten years. She took a sabbatical for a year to train and try out for the U.S. Olympics archery team and made first alternate. Eventually she left the accounting firm and set up a forensic accounting practice with her father. I never did understand the difference between forensic accounting and regular accounting. Anyway, I guess that didn't work out so she moved up here and started an accounting and consulting practice targeted at small businesses. That's when Harry and I met her. Oh, and of course she talked about her ex-husband and what a jerk and bad father he was."

"Women never have anything good to say about their ex-husbands," Harry volunteered.

"That's not true," Rona said.

Harry beat a hasty retreat. "I shouldn't have over-generalized, hon. I know that a lot of couples divorce and remain great friends."

"She had two children, right?" Pete asked.

"Yes. Her daughter, Melissa, lives in Seattle, and is having psychological problems as I think you know. Her son, Richard, lives in Los Angeles. I believe he's a screenwriter."

Pete said, "Does the name Laura Mati ring a bell with either of you?"

They talked between themselves briefly and then both said no. "Why do you ask?" Harry said.

"Because the Leelanau County sheriff found two driver's licenses in Lynn's purse. One was in Lynn's name and the other was in Laura Mati's name."

"Maybe she had a friend's license for some reason," Harry volunteered.

"Not likely. Lynn's picture is on both licenses. Plus the physical descriptions on the two licenses are identical."

"Why would Lynn have two licenses under different names?"

"That's why I asked," Pete said. "I thought something she said to one of you might shed light on it."

"Do you think the two licenses might have something to do with her death?" Harry asked.

"The sheriff doesn't see any connection, but it's strange, isn't it?"

"Yeah," Harry said. "She was old enough that she wouldn't need a fake ID to buy liquor or anything."

"No, she wouldn't," Pete said.

"What's the sheriff doing to check out the accident?" Harry asked.

"He's having the car examined to see whether there was a problem with the brakes and that sort of thing. And to determine why the air bags didn't fully inflate. Then he's going to check out the Washington State license in Laura Mati's name."

"This is a real shocker," Harry said.

No one spoke for a few moments until Rona said, "I assume Lynn's children don't know."

"Not that I'm aware," Pete said. "I wanted to talk to the two of you and decide who'd be best to call them."

"Rona and I won't be back for two more days. I don't think we should wait that long."

Pete said nothing, but sensed what was coming.

"Could you call them, Pete?" Rona asked hesitantly.

"I've never met her children," he protested.

"I don't think we have either, right hon?" Harry said.

"No, Lynn talked about them a lot, but they were never in the Frankfort area to my knowledge," Rona said.

"Do you have their phone numbers or addresses, Rona?" Pete asked.

"I don't think so." After a moment she added, "No, I'm sure I don't. Every time I called Lynn, it was on her cell phone. I asked for her address in Seattle a few times, but she always told me they were moving or something and that she'd send me the new address. She never did."

"I bet you can get the numbers from directory service," Harry said helpfully.

Pete took a deep breath and expelled air and said, "I'll try. Rona, do you know if Hawke is Lynn's maiden name or her married name? I don't want to be looking for her kids under the wrong name."

"I'm pretty sure Hawke is her married name because she was talking about her father once and referred to him as Armand Prentice. Or maybe it was Pruitt or something like that. I'd guess that the last name of her children is Hawke. It's hard to change a child's last name if the father is still in the picture."

"Was Melissa ever married?"

"I don't think so," Rona said. "But again, I can't say for sure."

"Getting back to Lynn," Pete said, "If her maiden name was Prentice, or possibly Pruitt as you say, she obviously wasn't carrying a second driver's license in a name that was derived from her maiden name. Mati isn't close to either of those names."

"No it isn't," Rona said. "For the life of me, I can't think of why she'd have two licenses with different names."

"Well," Pete said, "I'll try to get the phone numbers of her children and call them. I'm so good at these touchy-feely personal things."

"Thank you, Pete," Rona said. "I can understand why you're not thrilled to do this. When I get back, I'll take over arranging a memorial service unless one of the children wants to do it. You won't get stuck with that, too."

■ ■ ■

When Pete got to town later that morning, he parked in front of the building where his office was located. His Range Rover was the only car on the block. He looked down Main Street and saw small clusters of vehicles around Ebba's Bakery and the drugstore and Dinghy's Restaurant & Bar. Otherwise, it was like a ghost town. If the ancient town cannon were operable, it could have fired a volley through the business district without risk of maiming a soul.

It was his second winter up north, as the locals liked to say. He expected it to be quiet around the lake where the residents were almost all summer people, but he hadn't gotten used to how few people were in town unless something special was going on. In Chicago, where he commuted downtown every business day and most Saturdays for twenty years, the Loop crawled with traffic and bustled with people on all but the nastiest weather days. Oh well, "the season" was coming in a few months and then he'd be annoyed at not being able to find a parking place within two blocks of his office and could look forward to seeing tourists lapping triple-dip mint chocolate chip cones every time he stepped out the door.

The good news was that the weather had improved. The thermometer outside his cottage read twenty-four degrees when he left, but there was no wind to speak of. Even better, the sky was clear except for a few scattered clouds. On the drive to town, the trees sparkled like they were encrusted with millions of diamonds.

He let himself in and turned up the heat. Then he filled his new Mr. Coffee machine with water and added a package of Columbian-blend coffee. While it was brewing, he returned a couple of calls from his law office in Chicago. One was from his former partner, Angie DeMarco, who'd replaced him as managing partner of the firm. Angie's cheerful banter was one the things he missed most about leaving Chicago.

After he finished with law firm business, he turned to the task of coming up with the telephone numbers for Melissa and Richard Hawke. He decided to work on Melissa first. He dialed directory service and was patched through to an operator for the Seattle area. He knew that getting Melissa's number would be a challenge because he had neither an address nor any other identifying information for her. Just a name and no middle initial at that.

His concern proved well-founded. The first thing the operator asked for was Melissa's address. He pretended to fumble around looking for it and finally fibbed to the operator that he must have mislaid it. He was the family attorney, he explained, and was trying to reach Melissa to inform her of her mother's death. After repeated clucks of sympathy, the operator told him she showed one Melissa Hawke with an unlisted number. She gave him the number after emphasizing that she was breaching the company's policy only because of the tragic circumstances. Pete thanked her, and after listening to the woman some more and agreeing to pass on her heartfelt condolences to the family, he hung up and dialed Melissa's number.

The telephone rang about ten times before someone finally answered. The woman who came on the line sounded like she was in her senior years based on her voice and halting manner of speech. He introduced himself, and before they'd talked for ten seconds, it became clear that he hadn't reached the Melissa Hawke he was looking for. The woman proudly proclaimed she was seventy-eight years old, had been married to Ronald J. Hawke for fifty-two years, and had eleven grandchildren. Ronald, she added, had severe vision and hearing impairments and other maladies she chronicled in exquisite detail. The wrong Melissa Hawke completed the family saga by telling him her mother had passed away thirty years ago, but that she still visited her grave weekly just to chat and keep in touch. She concluded by telling him she was working on a family memoir that she expected to be a bestseller because they had such an exciting human story to tell.

When he finally got off the phone, he poured a fresh cup of coffee and decided to see if he'd have better luck getting Richard's number. He went through the calling routine again and when the operator said, "City please," he asked for Los Angeles and the number for Richard Hawke. She asked whether that was Hawk like the bird or Hawke with an "e." With an "e" he said. The operator told him she had numbers for seven Richard Hawkes, some of which were unlisted, and asked for the address of the one Pete was trying to reach. He pretended to look for the address again and tried his sympathy routine for the second time. It didn't work. The operator nearly froze his ear with her refusal to give out the numbers, death in the family or not. There was simply was no way she was going to risk having valued customers harassed with obscene calls, or nearly as bad, solicited to buy something.

As Pete sipped his coffee, he got an idea. He dialed Sheriff Bond's number and waited until the receptionist located him. When Bond came on the phone, he said, "Sheriff, it's Pete Thorsen. Could you do me a favor? I'm trying to get the telephone numbers of Lynn Hawke's children so I can notify them of her death. I'm having trouble and wonder if you could check the Washington State driver's license and tell me what address is shown."

Bond put the phone down and when he returned to the line, he said, "Here it is — 5314 22nd Avenue NW, Seattle, Washington."

"Thanks, I appreciate it. By the way, did you check to see if the license in Laura Mati's name is genuine?"

"Not yet. We've been backed up with all of the accidents. I'll make sure someone does it in the next day or two and we'll let you know."

"Thanks."

"Getting back to the phone numbers for the vic's kids a minute," Bond said, "how old are they?"

Pete thought for a moment. "I really don't know. Somewhere in their twenties, I'd guess."

"A lot of young people don't have land lines these days. They say it's for privacy reasons. Telemarketing calls and all of that stuff. But usually it's economics. They don't want to pay for a land line in addition to cell phone charges and they'd rather lose their left leg than live without a cell. Have you tried to get their cell phone numbers?"

"I thought you couldn't get those through directory service."

"Normally you can't. Law enforcement can usually get the numbers from the service provider, but I doubt they'd give out them out to a private citizen. You could try working the death angle. And there are services that claim they can get cell numbers."

"Thanks, that's good to know. This isn't my day job."

When Pete was off the telephone with Sheriff Bond, he tried directory service in Seattle again armed with more information. He got a different operator and gave her Melissa's name and the address on Lynn's duplicate license. After a few moments, she said, "We don't have a listing for a Melissa Hawke at that address. We do have a listing for a Melissa Hawke at another address."

He gave her the number for the lady he talked to earlier and asked whether that was what she had. She confirmed it was.

"Okay, thanks," he said. He sighed and mentally kicked himself for not leaving the contact duties to Rona when she got back to town.

FIVE

His plans for a quick lunch at Ebba's Bakery turned into an hour affair. Ebba bore in like a covert CIA operative working over a terror suspect and quizzed him endlessly about Lynn Hawke's death. After he answered "I don't know" forty-two times, she gave up and switched to other local gossip. She wouldn't let him leave until she'd packed a healthy chunk of blueberry cobbler for him to take along as a mid-afternoon snack. To keep his strength up, she said with an impish smile.

After storing the cobbler in a place where he wouldn't be tempted by it, he went back to his computer to see if he would have any luck finding the telephone numbers through channels other than directory assistance. He Googled the names Melissa Hawke and Richard Hawke. Numerous hits popped up, but further inquiry indicated they all related to different people with the same names. Then he surfed the social and professional networking sites to see if anything turned up there. Nothing did.

He was thinking about what to do next when he heard the door slam next door. It must be Brenda Lyons, the real estate lady who'd been handling rental of Lynn's house. He waited ten minutes to let her get settled and then walked next door.

Brenda looked up and smiled when Pete walked in. "Well, Peter, it's nice to see someone else is doing his part to keep commerce in northern Michigan afloat during this dreadful weather."

"Dreadful? Didn't you notice that fiery orb in the sky today?"

"I did, but I wasn't sure what it was. I have a question, though. What's that stuff coating the trees?"

"Don't worry, it'll be gone by tomorrow."

They laughed and exchanged small talk for a few more minutes. Then Pete said, "I'm sorry to have to tell you this, but Lynn Hawke was killed in an automobile accident two nights ago."

Brenda's eyes widened and she sat with her mouth open for a long moment. "No," she finally said. "What happened?"

"According to the Leelanau County sheriff, she was driving north on M-22 near Suttons Bay during the ice storm and either fell asleep at the wheel or lost control of her vehicle some other way. She ran off the road and piled into the rocks along the Bay. The sheriff said she died before they got her to the hospital."

Brenda continued to look stunned. "I didn't even know she was back," she finally said. "I talked to her on the phone two weeks ago and she didn't say anything about plans to be back here."

"She called you?"

"We talked about her house every few weeks or maybe once a month. Last fall, we decided to list it to see if we'd get any nibbles. The last time I talked to her, she told me she wasn't sure she still wanted to sell, but didn't actually pull the house off the market."

"Did she mention either of her children?" Pete asked. "I've been trying to reach them to break the news, but I'm having trouble locating them."

Brenda shook her head. "We didn't talk about family matters. She mentioned her daughter in the past. That's why she moved to Seattle, you know."

"I do know. Do you have an address or a phone number for either of her children?"

"No, all I have is Lynn's cell phone number. I've never met her children."

Pete thought for a minute and said, "Would you mind going with me to Lynn's house so we can try to find their addresses or phone numbers?"

"Today you mean?"

"Ideally, if you have time. I'm getting concerned that when we do reach the children, they'll be upset they weren't notified sooner."

"You caught me on a bad day," Brenda said. "Believe it or not, I have two showings this afternoon. In March no less. Both couples are looking forward to the season and want to get something lined up now. I'll be tied up the rest of the day." She appeared to think about it and added, "Why don't I give you a key? You and Lynn were close a while back and I know you've been to her house. No one's renting it at the moment."

"Makes sense," Pete said.

Brenda selected a key from a board behind her desk and handed it to him. "You probably don't know how to work the realtors' box," she said.

"You're right. I'll leave the key in your mailbox if you're not here when I get back."

"Pete," Brenda said as he was about to go out the door, "what was Lynn doing on the Peninsula during the storm?"

"I have no idea."

■ ■ ■

Lynn's house was located on a bluff overlooking the lake just outside of Beulah. There were no cars in the driveway, but when he peered through the side panels by the front door, he could see lights on inside. He knocked as a courtesy. As expected, no one answered and he used the key Brenda had given him to gain entry.

The heat had been turned up and it was comfortable inside. He stood in the foyer and looked around. The house had a peculiar silence to it. Empty houses were like that. The floorboards creaked more audibly than those of an occupied dwelling and the hushed atmosphere made a person want to whisper out of concern that normal speech might disturb the ghosts. He knew that was silly, but he still treaded quietly as he moved through the house.

He saw dirty dishes in the kitchen sink. That was unlike Lynn; when they were dating, she was fastidious and always put dishes in the dishwasher immediately after they were used. He pulled out the waste disposal drawer and saw a crumpled fast food bag. From the look of things, she'd grabbed something to eat and had been in a hurry to leave.

The colorful Navajo throw rugs he remembered still adorned the living room floors and a pair of metal sculptures rested on the end tables. Four of Lynn's paintings hung on the walls. Other than that, there were no personal items in sight. No family photographs, no artifacts from a child's growing up years. He tried to think back to times he'd been in the house, but couldn't remember seeing those things then either. Maybe he just hadn't noticed, or maybe Lynn had put them away.

He pulled out the drawers on a sideboard and found nothing of interest. Then he walked down the hall and peered into her bedroom. A table lamp was on and a scuffed leather carry-on with Louis Vuitton emblems emblazoned on the sides was on her bed. It was still zipped. He checked the dresser, the end tables, and the closet shelves. He found nothing that pertained to Lynn's children.

Lynn's studio was located at the end of a hall that was cordoned off by a velvet rope anchored by two brass posts of the kind you'd find in a restaurant or an art gallery. A neatly lettered sign dangled from the rope and read, "Private. Please Don't Use These Rooms." Pete moved a post so he could pass and entered the studio. Everything was draped with white coverings. The canvas panels on the two easels, the dozen or so other panels that rested against the studio walls.

Lynn's office was across from the studio. He remembered passing the office on his way to and from her studio. The furnishings were functional. A small desk occupied one side of the room and a bank of gunmetal gray file cabinets filled a wall. He tried the file cabinets and found them locked. He located a small ring with several keys among the mish-mash of office paraphernalia in one of the desk drawers. One of the keys fit the file cabinet locks.

He methodically checked each drawer. Most of them contained materials dealing with Lynn's accounting practice. He flipped through the client files and the billing records and the other materials you'd expect to find. Nothing that shed light on what he was looking for. In the last cabinet, he found papers and records relating to the house. Contractor's bills for improvements, tax bills, and the like. Once again, nothing that pertained to Lynn's children.

There was no Rolodex or similar device on the desk or the credenza, but that was not unusual in the tech age when people stored information in electronic address books on computers and cell phones. The only thing of interest in the desk drawers was a stack of business cards bound by a rubber band. He thumbed through the cards. Virtually all of them were from local businesses that were either Lynn's clients or had been gathered as potential clients.

He closed the office door and returned to the kitchen. He searched the drawer of a small desk that served as a telephone stand and found nothing that pertained to Lynn's children. He also looked through the kitchen cabinets and drawers and found only the usual things you'd expect to find — flatware, glasses, cooking utensils, napkins and placemats, books of matches.

Before he left the house, he gazed around the living room again and wistfully remembered. Then he pulled the front door closed and locked up.

SIX

Pete had an hour before he was scheduled to pick up Harry for breakfast. He decided to use the time to try one of the services that advertised cell phone number lookups in a last-ditch effort to locate Lynn Hawke's children. He selected a service that looked reputable based on endorsements by several prominent private investigators, including a former police detective who was a familiar face on television during the O. J. Simpson trial, and discovered he had to take out a trial subscription to proceed beyond the marketing come-ons. He was inherently distrustful of putting his credit card information on Internet sites, but decided to take a chance on the site's security and thirty-day cancellation promises.

He started with Melissa and entered her name and the address he'd gotten from Sheriff Bond. The search results flashed on his computer screen fifteen minutes later. Not located. He moved on to Richard and input various area codes in the Los Angeles area as he was permitted to do. He got several hits, but follow-up inquiries indicated that none of the numbers identified were for the Richard Hawke he was looking for.

He'd already scanned the social and professional networking sites. Then he had an idea. He knew nothing about Melissa other than that she had mental health problems, but he knew Richard was a screenwriter.

He Googled screenwriters organizations in the Los Angeles area and came up with three. He checked each organization's website, but found he couldn't access the membership lists unless he was a member himself.

He glanced at his watch; he was fifteen minutes late picking up Harry. He grabbed his coat and was on his way out the door when his telephone rang. He debated letting the call go to voicemail, but thinking it might be Harry, he decided he'd better answer.

"Mr. Thorsen, it's Sheriff Bond. I promised to let you know when we checked out Lynn Hawke's second driver's license. The one in Laura Mati's name? The DMV in Washington State tells us it's a validly issued license."

"I assume that means the license applicant established her identity in some acceptable way."

"Yes, and of course passed the vision test and whatever other tests were required."

"Hypothetically, could a person with false identification documents get a license?"

"Oh sure," Sheriff Bond replied. "It happens all the time. Of course, the documents presented would have to *appear* genuine. An appropriate seal on a birth certificate, no evidence of tampering, that sort of thing. But nothing is foolproof."

"How about the car? Anything on that yet?"

"Not yet. I expect it'll be a few more days."

By the time Pete hung up, he was a half-hour behind schedule, and if Harry wasn't upset before, he'd be boiling now. Being late was part of Harry's gene pool, but that didn't translate into tolerance for others. It was only five minutes to his house so Pete decided not to waste time on a call.

Harry's tirade began even before he closed the passenger-side door. Pete tried not to smile as Harry complained that his tardiness had eaten into his work day and jeopardized the schedule for getting out the next edition of his newspaper. As he continued to sputter and complain, the bay came into view on their right. Fragments of ice from the recent freeze nestled along the shoreline and a blanket of fog created by warmer air meeting the cold water hung over the area. Through the fog, Pete could see two things: the chartreuse color of the Bayview Grille on his left, their breakfast venue, and puffs of red and blue at the bottom of the bay along M-22.

Pete glanced at Harry and saw that he was also staring at the lights. "Looks like an accident or something," Pete said. "I'd suggest we go down for a look, but knowing how busy you are …"

Harry's eyes were barely visible under his purple stocking cap. He shot a disgusted look Pete's way and said, "Oh, suddenly you're in a big rush. This could be the biggest story of the winter and all you want to do is get to the Bayview to feed your face. I guess human misfortune doesn't interest you lawyers unless you can bill your time at some obscene rate."

Pete suppressed a grin and said, "I take it that means you'd like to have a closer look."

Harry jerked his head disgustedly in the direction of the lights.

Pete proceeded past the restaurant and turned right when they reached M-22. Harry continued his mutterings, switching from inconsiderate people who didn't call to say they'd be late to how the ethics of the legal profession had gone to hell, and how at one time, lawyers cared about their fellow man rather than just making a buck.

When they got closer, Pete could see that the light show was at the Port City Marina. A uniformed officer was standing in the middle of the highway fifty yards from the marina to slow the traffic which consisted of about one vehicle every two minutes. Pete pulled up behind a string of police cruisers with their light bars pulsing. Harry scrambled from the Range Rover before Pete came to a full stop and headed toward the marina parking lot at a fast waddle. Pete took his time and followed.

In the winter, the marina was a forsaken place even in the daytime. Rows of power boats four deep filled half of the lot. All of the boats had white canvas covers to protect them from the ravages of winter. The covers peaked up in the center and formed what looked like a small snow-capped mountain range that nestled eerily in the morning fog.

A cluster of uniformed officers was gathered near a civilian SUV on the opposite side of the parking lot. They stood in a circle and mostly stared down at the hulking shape on the ground that had been covered by a blue tarp. A boxy EMS vehicle with flashing lights was parked nearby. Intermittently, its lights bathed the tarp and officers in bursts of color.

Harry was engaged in an animated conversation with an officer who was none other than Sheriff Franklin Richter. Richter wasn't hard to spot. Of all of the officers on the scene, he was the only one without headgear. He used his palm to slick back one side of his carefully moussed hair as he listened to Harry.

Pete groaned. The last thing he wanted was to have another confrontation with Richter just now. He was debating whether to return to his Range Rover and wait for Harry when Richter turned and saw him. The sheriff stared at him for a long moment then began to laugh and waved him over.

"Mr. Thorsen, a crime scene isn't complete without you here. You came to tell us how we should conduct our investigation, right?"

"It's a small town, Sheriff. We were just going to breakfast when we saw the lights. Harry wanted to come down to see what was happening. Nothing more than that."

Richter looked at Harry and said, "Does he work for you, now?" Harry seemed uncomfortable, and in his dumpy cold weather attire, looked like a street person next to the crisply dressed sheriff. Richter turned to Pete again and said, "Do you have press credentials, Mr. Thorsen? If not, I think it's best if you move on."

"You're kidding."

Richter's expression and demeanor made it clear he wasn't.

Pete debated whether to argue with him, but decided against it. He said to Harry, "You heard the sheriff. I've been told to move on. I'll wait for you in the car." He turned and started back to his Range Rover.

As he was about to get in, he heard, "Pete! Hold on!" He saw Harry waddling toward him like an over-energized penguin.

Harry caught up and between gulps of air said, "A man was killed last night. They're waiting for the photographer to come and shoot the crime scene. I have an idea. I'll call Rona and have her meet us at the Bayview. Then the two of you can have breakfast and decide what to do about Lynn. I'll take Rona's car and come back to get the details from Richter. Okay?"

"Sounds like a plan," Pete said. "I'd rather have breakfast with Rona anyway. She doesn't complain as much."

Harry was already on his cell phone to Rona. He gave her detailed instructions while gesturing excitedly with his hands. When he finished, he said to Pete, "She's going to meet us at the restaurant. Let's hurry so we don't keep her waiting." He was already looking at his watch impatiently.

As they circled back to the Bayview, Harry looked at Pete from under his stocking cap and asked pointedly, "When are you and Richter going to patch things up? It's time you two started acting like a couple of adults. This is a small community, and in the future, you're going to bump into each other a lot, him being the sheriff and you being the only decent lawyer in town and all."

Pete looked at him and said, "Maybe you can suggest to your new friend that he can jump start rapprochement by apologizing for the way he hounded me in the Cara Lane case."

"Can't you just forget about that, for God's sake? That happened almost two years ago. It ended up alright, didn't it?"

"Did it end up alright because of us or because of Richter?"

Harry shook his head disgustedly as Pete pulled into the Bayview lot. Jill was there as usual. She was about to give Harry a hug when he began to spew out the morning's hot story like rounds from an old time Gatling gun. She looked horrified as Harry told her every scrap of information he knew about the shooting plus a few embellishments of his own. Pete left them to their animated conversation and found a table in back and started to peruse the menu. Whenever Pete glanced up, Harry was still scorching Jill's ear with a torrent of words while checking his watch every ten seconds.

As soon as Rona walked in, Harry was on her like a puma. He pecked her on the cheek, snatched the car keys from her hand, and was gone. Rona talked to Jill for a few moments and then went to where Pete was sitting.

"Whew," Rona said. "Now I know what whirling dervish means."

Pete smiled. "Newspapermen aren't nearly as courtly as lawyers."

"From what I could understand, a man was shot at the marina."

"Last night," Pete said.

"Who, do you know?"

Pete shook his head. "Richter wouldn't disclose any information as long as I was around." He grinned. "He thought I might be there to take over his investigation."

"You two," Rona said with a disapproving look. She knew about the bad blood between Pete and Sheriff Richter and didn't say more.

They placed their orders and switched the conversation to Pete's efforts to get in touch with Lynn's children. He told Rona everything he'd done to try to locate them.

"What do you suggest?" Rona asked.

"I'm out of suggestions. I've tried everything I know."

"We have to get in touch with her children somehow."

Pete shrugged. "Feel free to try if you'd like."

Rona took a bite of her French toast and then a sip of her coffee. "The only other thing I can think of is to contact Lynn's father to see if he can help."

Pete frowned. "He has Alzheimer's, doesn't he?" He recalled a conversation he'd once had with Lynn when they were talking about their fathers.

"Yes, but he might remember something about his grandchildren. Don't you think?"

"Unlikely," Pete said. "My father has Alzheimer's, and most of the time he doesn't even know who I am."

"Is it worth a try?"

Pete sighed and said, "I suppose. He's in a facility downstate as I remember."

"Grand Rapids. I have the address at home. I sent him a birthday card once. I checked his name. It's Pruitt. Armand Pruitt."

"Mmm," Pete murmured. He sat quietly for a long moment and then said, "You've had a while to think about this. Anything occur to you about why Lynn would be driving around on the Leelanau Peninsula in an ice storm and have two driver's licenses under different names? Or why she didn't tell anyone that she planned to be back?"

Rona looked at him for a long time. "Maybe we didn't know her as well as we thought we did. That's what you were getting at on the phone, weren't you?"

"Yeah, that's what I've been thinking."

Harry burst in the restaurant just as the waitress was clearing the dirty dishes from their table. He plopped into a chair by Rona and said breathlessly, "It's Arne Breit." Simultaneously, he grabbed the waitress by the elbow and began peppering her with detailed instructions for the chef. He'd like three eggs, he explained between gulps of air, scrambled with cheddar cheese mixed in and crispy bacon and hash browns and two English muffins with plenty of butter.

Pete tapped impatiently on the table with a spoon as he waited for Harry to finish with the waitress. As soon as she turned away, Pete said, "Did I hear you right? That's Arne Breit in the marina lot?"

"That's what Richter said."

"Arne Breit's the man who runs charter boats, isn't he?" Rona asked.

"Yes," Harry said, finally beginning to get his breath back.

"That's incredible," Pete said. "What was Arne doing in a vacant marina parking lot at night in the winter?"

"No one knows," Harry said. "But according to Richter, there's no doubt it's Arne."

"Did he say anything else?"

"Just that their preliminary assessment is that it was a stick-up gone bad."

Pete stared at Harry for a long moment and said, "That doesn't make sense."

Harry spread his arms in a gesture of helplessness. "I'm just telling you what Richter told me."

"Think about it, Harry. An out-of-the-way spot at night at this time of the year? Even if Arne had some reason for going to the marina, that's not exactly the venue a robber would pick to lie in wait for someone."

"Why are you attacking the messenger?"

"I'm not attacking you. I'm just saying it doesn't make sense."

"How do you explain this, then?" Harry said, showing indignation at Pete's challenge to what he obviously regarded as his superior knowledge of the facts. "They found Arne's wallet on the other side of the parking lot near the boats. There was no cash in the wallet and Arne's credit cards were gone. Assuming, of course, he had credit cards. Other stuff that was in the wallet — slips of paper, his driver's license, that sort of thing — was scattered around the lot. Like the perp or perps," he said, lapsing into cop-speak, "panicked, ripped the stuff out, and were in a hurry to get out of there."

Pete continued to stare at him.

"Richter seemed to be on top of the case. He told me that one of the first things they intend to do is trace Arne's movements last night to see if they uncover anything that leads them in a different direction. But right now he said it looks like a robbery gone bad."

Pete didn't know Arne Breit well, but had represented him a few years earlier when a member of his fishing party filed assault charges against Arne for roughing him up when he allegedly refused to release an under-sized salmon. The charges were dismissed when other members of the charter party declined to testify against Arne. To a man, they denied that they'd witnessed the incident. Pete had seen Arne only intermittently since that time, but had a good relationship with him and liked the guy and chatted with him whenever he saw him around town.

"Have they considered whether someone might have had it in for Arne and deliberately left signs at the scene making it look like a robbery?" Pete asked.

"Like who?"

"I don't know, Harry. I'm not the sheriff, remember?"

"I'm sure they'll look into all of the possibilities. But at this point, they're focusing on the robbery theory."

"Of course," Pete said caustically. "We know what a deep thinker Sheriff Richter is. The first thing that pops out at him is always the answer."

"Pete, we're friends and everything, but on this one, I think you may be letting your personal view of the sheriff color your thinking."

"Maybe," Pete said.

Harry finished his eggs and heaped orange marmalade on one of the English muffins that was already dripping with butter. He took a healthy bite and pointed the remainder of the muffin in Pete's direction and said, "If something personal were behind the shooting, what do you think it might be?"

"I thought you were absolutely, positively sure it was a robbery."

"I am," Harry said confidently. "I'm just talking hypothetically now."

"Hypothetically, I have no idea."

"Any guesses?"

"Harry, are you deaf?"

"Okay, no call to jump on me. But hypothetically, do you think it might be someone like that guy Romer we helped put away on meth charges a couple of years ago? You said he and Arne didn't get along very well."

"That was two years ago. Anyway, if Romer came after someone, don't you think it more likely that it would be one of us? We turned him in."

"That's probably true," Harry said. "But I think you're right on the bigger picture. They should check out grudge killing as a possible motive. How do you think we should communicate this to Richter?"

"What do you mean, how should *we* communicate this to Richter? I have no role in this case and don't want to have a role. Besides, if I made a suggestion to Richter, the first thing he'd do is start looking my way. I think I'll sit this one out and just be a spectator."

"Point taken," Harry said. "Maybe I'll say something to Richter myself. I was the tipster who brought down Romer and his pal, remember?"

"I do remember," Pete said dryly. "You were the unsung hero of that case."

Harry's eyes grew wistful and he appeared to think for a few moments. "I guess I was kind of the linchpin of the law enforcement effort. But for my tip, Romer and friend would be running an even bigger meth operation down in Alabama or somewhere."

"As I said, you were the unsung hero." Pete rolled his eyes. "Now, to wrap this up," he said, looking at Rona, "I suppose I'm nominated to talk to Lynn's father to see if I can get anything out of him regarding his grandchildren."

Rona had been sitting quietly while Pete and Harry went back and forth at each other over the Arne Breit killing, but now said softly, "If you could. I'll find the address of the home Mr. Pruitt's in and call you. After that, I'll take care of things," she added.

"Okay," Pete said, "Driving to Grand Rapids is always high on my list of things to do. After that, I have to get back to other things." He looked at Harry. "Did I tell you I'm doing a five-part series for *The Fjord Herald* about the civilizing influence of the Vikings on various parts of Europe?"

Harry gave him a baleful look. "Only about ten times. I don't know what you're going to write about in the last four parts of that series. A few paragraphs in the first story should pretty much exhaust the subject."

Pete looked at Rona and winked.

They all stood. Harry looked deep in thought and said in a quiet voice, "You don't really think Romer will come after us, do you?"

SEVEN

On the drive to Grand Rapids, Pete thought about his father and knew he had to schedule a visit to the facility in southwestern Wisconsin where he was living out the final months of his life. Not that it would do much good. He'd come away from his last trip there feeling empty and depressed. Throughout the visit, his father showed no sign he recognized him. Pete tried to talk about many things, but it was like speaking with a stranger rather than a person with whom he shared a familial bond and many memories even if not all of them were fond.

He wondered if his visit with Armand Pruitt would be any different. When Lynn spoke of him, she always told of his days with the FBI, or later, when they had their forensic accounting practice together. Thinking back, Pete couldn't recall her telling much about her father as a person other than that he once saved her life by calling to warn her the morning both of their cars were bombed. He knew almost nothing else about Pruitt. What he liked to do, whether he was driven by ambition in his younger years, whether he loved music or liked to read or enjoyed baseball.

As Pete passed through downtown Grand Rapids on the way to Sunrise Manor on the east side of town, he thought about how he should raise Lynn's death with Pruitt. Did he have good days and bad days, or was every day part of the growing and deadly fog of dementia? He was reminded again of the fact he wasn't very good at wrenching personal things. He was a corporate guy. Complicated deals with big money at stake, that's what he was good at.

He located Sunrise Manor and pulled into the visitor's lot. After some thought, he'd decided not to call the facility in advance, but to show up between mealtimes, talk to the manager, and try to see Pruitt. He felt that gave him the best chance of avoiding being put off by the facility's gatekeepers.

He identified himself as the Pruitt family attorney, realizing that was more than a slight stretch, and asked to see the manager. He emphasized that he wasn't there to complain about Mr. Pruitt's care, but rather to deal with a tragic family matter. After ten minutes, a stout woman with gray curls wound so tight they could have been spring-loaded appeared in the waiting room and approached him. She looked barely five-two and held one bow of her silver-rimmed eyeglasses in her left hand even though the glasses were already secured by a beaded strap around her neck. She looked like she was getting ready to sit for a portrait that one day would hang in the entrance hall to commemorate her service to her profession and humanity.

"I'm Dr. Blake," the woman said in a formal voice. She extended her free right hand. "How may I help you?"

"Pete Thorsen," he said. "I'm the attorney for the family of one of your residents, Armand Pruitt." He gave her one of his business cards. "Can I speak to you in private for a few minutes?"

Dr. Blake fussed with her glasses and seemed to be collecting her thoughts. "What about, Mr. Thorsen?" she asked.

"As I told the receptionist, it's a family matter."

"I see. If it has legal ramifications, I suggest we set up a time when I can have our attorney present."

"No legal ramifications. But I'm afraid I have some bad news about Mr. Pruitt's daughter. Could we go back to your office, please?"

Dr. Blake gave him another quizzical look and said, "This way please."

Her office was an edifice to her professional life. It was lined with book-cases filled with medical textbooks and psychological treatises and leather-bound biographies of the giants who'd preceded her. Professional journals were neatly arranged on a coffee table and more certificates than he could count filled her walls. When they were seated, Dr. Blake looked at him with studied concern and asked, "What's the bad news, Mr. Thorsen?"

"Mr. Pruitt's daughter, Lynn, was killed in an automobile accident."

Dr. Blake looked at him for a moment and then exclaimed, "Oh, that's *terrible*." She shook her head and donned a sorrowful expression that must be a hallmark of professionals in her field because he'd seen it before.

"I'd like to talk to you about how we convey this news to Mr. Pruitt," Pete said.

Her clinical expression and body language suggested that she thought Pete must be truly naïve when it came to dementia. "He won't understand anything you say, Mr. Thorsen," she said with an aura of superior profes-sional knowledge.

"Don't you think we still need to tell him? If he doesn't understand, he doesn't understand, but that's no reason not to tell him."

"Mr. Thorsen, I don't think you understand Alzheimer's. I work with …"

Pete cut her short. "I understand a little about Alzheimer's. My father's in a facility in Wisconsin with the disease. I may not be an expert like you, but I know something about it. Every now and then, something you say gets through to him. That may be true of Mr. Pruitt as well."

"Still …," Dr. Blake said.

"Will telling him that his daughter is dead harm him in any way?"

"I don't think so, but …"

"Then I'd like to see Mr. Pruitt and do my duty to the family."

Dr. Blake sighed, "Okay, I'll have a nurse see if he's awake."

"Before you do that," Pete said, "could you tell me if Mr. Pruitt's file lists any contact person other than Lynn and if it shows the last time a visitor was here to see him?"

Dr. Blake said nothing, but picked up the phone and asked the person at the other end to bring in Armand Pruitt's file. A nurse arrived five minutes later and Dr. Blake slipped her glasses on and briefly looked through it. She peered at Pete over the rims and said, "The only contact information we have for Mr. Pruitt is his daughter, Lynn."

"What do you show for a phone number and address?"

Dr. Blake looked down again and read the information to him. It was Lynn's cell phone number and her address in Beulah.

"How about Mr. Pruitt's grandchildren? Do you have contact information for them?"

She glanced at the file again and shook her head sadly. "There's no mention here of grandchildren."

Pete bit the inside of his lip and thought for a moment. "How about my other question? Can you tell from the file when Mr. Pruitt last had a visitor?"

Dr. Blake stoically paged through the file again and pulled out a sheet that appeared to be a visitors' log and studied it. "Lynn was here to see him in late November last year, right after Thanksgiving," she said.

Pete wanted to shake his head when he heard that.

Dr. Blake sat behind the barricade of her mahogany desk and gazed at him. Her expression suggested that she hoped he would give up and go away.

"Okay," he said, "why don't you call and see if Mr. Pruitt is awake."

She looked at him like the weight of the world had descended on her shoulders and slowly reached for the telephone again. She waited on the line and then cupped a hand over the mouthpiece and said to Pete, "Mr. Pruitt's awake. I suggest we have the nurse bring him to the lounge instead of going to his room." Pete nodded his agreement and listened while Dr. Blake instructed the nurse.

The only people in the lounge were a middle-aged couple sitting next to an elderly woman in a wheelchair. The woman bowed so far forward in her chair that her head nearly rested on her knees. She showed no awareness of Pete and Dr. Blake when they entered the lounge and seemed not to hear the couple speaking to her in soothing tones. Pete had witnessed a similar lack of awareness when he visited his father.

They staked out a seating area in an opposite corner of the room and waited. Neither spoke even though it was evident that they wouldn't have disturbed anyone if they had. Five minutes later, a nurse pushed a wheelchair into the lounge. The man seated in the chair was dressed in a red and black checked shirt and khaki pants and had silver hair that was slicked straight back. He gripped the armrests of his wheelchair and stared out at the room. The distracted look in his eyes telegraphed that he wasn't well, but he looked positively robust compared to the woman in the opposite corner.

The nurse wheeled Pruitt to where Pete and Dr. Blake were sitting. Dr. Blake rose and folded her hands around his and said, "I brought you a visitor, Armand. This is Pete Thorsen, your family's attorney."

Pete extended his hand close enough for Pruitt to seize it. No reaction from him, no sign that Pruitt even recognized Pete was there. "Nice shirt," Pete said, hoping his voice sounded reassuring. "It looks good on you." Pruitt continued to stare straight ahead.

Dr. Blake moved closer to Pruitt and held his hand. His head was down and he was mumbling something, but Pete couldn't understand what he was saying. Dr. Blake moved even closer and shook her head a couple of times. Pruitt's lips continued to move. Finally Dr. Blake looked at Pete and said, "I think he believes you're someone else."

"Who?"

Dr. Blake hesitated a moment and then said, "I thought he said something about a person the FBI is looking for."

Pete frowned. "Could you explain to him again that I'm his family's attorney?"

"I'll try."

Dr. Blake spoke to Armand Pruitt in her soothing tones again. Pruitt didn't respond and continued to stare straight ahead.

Pete said to Dr. Blake, "Can I speak to him directly?"

"Yes, but don't frighten him."

"Armand, my name is Pete Thorsen. I'm an attorney. I represent your family." He took another business card from his wallet and reached over to hand it to Pruitt. Pruitt just sat there staring at Pete with the same distracted look.

Pete put the card back in his pocket and continued, saying, "I have a message from Lynn. She's gone to Heaven. She said she'll see you there and asked Dr. Blake and me to look after you until then." There was no sign Pruitt heard or understood anything Pete said.

Pete went on. "Your grandchildren, Richard and Melissa, asked me to say hello. They'll be here to see you soon." Still no cognitive response of any kind.

Dr. Blake took over and talked to Pruitt once more in a soft voice. Pete decided she sounded much more comfortable and compassionate than he had. She talked about what the center was serving for dinner that night and what activities were on the agenda. She described the Easter egg hunt that was coming up. Armand Pruitt sat impassively through it all and didn't bat an eye. Occasionally, his gaze would wander toward Pete, but Pete wasn't sure he was really looking at him.

Dr. Blake whispered to Pete, "I think we should wrap this up." Pete nodded his agreement and Dr. Blake signaled the nurse to take Pruitt back to his room. As the nurse rolled the wheelchair across the lounge, his head was cocked to one side and he appeared to be aware of no one in the area.

They walked back to Dr. Blake's office and settled into the same chairs they'd occupied earlier. Dr. Blake said, "Now do you believe me, Mr. Thorsen?"

"I never expected him to suddenly become lucid just because I was there. I just felt I had to see him to do my duty to the family."

"Mr. Thorsen, I have someone coming in in a few minutes, but I have a question. Why did you mention grandchildren again? I told you, we have no record that Mr. Pruitt has grandchildren."

Pete debated how much to tell Dr. Blake, but finally decided that there was no harm in coming clean with what he was doing. "Lynn told everyone that she had two children, but we've been unable to locate them. I thought my comment might trigger a response from him. I was wrong."

"He didn't understand anything you said," Dr. Blake said. Her comment dripped with an "I told you so" message. "The only thing that seemed clear," she added, "was his conviction you're on the FBI's wanted list. It's not unusual for people with advanced Alzheimer's to have paranoid emotions, but do you understand why he reacted that way to you? I've never witnessed that before."

"I think I know. Armand spent twenty years with the FBI. He must have some memory of those years."

"I have to present a paper to our regional association in two months. I think our members would be very interested in this as a case study."

"Would you like me to appear to support your presentation? I could play the part of the guy whose picture is on the Post Office wall."

Dr. Blake stared at him with a horrified look. She obviously wasn't used to someone with his sense of humor.

Before he got in his Range Rover, Pete looked around the grounds of Sunrise Manor. It was a nice facility. Maybe he should look into moving his father so they'd be closer.

EIGHT

Pete broke the seal on the CD he'd purchased after leaving Sunrise Manor. It was the audio version of the "American Pie" video that a group with Grand Rapids roots had produced to counter the notion that the city was a dying community. He couldn't play it on the drive north because his CD player was on the blink. First the heater and now the CD player. He hated to part with the vehicle he'd grown so comfortable with, but after twelve years maybe it was time.

He slipped the disc in the player and the Don McLean song drifted out. He turned up the volume and listened to the familiar lyrics. The part about how a long, long time ago, the music made him smile. The part about February making him shiver, which he certainly could relate to. The part about driving his Chevy to the levee. The part about asking whether you believed in rock and roll. And of course, the rousing chorus with "Bye, bye ..."

Pete wasn't even born when Buddy Holly, whose death the song supposedly commemorated, died in a plane crash together with some other prominent musicians of the time, but he'd learned to love Holly's music thanks to Jimmy Ray Evans. He played the CD a second time.

He sighed and turned off the player. He knew he couldn't delay the inevitable any longer. He dialed his stepdaughter, Julie's, cell phone number and waited. Soon he heard some female pop singer's screechy tones followed by Julie's bubbly voice.

"I'm glad you called, Dad. I was about to call you."

"See, I saved you minutes you can now use to call your friends."

She either didn't hear his comment or chose to ignore it and said breathlessly, "I just got accepted to art school in Paris this summer. I'm so excited!"

"That's great, Sweetie! Congratulations!"

"It's too late to back out now, huh?

"I think it is. Are you nervous?"

"A little." Then she added a bit apprehensively judging from the tone of her voice, "It would help if Mikki could go."

"Has she changed her mind about going?"

"She hasn't heard from the school yet. She's really afraid she won't be accepted."

"I bet she will."

"If Mikki doesn't go, I don't know what I'll do. Without a friend to do things with, I'll just be sitting in my room. Maybe that's why some artists produce those black paintings. They don't have any friends."

"Come on, Julie. Be optimistic. I'll bet she gets accepted. But if she doesn't, you'll probably make five new friends the first day you're over there."

"It will really mess up our publishing plans if she can't go."

"Publishing? Aren't you going to study art?"

"Well yeah, but remember last year I told you that Mikki and I were thinking of writing a book about our experiences when we got back? Julie and Mikki in Paris? We decided we're definitely going to do it. Now that idea will be down the toilet, too, if Mikki doesn't go."

"I'm sure everything will work out."

She abruptly switched gears and asked, "Is Lynn back from Seattle yet? I'd like to talk to her about her experience when she went to art school in Paris. What kind of clothes she took with her, things like that. Whether the girls wore makeup and shaved their legs or ran around looking like a bunch of Bohemians. Of course, I know a lot has changed since older people like you and Lynn went to Europe."

Pete clinched his teeth at the reference to age. "That's why I'm calling, Julie. I have bad news. Lynn had an accident during the big ice storm. I'm afraid she didn't make it."

Julie said nothing. Pete became uncomfortable with the silence and added, "I'm sorry."

More silence, then Julie said between sniffles, "Is that all you can say? You're sorry?"

"What more do you want me to say, Sweetie? Her death was as much of a shock to me as it is to you."

More silence, then Julie, who obviously was crying, asked, "When did you say this accident happened?"

Pete told her again.

"And you're just telling me now? What took you so long? Did you just remember your daughter has a telephone?" She sounded angry.

"I'm sorry, I should have called sooner. We've been trying to locate Lynn's children and …"

"And you couldn't find two minutes in your busy day to call me?"

"Julie …"

"It's no wonder the two of you broke up. With your communication skills … The first woman I've felt any bond with since Mom died, and now she's gone, too."

"I know how you feel, Julie."

"Do you really, Dad? I've got to go. I'll call you later."

The phone went dead. Well that was a minor disaster, he thought. Maybe it had been a mistake to put off calling Julie for as long as he had, but he was afraid of her reaction. In retrospect, he might have made matters worse by not telling her sooner. He sighed. Now that the news was out, maybe he could have a rational discussion with her the next time they talked.

■ ■ ■

Rona's Bay Grille had only a scattering of customers on a week-night during the off-season. Rona was attending to her restaurateur duties, but joined Pete and Harry at their usual table when she was free.

"How did it go in Grand Rapids?" she asked.

"As I just told Harry, I'm not sure Pruitt processed anything I said during my visit. The bottom line is I found no evidence of Lynn's children there, either. Lynn is the only contact person Sunrise Manor has on file for her father. They have no record of Melissa or Richard or any other relative."

"What's your take on it after all of the looking around you've done?" Harry asked, looking thoughtful.

"I don't know, but as I said before, I'm beginning to wonder if Lynn really had children."

"That can't be true," Harry said. "She talked about her children with all of us."

Pete shrugged and said, "If they exist, they must be ghosts."

They sat quietly until Rona asked, "What do we do now? People continue to ask about a memorial service. We have to decide one way or the other."

"Sometimes memorial services are held weeks after the death," Harry volunteered. "We can't very well schedule something without giving Lynn's kids a chance to attend."

Pete looked at Harry and then Rona. "The only thing we have to go on is the address in Seattle that's on her duplicate driver's license."

Harry stared at him for a long moment. "Are you suggesting we have someone check the apartment?"

"Yes, me. I already have my ticket."

Rona looked at Pete with a sympathetic expression. "Pete, you don't have to do this. You've already done more than anyone could expect."

"There's something wrong, Rona. Lynn being back here without telling anyone, where she was when the accident occurred, no sign of either of her kids. Besides, my trip is going to do double duty. I'm having dinner with the managing editor of *The Fjord Herald* tomorrow night to discuss my articles and explore some ideas I have for a book."

"Rona's right," Harry said, "you've already done a lot."

"I wouldn't go just to see if I can find Lynn's kids. The trip is going to do double duty as I just said."

"Are you sure your meeting with that newspaper isn't an excuse for you to play detective again?"

"I'm not playing detective. I'm trying to find two young people Lynn mentioned to all of us many times."

Harry studied Pete for a moment. "I've learned it's useless to argue with you when you've made up your mind," he said. "Anything we can do?"

"Not unless you've got Melissa's current address and telephone number. Then I can spend all of my time talking Norwegian stuff with the newspaper's editor."

When Rona left the table to check on operations, Pete asked, "Have you heard anything new about the Arne Breit investigation?"

"Nothing really new," Harry said. "I guess they're trying to reconcile the robbery theory with the way Arne was killed. Two shots to the head. It doesn't seem like something a panicked robber would do, does it?"

"No it doesn't. I'm surprised that your new friend Frank Richter hasn't been investigating to see whether any handguns are registered to me. With him, the fact I represented Arne a few years back would usually be enough to make me a person of interest if not an actual suspect."

"I can send him over if you like," Harry said with a deadpan expression and a mischievous gleam in his eyes. "I have influence with him these days, you know."

"Don't bother. Oh, but you can assure him that when I leave tomorrow, I'm not fleeing the state. I have every intention of returning."

"You might have to post a flight bond," Harry said, feigning a thoughtful look.

Rona came back to the table and interrupted their banter. Pete asked her, "If I can't find Melissa when I'm in Seattle, when do you propose to schedule the memorial service?"

"In a week or two, I would think. I'll have to line up a church and get a notice in the *Sentinel*."

Harry ordered a piece of key lime pie and looked disappointed when Rona asked the waitress to bring three forks. Harry's diet and workout regimen of the previous summer had gone the way of the summer sun and balmy breezes and he'd regressed to his old ways. Pete kidded him about it once and Harry reminded him that it was winter and the human body needed extra calories to ward off influenza and other bugs that floated around the community in cold weather. Always an excuse when it came to food.

When the waitress brought the pie, Harry offered it to Rona first in a chivalrous gesture. She took a forkful and passed it to Pete. Harry's ravenous eyes followed the dessert as it made its way around the table. Pete took a small bite and savored it, closing his eyes in mock pleasure, then took another bite. He took his time passing the pie back to Harry. Harry's fork was poised in the attack mode and he gouged out a chunk of pie before the plate came to rest and shoveled it in his mouth. He didn't pass the pie around the table a second time.

"Have you told Julie about Lynn's accident?" Rona asked. "I remember your saying that the two of them hit it off pretty well."

"Yes," Pete said, "I told her when I got back from Grand Rapids and it didn't go well. Here was a woman who essentially dumped me and my own daughter inferred, as she has in the past, that it was my fault. She accused me of lacking communication skills and not knowing how to share my feelings. Then she took me to task for not telling her about the accident sooner. I don't know, maybe she thought I should have taken her with me to the morgue or something."

Rona looked sympathetic and said, "I'll talk to her if you want."

"Everything should be okay when she gets over the shock of the news."

Harry seemed to sense an opportunity to get back at Pete for his antics with the pie. "Some men aren't as sensitive as they could be about these things," he said solemnly. "They give the rest of us a bad reputation. Like that time we went shopping at Crystal Crate & Cargo for your birthday gift, hon." He placed his hand over Rona's. "I took Pete along for company thinking he'd maybe have a few thoughtful ideas, but all he did was give me grief for looking around the store instead of going straight to the glass counter where the jewelry is. I know a lot of men would have done that. Go in, spend just enough money to keep the little lady happy, and get out as fast as possible. But I'm different. I wanted my girl to know I spent time looking for something really special and didn't just jump on a hint she gave me."

Pete nodded his head and said, "You taught me some valuable lessons that night, Harry, and I'm forever grateful. First, whenever you're shopping for your girlfriend or wife, thoroughly canvas the store for gift options. Second, weigh those options carefully. I can't fault your decision to buy the silver bracelet with imported stones that you ultimately bought for Rona, but I wonder if you really gave that cherry-pitter you spent fifteen minutes admiring a fair shot."

Rona did everything but stuff a napkin into her mouth to stifle her laugh.

NINE

As Pete packed for his trip, he thought about everything he'd done in the past few days to find and notify Lynn's children of her death. It troubled him more than he let on to Harry and Rona that he'd come up empty. The Seattle trip, which they already suspected was unnecessary, was his best shot at finding out what was going on.

The telephone rang. It was Dr. Blake returning his call from earlier that morning. "Maybe you know the answer to this off the top of your head," he said, "but if not, I'd appreciate it if you could have someone check. Armand Pruitt. Does he have any family photographs in his room?"

Pete thought he heard a sigh at the other end. Then Dr. Blake said, "Is this about his grandchildren again?"

"Yes."

"I thought we settled that."

"I know what you said, but I'm just trying to be thorough. If Lynn had children, the last thing we want is to schedule a memorial service and discover later that we didn't notify all family members."

"Okay," Dr. Blake said, not even trying to disguise her weary tone, "I'll have someone check."

"That's great. I'm leaving for the airport at noon and I'll be gone for a couple of days. Could your person do it before then?"

"We'll do our best, Mr. Thorsen. Any other requests?"

"No," he said, thinking she was a pompous pain in the ass, "that's it. You've been very generous with your time. We're just trying to do the right thing by the Hawke family."

Pete finished his packing and added a folding umbrella to his luggage. He had a feeling he'd need it. Shortly before noon, Dr. Blake's assistant called back to report what he already suspected. The only photograph Armand Pruitt had in his room was the one of his daughter, Lynn.

■ ■ ■

Pete caught a taxi at Sea-Tac International Airport to take him downtown to his hotel. A steady drizzle was falling and the low-hanging gray clouds reminded him of Michigan in March. It was warmer, though. Fifty-four degrees and West Coast residents didn't have to endure the same dramatic plunges in temperature that folks in the Middle West did. Except for the annoying squeak of the wiper blades, he enjoyed the ride in. It was almost like old times when he would fly into a city and experience an adrenaline rush as he geared up to do battle with the other side on some new deal.

The taxi pulled up in front of the Doubletree Arctic Club Hotel. Harry recommended the hotel as *the* place to stay in Seattle and Pete liked enough of what he read in a guidebook to book a room there. The Arctic Club had been one of the most famous men's clubs in the northwest before it was converted into a hotel and he concluded it would be a good place to soak up some local color. As usual, Harry was a bit behind the times when it came to the hotel's current full name, but he was right about the hotel's imposing exterior and general ambiance.

Pete checked in and was shown to his room. It was on the dark side, but the décor fit the rest of the building. He particularly liked the leather chairs, the trunks for bedside tables, and the dark wood crown molding.

When he saw the bottle opener with a miniature walrus head at the end, he smiled and knew he was staying at the right place.

After a long shower, he unpacked and dressed for dinner. Harry emphasized eleven times that Seattle was a casual town, so even though he was meeting Kjersti Aarvik at a nice restaurant, he donned a pair of wrinkled khakis and the only black shirt he owned. Not exactly Seattle grunge, but not formal either.

He had an hour to kill before he met Kjersti. He grabbed the folder with his notes, took his jacket and folding umbrella, and went in search of the Polar Bear Lounge Harry had told him not to miss. The name of the watering hole turned out to be the Polar Bar, but it was every bit as charming as Harry had described. He found a table in the corner and ordered a glass of tonic water with two slices of lime and no vodka and studied his notes. Melissa Hawke drifted in and out of his thoughts and he wondered if he'd have any luck locating her.

He left money for his drink and a tip and caught a taxi to the Steelhead Diner to meet Kjersti. It was an unpretentious place, which suited him just fine. He scanned the dining area, but didn't see anyone who looked like Kjersti based on how she'd described herself. He opted to wait at a table looking out at Pike Place Market. The Market had a peaceful look in the rain. In nice weather, it reportedly was all hustle and bustle and teeming with tourists. He was glad he was there at a quieter time.

A woman with medium-length blonde hair walked in and surveyed the room. Pete stood and waved. Kjersti crossed the room with the stride of an energetic woman who enjoyed the outdoors and said, "Pete?"

"Yes," he replied. "You described yourself to a 't.' I picked you right out of the crowd."

She gave him her best Colgate smile. "You're a real Scandinavian detective. Of course, it helps that I'm the only blonde woman in the place."

Pete laughed. He liked her already. The infectious personality that came through in her e-mails was magnified when he saw her in person.

"So," she said brightly, "your first time in Seattle, huh?"

"First time. But the city is living up to its reputation. The bellhop at the hotel told me it's been raining for three days and it's expected to rain for two more."

Kjersti looked at him in mock horror and said, "A Michigander complaining about the weather in Seattle? I saw the weather report a few days ago and it said you people had a little rainstorm of your own. From what I heard, it froze and coated the trees and everything else with an inch of ice. Look out the window, sir. Do you see any ice?"

Pete laughed. "Not so far."

They both ordered a glass of Sauvignon Blanc from her home state and scanned their menus. Kjersti put hers down first, and as soon as he did, asked, "So, how are you coming with our articles?"

They spent the next half-hour discussing the pieces he was writing for *The Fjord Herald*, pausing only to get their orders in. She reviewed his rough outlines and made some suggestions. He dutifully noted her comments. When they finished talking about the articles, Pete told her about the book he had in mind. She reminded him that the *Herald* didn't publish books, which Pete already knew, but said she would introduce him to the editors she knew at a couple of publishing houses.

They both ordered a second glass of wine with their meals. He'd splurged and ordered the Pan Roasted Alaskan Halibut, one of the more expensive items on the menu. She had the Sauteed Oregon Petrale Sole. From the way both of them attacked their dinners, it was apparent either that they shared a passion for food or were famished. The latter pretty much described him since he'd spent half the day on an airplane with only two bags of Goldfish crackers to tamp down his hunger pains.

"You said you have another mission in Seattle. Anything I can help with?"

"Actually, you can." He fished the piece of paper from his wallet with the address Sheriff Bond had given him and handed it across the table. "Do you know where this is?"

Kjersti stared at the address for a few moments. Then she said, "Ballard, I think. Yes, I'm sure it's in Ballard."

"Where's that?"

"It's a neighborhood north of here. It was settled by the Scandinavians. Actually, I was thinking of suggesting we have dinner there at the Copper Gate. But I thought better of it when another person in my office said it might not be the best venue to have an inaugural dinner with a gentleman who's going to be one of our contributing editors."

"And the reason for that would be?"

"Well, it has a replica of a Viking ship for a bar, which is all fine and dandy, but then there are these photographs and artifacts all over."

"The way you said that makes me think I should make further inquiry, as a lawyer would say."

Kjersti giggled. "What's the word? Bawdy? Racy?"

"Ah, I'm beginning to get the picture. Maybe I'll check the place out when I'm in the area tomorrow."

"Don't say I didn't warn you."

"I'll complain only if it turns out you steered me wrong about the décor."

After a couple of minutes, Kjersti said, "I don't want to pry, but who are you looking for at that address and why did you come way out here to look for him? Or her."

Pete told her the whole story, beginning with how he knew Lynn Hawke, her temporary move to Seattle, and her death back in Michigan during the ice storm. He added a summary of his efforts to find Lynn's children.

"Can you think of anything else I could have done?"

"No," Kjersti said, shaking her head, "You were more inventive than I would have been." She looked at him and said, "Reading between the lines, I get the feeling you don't think the 'accident' was really an accident."

"I wouldn't go that far, but there are some things about Lynn's death that don't compute."

"You sound more like a detective than a corporate lawyer turned Viking history buff. Do you read Jo Nesbø?"

"I'm becoming a fan. I finished *Nemesis* and now I'm reading *The Redbreast*."

"You'd make a good Harry Hole," she said, referring to the lead character in Nesbø's mysteries.

"That's what I tell my friend Harry McTigue. He's always chiding me for getting involved in police investigations. I told him I can't help it; sleuthing comes naturally to Norwegians."

"Maybe you should scrap the book you're considering and come up with a crime fiction plot. Scandinavian mystery writers are hot these days."

"I've thought about it. The problem is, all my ideas are so dull that I couldn't get anyone to read beyond the first page."

"You know the old saying. Write what you know. It sounds like the situation you're investigating would make a great plot for a book. Maybe you could spice it up a little. Throw in a few clandestine meetings at the Copper Gate. Add a little sex."

Probably a lot of sex, he thought. But she was right; the mystery surrounding Lynn Hawke was more intriguing than most fiction he'd read.

They fought over the bill and finally agreed to split it. Kjersti's parting shot was to give him an impish grin and say, "Don't forget about the Copper Gate tomorrow if you're not too busy sleuthing. They actually serve food in addition to treating you to an art show."

TEN

To orient himself, Pete located 5314 22nd Avenue NW on the city map he'd purchased in the hotel lobby gift shop. It was in Ballard just as Kjersti had said. He checked his bag with the hotel and caught a taxi north. He alternated between admiring the scenery and scanning his pocket guidebook.

Ballard had a colorful history and was known as much for its gritty nightlife as for its Scandinavian flavor. From all reports, it still had bars where patrons drank the night away only to go into the back alley in the wee morning hours to upchuck before returning to the bar to greet the day with a fresh round of shots. The artists and young professionals who'd discovered the area added a hip atmosphere.

Pete paid the driver and got out in front of the three-story structure. It was a solid building, but not exactly architecturally novel. The outer door was propped open. He walked in and scanned the board that listed the names of the tenants. Neither Lynn Hawke nor Laura Mati was listed. Melissa Hawke was not listed either. None of the names that were listed meant anything to him.

A plaque on the opposite wall announced that the rental agent for the building was an outfit named Greater Sound Realty with offices throughout the Seattle area. One was on Ballard Avenue a short distance away. It seemed unlikely that the board would have been changed so soon to delete Lynn's name if she had been a tenant. Checking with Greater Sound seemed like his best option.

He looked at his map again to find the shortest route to the real estate firm's office and headed in that direction. After a block, his hair was matted from the cold drizzle and a trickle of water that ran down his back sent shivers through his body. He pressed the button on his umbrella and zipped his jacket tight around his neck. He turned left on Ballard Avenue and found the real estate office two blocks up. A melodic chime sounded when he opened the door.

The only occupant was a man of about forty who had his feet propped up on his desk and was either dozing or staring transfixed at the Jimi Hendrix posters on the wall and dreaming of concerts past. A two-inch swath of purple was burned into his shaggy dark hair, and he wore black-framed rectangular glasses that were barely eyeball deep. His waist-length black jacket was adorned with an eye-numbing collage of Mayan sunbursts and purple swirls and lush green leaves that Pete assumed belonged to the cannabis family. It was all topped off, if that was the right expression, by sequined black jeans and pointy-toed cowboy boots adorned with serpents and yellow roses.

The man opened his eyes when Pete walked in and dropped his feet to the floor. He gave Pete the once over with studied disinterest. "If you're looking for an apartment, dude," he said, "I'll save both of us time. We're booked up in this part of the city. You can try our other offices." He put his feet back on the desk and reclined in his chair again.

"I'm not looking for an apartment," Pete replied. "I'm looking for information." He fished out one of his business cards and handed it across the desk to the man. The man stared at the card, but made no effort to take it. Pete hated insolence and was tempted to walk around the desk and yank the gold hoop from the prick's ear.

He tried the soft approach instead. "I don't believe I caught your name," he said.

The man looked at Pete, then at the Jimi Hendrix posters, then back at him. "Jimi," the man said. "That's J-I-M-I." From the smirk on his face, he obviously thought he'd come up with the one-liner of the year.

"Okay, Jimi, maybe you can help me. I'm looking for two people. One is a woman named Lynn Hawke, and the other is her daughter, Melissa. Are they tenants of yours?"

Jimi gave a little shrug and said, "Do you see a sign that says 'Information'? This ain't the city tourist bureau."

Pete stared back at him and said, "Here's how the game is played, Jimi. I ask you a civil question, you give me a civil answer. Simple, huh? So let's start over. Are Lynn Hawke or Melissa Hawke your tenants?"

Apparently sensing that Pete's fuse was lit, Jimi swung his feet to the floor again and said in a slightly less cocky voice, "Can't say. I don't have the names of all of our tenants at the tip of my tongue. Besides, we don't give out confidential information like that to any old dude who walks in off the street."

"I'm not any old dude," Pete said. "I'm the attorney for the family of a woman who was killed in an automobile accident. I'm trying to get in touch with her children."

Jimi squinted through his miniature glasses and yawned. "You caught me at a bad time. I was about to hunt up an ATM and get some scratch. Then I got errands to run. Maybe you'd like to come back next week when I have more time." He pulled out his wallet and began to count his cash as though Pete weren't there. Pete saw a five and three singles.

Pete was beginning to get the drift. "You do seem to be a little short," Pete said. "I stopped at an ATM this morning." He extracted a crisp fifty dollar bill from his wallet and laid it on the desk. "I believe in helping my fellow man. This should eliminate the need for you to hunt up an ATM in this nasty weather."

Jimi's eyes flicked toward the bill and then back at Pete. "I got big plans for tonight. I'm not sure that will cover everything I have in mind."

"How much are those plans going to cost you?"

He shrugged. "Who knows, man. Two of those maybe?"

"Sorry," Pete said. "I didn't understand your cash needs and it is raining out." He took out another fifty and put it on top of the first one.

Jimi finally reached for the bills, tapped them on the desk top to align them, and stuffed them in his wallet. "You know," he said, "I could get in trouble for giving out confidential information about our tenants."

"You could also get in trouble for engaging in, how shall I say, financial transactions on the side?"

Jimi looked at him for a moment and took his time logging on his computer. After accessing a page that looked like a list of tenants from where Pete stood, Jimi began to scroll down. He looked up at Pete after a minute and said, "Sorry, dude, no Lynn Hawke listed. What was the other name?"

"Melissa Hawke."

He scanned the list again and shook his head. No Melissa Hawke either. You sure you got the name right, pal? You sure it's not Lynn Falcon and Melissa Falcon?" He grinned at his second big one-liner.

Pete ignored the lame humor and asked, "How about Laura Mati? Do you have anything on her?"

Jimi smirked and shook his head. "You sure do have a lot of ladies' names in that noggin of yours. I'd like to see your little black book sometime." He grinned again and stroked his scruffy chin hair.

"Do you?" Pete asked. "I'd hate to have to reverse that withdrawal."

"Hey, man, you saved me a trip to the ATM and I gave you information I'm not supposed to give out. That makes us even."

Pete's fuse was sizzling now. He moved to within a few feet of Jimi and glared down at him. "We'll be even when you tell me if Laura Mati is one of your tenants."

Jimi scooted his chair back and looked at Pete warily. Pete stepped forward again.

"Okay," Jimi said. "Gimme some room to get to my computer, huh?" Pete stepped back and continued to watch him. Jimi edged over, keeping an eye on Pete, and scrolled down the names a third time. When he finished, he shook his head and said, "No Laura Mati, either." It must have concerned Jimi that a man who was five inches taller and forty pounds heavier was looming over him because he added, "But to show you what a cooperative guy I am, I seem to remember that a broad named Laura lives in our building, but she's not an official tenant, if you know what I mean."

"No, I don't know what you mean. Speak English."

"This Laura I'm thinking of is the squeeze of one of our other tenants if that gives you a better picture."

Pete's eyes never left Jimi's face, but a hollow feeling crept into his stomach. "Is this squeeze, as you call her, about five-seven with long honey-brown hair and a good figure?" he asked.

"Yeah, man, that sounds like her. A hot babe even if she has some miles on her." He appeared to relax again. He leered at Pete and asked, "Is that what this is all about? Is this Laura chick your woman?"

"Not exactly," Pete said. "What's the name of the tenant she lives with?"

"Whoa, man. I told you too much already."

"What's his name?" Pete demanded. His expression made it clear he was finished fooling around.

"Hey, man, don't get mad at me. His name is Bartholome. Gil Bartholome, but you're too late if you're looking for him. He split a few days ago, not long after that Laura babe left."

"How do you know he split?"

"One of our workmen saw him loading stuff into his SUV. No one has seen him since."

"Have you checked his apartment?"

"Well sure, out of curiosity, you know. His personal stuff is gone. The babe's clothes are still there."

Pete thought about it for a few moments, and then asked, "How long have Bartholome and Laura been together?"

"I don't know, man. I'm the building manager, not his social secretary."

"How long, Jimi?"

He eyed Pete warily again and said, "She moved her ass in about two years ago. She was out here off and on for years before that."

Two years, Pete thought. It would be two years in August that Lynn had told her friends back home that she was going to Seattle to be with her daughter, Melissa. The timeline fit. A picture had emerged and he didn't like what he was seeing.

"I changed my mind," Pete said, "I am interested in an apartment. I'd like to see Bartholome's unit."

Jimi peered at him through his small glasses for a few moments. "I don't think I can show you that unit, man. It's leased to Mr. Bartholome and his rent is paid to the end of the month. I can't just let anyone on premises that are kind of like private property, you know?"

"Look, Jimi, I'm getting tired of this bullshit. I just told you I might want to lease that unit if Bartholome doesn't come back. I'd like to see it."

Jimi gave him another skeptical look and said, "I don't know. You're asking me to violate company policy again."

"Look, pal, you don't have a choice. I'm sure taking bribes is against company policy as well, so you already have a problem. Either you let me see the apartment, or I'm going to call your boss and tell him you've been extorting money from prospective tenants. Then I'm going to call the police. Laura is dead and Bartholome might have had something to do with it. I know cops. When they hear two minutes of my story, they're going to think you're complicit in the crime and are trying to cover for him. Then they're going to be on the phone with the authorities in Michigan and before you know it your ass will be extradited back there. You won't even have time to touch up the purple in your hair."

Jimi's eyes grew larger and he said, "You can't do that. I had nothing to do with Bartholome or his squeeze. I just rented them some digs."

"Tell that to the police." Pete grabbed the telephone on the desk, whirled it around, and punched in 411 for directory assistance. He asked the operator for the telephone number of the Seattle Police Department.

"Wait," Jimi said. "Maybe we can work this out. I need to make another ATM withdrawal tomorrow. If you can save me a trip, I might be able to let you in as long as I'm there, you know, at the same time."

Pete returned the phone to its cradle. "What's your daily withdrawal limit?" he asked.

"Two bills."

Pete checked his wallet and looked up at Jimi. "I understand that some of the recent deposits to your account have been questionable and the bank is cutting you back to a hundred dollars a day. If that will work, I think we can make a deal."

Jimi stared at the five twenties in Pete's hand. "I think that will hold me."

Pete handed him two twenty dollar bills. "The machine is temporarily low on currency. I'm sure it'll be restocked by the time we leave the apartment."

Jimi seemed to consider Pete's proposition. Then he said, "And I get the other sixty after you've seen the apartment?"

"I'm sure the ATM will be up and working by that time."

"Okay," Jimi said, "but we have a deal, right?"

Pete nodded.

Jimi picked up the phone and dialed a number. Within ten minutes, a fresh-faced kid whose dress and demeanor were the antithesis of Jimi's burst into the office. Jimi gave instructions as the kid stood in front of him at attention like a recruit in boot camp. Then Pete and Jimi left and walked to the 5314 building. They climbed the stairs to the second floor where Jimi used a master key to let them in.

The living room was spacious with polished hardware floors and Oriental rugs. But messy. Bartholome must have left in haste without bothering to pick up the newspapers and other clutter in the room. Pete looked in the kitchen and saw a stack of dirty dishes in the sink. The master bedroom in the rear of the apartment was a mess, too. The bed was unmade and some of the dresser drawers were open and dirty clothes were on the floor. The largest closet was filled with a woman's clothes, as was one of the dressers. The smaller closet was empty. A framed black and white photograph of a younger Armand Pruitt was on a nightstand; there were no other photographs.

The room next to the master bedroom had been converted into an office. It had a built-in desk along one wall with slots for two people to work. A router and modem were on top of the desk, but he didn't see any desktop computers or laptops. He flipped through the papers on the desk and looked in the waste basket that was half-full with discarded paper. The small room in back didn't have sheets on the mattress and appeared to be used for storage.

The bathroom had a double sink and roomy marble shower and a Jacuzzi in one corner. It was as messy as the rest of the apartment. Pete stared at it for a few minutes and then went to the kitchen and found a small plastic bag. Jimi was sitting on the couch reading a week-old newspaper and glanced at him when he passed. Pete returned to the bathroom and picked up a can of shave gel with two fingers, using a piece of tissue, and put the can in the plastic bag and pressed the seal. He put the bag in his jacket pocket.

"Hey," Jimi complained from the doorway, "you can't come in here and take Mr. Bartholome's things!"

Pete glared at him for a moment and said, "You're objecting to me cleaning up some of this garbage? The can is empty. Bartholome threw it out."

"You still shouldn't be taking things that don't belong to you."

"Jimi, if this continues, I have a feeling that ATM is still going to be short on cash when we finish."

Jimi muttered to himself and then asked impatiently, "How much longer do you need? You've seen the unit. It's only five rooms, for Christ's sake. You wouldn't be buying the *building*. This is *rental* property."

"I'll be done in five or ten minutes. I'm trying to decide how the place would lay out if I rent it."

"You're not interested in renting this place," Jimi scoffed. "You're just trying to find dirt on Mr. Bartholome because he stole your woman."

"Jimi ..."

Jimi returned to the living room, still grumbling, and Pete went back to the office to check it more carefully. He sat in one of the chairs and scanned the corkboard mounted on the wall above the desk. The usual potpourri of items was pinned to the board — cards, carryout menus from restaurants, notices of various cultural activities in the Seattle area, several travel brochures. Among the clutter was a scrap of paper with a telephone number; it had a 231 area code. No name, just the telephone number. He removed the tack and put the piece of paper in his wallet.

He checked the desk. In an upper drawer, he found an imitation leather address book that must belong to Lynn judging from the names and numbers. He was in the book, as were Harry and Rona and Armand Pruitt. There were no entries for either Lynn's son or daughter. He looked over his shoulder and didn't see Jimi. He slipped the address book into his other jacket pocket.

Pete pulled out the opposite drawer and saw two passports. One was issued to Laura Mati but had Lynn's photograph and physical description. Judging from the stamps, the passport had been heavily used. Many of the stamps were from India with a scattering from places like Hong Kong and South Korea.

The other passport was in Lynn Hawke's name. As with the one issued to Laura Mati, it contained numerous stamps from Asian countries. He returned both passports to the desk drawer and looked through the other drawers, but found nothing else of interest.

When Pete told Jimi he was ready to leave, he seemed relieved, as though he were fearful that Bartholome might return to the apartment and catch them snooping around premises that were still under lease to him. When they were outside the building, Pete raised his umbrella and withdrew three twenty dollar bills from his wallet. Jimi reached for them, but Pete drew his hand back.

"What does this guy Bartholome do for a living?" Pete asked.

"I don't know, man. We made a deal. I want the rest of my money."

Pete held the bills away from him. "He lived here for what, five years? Don't tell me you don't know what he did."

"I tell you, I don't know! I don't keep track of what all of our tenants do!"

"Well, you just saved me some money." He put the bills back in his wallet. "Pity that ATM never got back up the way I thought it would."

"We had a deal!"

Pete shook his head and said in a resigned tone, "They really have to do something about those ATMs. They're so damn unreliable."

"I think he's in some kind of international business," Jimi muttered. The steady rain had soaked his hair and flattened the purple streak against his head.

"Trade deals?" Pete asked. "Import/export?"

"Something like that."

"Anything else you want to share with me?"

"No. I told you everything I know."

Pete gave him the money and watched him trudge up the street. A half-block away, he glanced over his shoulder to see what Pete was doing and kept walking. The rain started to fall harder, and as Pete looked for a taxi, he wondered if Jimi would offer a sacrifice to the sun god depicted on his gaudy jacket when he got back to the office. More likely, he'd pray to the man who cultivated the green leaves.

He saw a taxi coming down his street and waved a hand. After he gave the driver instructions to stop at his hotel to pick up his bag and then go on to the airport, he settled back and stared out the window. Subliminally, he really hadn't expected to find Melissa, but what he did find was more depressing. Why had Lynn lied?

ELEVEN

"You look tired," Rona said.

"Flying half-way across the country and getting home at midnight will do that to you."

"Have a cup of coffee," Harry volunteered, pointing to the small pot on a hotplate in the corner of his office. "The caffeine will perk you up."

"No offense, but I think I'll pass on your sludge today."

Harry looked hurt. "I don't think my coffee is so bad. Besides, I'm using a new blend I picked up in a shop in Traverse City over the weekend."

"Was the shop having a going out of business sale?" Pete asked, winking at Rona.

"No, wise guy, they were selling a special blend that was flying off the shelves. Coffee buffs from all over the area were there snapping it up left and right. I was damn lucky to get a few packages."

Pete relented and said, "Okay, I'll try some." He filled a mug and took a sip, then another. "This *is* better than your normal stuff," he said. "It might help, though, if you'd wash that pot of yours now and then."

"Hey, friend, I rinse that pot every morning. You don't want to use a lot of soap on coffee pots because it leaves a film and ruins the taste of the coffee."

Pete shot Rona another glance. She had an amused look on her face, but also seemed impatient to hear about his trip to Seattle. Pete continued to sip his coffee.

"Well," Harry said, smoothing the fringe of hair that ringed his head, "are you going to tell us what you learned or are you going to keep us sitting here all day? Some of us have day jobs, you know."

Pete took another sip of coffee and looked at Rona and then back at Harry. "I learned only one thing that matters," he said. "Our lady friend was a liar."

Harry sat with a blank look. "What does that mean?" he asked after a long moment.

"She lied to us about everything," Pete said. He proceeded to tell them about his conversation with Jimi and how Lynn had been living with a man for two years and was seeing him before that. Then he pulled out the address book he found in Bartholome's apartment and flipped it on the desk in front of Harry. "If she had children, don't you think they'd be in here? All three of us are in that book, but there's no mention of her alleged daughter in Seattle or alleged son in Los Angeles."

Harry and Rona sat speechless. After a few moments, Harry reached for the address book and paged through it. When he was finished, he laid the book on the desk again.

"You said Lynn was living with a man," Rona said, sounding hesitant to get into the subject. "Did you find out anything about him?"

"According to the rental agent, his name is Gilbert Bartholome. I guess he's in some kind of international business. Lynn apparently was helping him. She had two of everything — passports, driver's licenses, the whole ball of wax. In Seattle, she went by the name Laura Mati for some reason."

No one spoke for a minute. Then Pete asked Rona, "When you first met Lynn, was she traveling to Seattle a lot?"

"Now and then," Rona answered, "To see her daughter."

"To see her daughter," Pete repeated disgustedly.

Rona's eyes flicked toward Harry and then back to Pete. She said almost in self-defense, "She hadn't been out there for months when we introduced you. I thought the crisis with her daughter was over."

"She doesn't have a daughter, Rona."

"I know it looks that way now, but back then …"

Pete shook his head disgustedly and shoved his empty coffee mug to one side. "I guess it explains why she didn't want me to come to Seattle to see her, doesn't it?"

As if to ease the awkward silence that followed Pete's comment, Harry said, "While you were gone, I heard something interesting. The feds are now involved in the Arne Breit case."

"Really?" Pete said, only half paying attention.

"Cap told me, but I'm not supposed to know." Cap was Ernie Capwell, the senior deputy in the sheriff's department who'd been frozen out of everything meaningful by Sheriff Richter because he suspected him of being the one who leaked information about what was going on in the department.

"The more investigators the merrier," Pete said. "Maybe Richter will learn a thing or two from the feds." He stood to leave.

"I'll start arranging a memorial service," Rona said.

"It's in your hands," Pete said.

■ ■ ■

Pete caught up with his e-mails and scanned the two issues of the *Traverse City Record-Eagle* that had arrived while he was gone. As always, he checked the sports page first. There was seemingly endless spring training news about the Detroit Tigers, but nothing about the Chicago Cubs. The "Transactions" column didn't even list the players the Cubs had cut to get down to the regular season roster. He sighed, gave the rest of the papers the once-over, and tossed them in the box that served as his recycling bin.

He propped his feet on his desk and stared out at the bay. He had plenty of time to think about things on the flight back from Seattle and his conclusion reinforced what he had already realized. It would have been easier to put Lynn Hawke out of his mind again if he'd just learned of her death in an automobile accident and not seen her body in the morgue. And if he hadn't learned of her duplicity. When he'd gotten involved in investigations in the past, it was usually to see that justice was done. Lynn Hawke's death was different; there was a personal element to it.

Pete called Emory Bond. "Sheriff, it's Pete Thorsen. I've been out of town for a few days and was wondering if you'd reached any conclusions about Lynn Hawke's vehicle."

"Your timing is good," Bond said. "I spoke to the mechanic this morning. He hasn't prepared a written report yet, but he told me he found no evidence of tampering and no serious malfunctions. Nothing with the brakes or the steering mechanism or any other component that would lead to loss of control of the vehicle. He said he didn't find any problem with the seat belt or the air bags, either. It's an older vehicle, and I guess that sometimes affects the air bags, although the manufacturers deny it."

"It sounds like you intend to classify Lynn Hawke's death as an accident."

"That's all we can do," Bond said. "With the caveat that what caused the vehicle to go into a skid is unclear. We continue to believe that the vic either fell asleep at the wheel or lost control for some other reason in the slippery conditions, but that's just conjecture. We can't see any other possibilities."

"And after thinking about it, you don't feel the two driver's licenses and the fact Lynn must have been on the Leelanau Peninsula during the ice storm for some purpose are reasons to look into it further?"

"As I told you before, those circumstances certainly raise questions, but without evidence linking them to her accident, I don't see what more we can do."

"When I was in Seattle, I found out that the guy Lynn was living with disappeared right after the accident. Does that help?"

"Tell me a little more."

Pete gave him an abridged version of what he'd discovered on his trip to Seattle.

"If we can establish that Bartholome was in our area the night of the accident, we might have something. Do you have proof that he was?"

"No, just the opposite. It looks like he left Seattle *after* the accident occurred."

"Then I don't see a connection between him and the accident."

When he was off the telephone with Bond, he removed the scrap of paper with a 231 number from his wallet and dialed the number. His call rang and rang and didn't go to voicemail. He hung up.

His last call was to Angie DeMarco to talk her into doing another favor for him. Besides being his successor as managing partner of their law firm and a close friend, Angie had kept up her contacts with people she knew in law enforcement from her days as a prosecutor. He'd drawn on those contacts in the past.

"This is the Stud of the North," he said, using a nickname he'd previously given himself in jest that he knew Angie would remember, "calling to chat and ask a favor."

"Let's take the favor first, Mr. Stud. My reaction to that will determine whether I want to chat with you or not."

"This is a little awkward," Pete said.

"Oh goodie. I can almost see you squirming right now."

"Remember two summers ago when I was caught up in that Cara Lane case?"

"Sure," Angie replied. "How could I forget? One of your bimbos up north drank too much lake water and a deputy sheriff was pounding on your door and accusing you of over-serving her."

"Something like that. Anyway, there's another woman up here that I took out a few times and ..."

Angie interrupted and said, "Oh spare me, Pete. You know, it's time for you to become monogamous and settle down with a good woman who'll take care of you. I'm available for consultation if you ever live up to your promise and come to Chicago for a quiet one-on-one dinner."

Pete forced a laugh and didn't bite on her innuendo. He continued, "Anyway, the woman was killed in an automobile accident and I'm trying to check out her boyfriend. Don't worry, I'm not a suspect or anything."

"I think I'm beginning to get the drift. This unnamed woman threw you over for some other guy and now you want to check him out. Do I have it right? What's this called, *post mortem* revenge?"

Angie was obviously at the top of her game today and he was ready to run up the white flag to get what he wanted.

"You certainly have a fertile imagination," he replied with a sigh. "No, nothing as dramatic as what you're suggesting. There's just something screwy about the guy and I'd like to find out about his background."

"And just how do you propose to do that?"

"I have a can of shave gel he used. Could you ask one of your friends at Chicago PD to lift his prints from the can and run them through their computer to see if anything pops up?"

"What do you do up there?" Angie asked. "Follow people around and pick up their water bottles and cans of shave gel so you can investigate them?"

"I was right about the guy with the water bottle, wasn't I?" he said.

"Okay," Angie said. "How are you going to get this shave gel can to me? I'd like to get the details out of the way so we can talk about compensation."

"I'll overnight it to you. And as far as compensation is concerned, how about the usual? Dinner at Gibson's the next time I'm in Chicago. And of course, all the Pinot Noir you can drink."

"Is one of those gooey chocolate desserts included in your bribe?"

"Any dessert you want, love."

"Oh, I love it when you talk dirty to me, Mr. Stud. Now let me bring you up to date on what's been happening at your old shop."

He felt run through the ringer after he was off the phone with Angie. He took a few minutes to recoup his energy and then tried the 231 number again. Same result.

TWELVE

The telephone rang while Pete was struggling with the lead for his first article for *The Fjord Herald*. His caller ID showed an unknown number. He was tempted to ignore it, but since he was experiencing writer's block, he thought a break might do him good. "Pete Thorsen," he said.

"Mr. Thorsen, this is Special Agent Keegan Harris from Homeland Security. Am I catching you at a bad time?"

Homeland Security? Pete thought. *What was this?* "No," he said slowly, "it's okay. Go ahead."

"I'm in your neighborhood," Harris said. "Do you have some free time this afternoon? I'd like to stop and talk to you. It shouldn't take more than an hour."

"Is this about Arne Breit?"

"Yes," she said, sounding mildly surprised. "How did you know?"

"His death is big news in a small town. A rumor around town is that the federal government is involved in the investigation."

"A murder is big news in any town, Mr. Thorsen."

"I'm not sure what I can tell you that will help with your investigation," Pete said. "I didn't know Arne that well."

"Detective Tessler, who I believe you know, says you've done legal work for Mr. Breit. We're talking to everyone who knew him."

Pete glanced at his desk calendar which was as free of appointments as the March beaches were free of sun worshippers. "Okay," he said, "what time?"

"Two o'clock work for you?"

"Two would be fine. I'm on Main Street, just down from …"

"I know where your office is, Mr. Thorsen. I'll see you at two."

At the time Harry raised the federal involvement in the case, Pete viewed it as just a ploy to get him off his high horse about Lynn's deceit. In retrospect, he was glad he'd heard the scuttlebutt before the Special Agent called; he didn't like to be surprised. He dialed Harry's number to see if he could provide more information.

"Harry McTigue here," he answered. "All the news from Up North that's fit to print."

"Some people might argue with that."

"Ha!" Harry said. "Show me a weekly that turns out a better product than we do."

"You've got me there. When I was in your office yesterday, you said that the feds are involved in the Arne Breit murder investigation. Anything else you can tell me?"

"Nope," Harry said. "Just reporting what I heard. That's what reporters do. Report the news. In this case, report it confidentially to an audience of one."

"I just got a call from Special Agent Keegan Harris of Homeland Security. She's coming to see me at two this afternoon."

"Really?"

"Joe Tessler gave her my name."

"What does she think you can tell her that she doesn't already know?"

"No idea. I already warned her that I don't know that much about Arne. It'll be a short meeting."

"Don't you have to be a little careful? You lawyers have that confidentiality thing with clients, don't you?"

"We do, but I don't see how that would be an issue here. The allegations and the outcome of the assault case, which I assume is one of the things she wants to talk about, are public knowledge."

"You told me Arne admitted he did it."

"I never told you that."

"You as much as told me. When I asked you off the record whether Arne was really guilty of assaulting that guy, you gave me that lopsided grin of yours."

"There's nothing in our professional code of ethics that governs the kind of grins a lawyer can use."

"Maybe she wants to question you about other things."

"Could be. I don't know."

Harry was silent for a few moments. Then he said, "You're a lawyer. What kind of federal crime do you think they suspect Arne of?"

"I haven't the foggiest. Last I heard, it wasn't a federal offense to keep an undersized salmon."

"If you like, I can call Cap and try to get more information."

"No," Pete replied, "I'll know soon enough. Want to grab a bite to eat before I meet with the forces of righteousness?"

■ ■ ■

Pete spent a half-hour clearing off his side chairs and tidying up the rest of his office in anticipation of his guest's arrival. When he finished, he surveyed the room with a critical eye. The walls were bare except for a pair of pastels he'd hung before he went to Seattle, but looking at them now, he wasn't sure that even they were in the right place. His law certificates, three watercolors of local scenes, including one by Lynn Hawke, and a large framed photograph of Julie on the soccer field still rested against the walls.

His office at his law firm in Chicago was always a showpiece with a minimum of mess and clutter. Books were shelved, walls were adorned with art and professional certificates, the papers on top of his desk and credenza were stacked in neat piles. And there, he really didn't have to worry about his office's appearance because he had a spectacular view of Millennium Park that drew a visitor's eyes from the moment she walked in. And if the park didn't command a visitor's attention, farther out there was Lake Michigan with fascinating ice formations in the winter and scores of sailboats and other vessels in the warm weather months. His Frankfort office was more modest, but at least it had a nice view of Betsie Bay with its outlet to Lake Michigan.

Promptly at 2:00 p.m., he heard the outer door to his two-room office suite open. He rose from his desk chair, hitched up his jeans, and headed out to greet his Homeland Security guest. She was standing with her back to him unwinding a long purple scarf from her neck and taking off her white quilted parka. She hung both on the clothes tree, fluffed her curly dark hair, and placed her hands on her face.

"Chilly out there, huh?" he said.

Her cheeks were flecked with red. "The wind," she said, patting her cheeks again. Her penetrating green eyes looked unusually vibrant above her rosy cheeks. She stepped toward him and extended her right hand in a businesslike gesture. "Keegan Harris, Mr. Thorsen." She fished her badge and an identification card from her purse and showed them to him.

She took him up on his offer of coffee and cradled the mug in both hands and wrapped her fingers around it as though soaking up its warmth.

"By the way, everyone calls me Keegan."

"Isn't there a professional golfer with that name?"

"There is," she said. "Keegan Bradley. I get razzed all the time. You've got a boy's name."

"Must get irritating after a while."

"I don't mind. I tell everyone that the golfer must have stolen the name from me because I had it first. Actually, it's pretty simple. Keegan was my fraternal grandmother's maiden name. My father liked the name so that's how I wound up with it."

Pete smiled and nodded.

Keegan glanced around his office and added, "Nice space. I'll bet it's interesting to watch the boats come and go during warm weather."

"The finest view Frankfort has to offer," he replied, grinning. "Different from my old digs in Chicago which looked down on the Lake Michigan waterfront, but still a respectable view."

"Chicago is a beautiful city."

"Have you ever been there in the winter?"

"Many times."

"Then you know about what we call The Hawk. It comes out of the north and cuts through you like a saber slashing into the enemy during a cavalry charge. I was born in the wilds of northern Wisconsin where temperatures can get pretty brutal, but I've never been colder than when I walked from Union Station to my office in January."

A faint smile creased her face. "Let's see," she said, "Sears & Whitney for twenty years. Corporate lawyer who got bored with what he was doing. Moved north. Likes to get in the local sheriff's hair when there's been a crime he thinks isn't being investigated properly. Writes about his Norwegian heritage."

"My, my. You've been doing your homework." His old boss with the army's CID always said there were two kinds of people in the world. Gathers who collected every scrap of information no matter how inconsequential it might seem at the time and then sifted and winnowed it after they had everything, and those who focused only on what was in front of them. It looked like he'd met a fellow gatherer.

"It's my job," she said. "But in this case, I just talked to Detective Tessler who told me everything I needed to know."

Pete smiled sheepishly and said, "Maybe you got a skewed point of view."

"Actually, he was quite complimentary. But I'm sure you're busy so I won't waste your time. Can we talk about Arne Breit?"

"I have a feeling you already know more about him than I do."

"Maybe, but I understand you represented him so let's see what you can add."

"I think Arne regarded me as his lawyer, but I only actively represented him in one matter."

"I know about the assault case against him for roughing up that guy in his charter party, so I'd like to talk about other things. Starting with his friends. What can you tell me about them?"

"Not much. Arne was a jolly guy who looked like he should be running a *bierstube* in Bavaria. He seemed to know everyone in town, but I'm not sure who his real friends were. He was divorced and hung around the bars a lot when he wasn't working. I can't tell you much beyond that."

"He liked to gamble I understand."

Pete just shrugged and shook his head.

Keegan refilled her coffee mug, and when she sat down again, said, "You don't know anything about his gambling activities?"

"I really don't," Pete said.

"I'm told he was a fixture at the casinos in Manistee and Suttons Bay."

"Lots of people go to the casinos," Pete said. "Including some senior ladies I know."

"Mr. Breit didn't go there to play the nickel slots."

"If I had to guess, I'd say you're inferring that he had a gambling problem. Do you think that had something to do with his murder?"

"Maybe. Money is behind a lot of crime."

"I agree, but I thought gambling was regulated by the states. Even if he had a gambling problem, the casinos in Manistee and Suttons Bay are both in Michigan the last time I checked. He wouldn't have to cross state lines to get there. Plus, Homeland Security doesn't get involved in gambling activities, does it?"

"Not usually."

"And Arne never struck me as a terrorist."

"Terrorism isn't the reason we're investigating his murder, but I'd prefer not to get into the details of our case."

"Now you have my interest piqued."

"You'll have to put your interest on hold until this is over," she said. "Getting back to Arne Breit, do you know anything about his travels?"

"In what respect?"

"For example, was he gone for periods of time?"

Pete thought about her question for a few moments and said, "When you say gone, do you mean overnight or for a week?"

"Two or three days, let's say."

"I know he marketed his charter business both as half-day outings and longer trips. On his longer trips, I assume he was away overnight or maybe even for a couple of days. That's just a guess. The guy who owns the Port City Marina might be able to tell you more."

"I'm seeing the marina owner tomorrow. If you don't know anything about Mr. Breit's travels, I assume you don't know anything about where he went or the people who went with him?"

"I really don't," Pete said.

"There's usually a motive for murder. Jealousy, passion, hatred, money, a business rivalry. Can you think of anyone who might have wanted Arne Breit dead? Anything he ever said, or that you might have heard from others for that matter, that raised a question in your mind?"

"Not really. Someone once called him affable Arne. I never associated him with any of the emotions you just described."

"Not even money?"

"That's a leading question. Your gambling question is, too. Are you suggesting Arne might have had problems that none of us knew about?"

"I'm not suggesting anything. I'm just trying to stimulate your thought processes in hopes you might remember something."

"I'll think about it, but nothing occurs to me offhand."

"Did Arne have partners in his charter business?"

"I don't think so. He owned the boats himself as far as I'm aware."

"No disputes with business partners you know of that might constitute a motive?"

"Not that I know of."

"How about conflicts with other people?"

"Arne probably had minor dust-ups with a few people — like the guy in his fishing party — but nothing particularly serious that I know of."

"I understand that the guy he allegedly roughed up bad-mouthed Mr. Breit for a year after. It sounds like he held a grudge, doesn't it?"

Pete stared at her in amazement. "Why are you wasting your time interviewing me? You already know everything I know and more."

"I didn't start working this case this afternoon," Harris said.

"Apparently not. But let me ask you something. The sheriff thinks Arne's death was due to a robbery that went bad. Your questions seem to suggest it was something else."

"It could have been a robbery."

"But you don't believe it was."

"I haven't decided what I believe or don't believe. I'm just investigating at this stage."

"If you thought it was just a robbery gone bad, though, you wouldn't be investigating, would you?"

Keegan Harris said, "Probably not. But to get back to my question, you're saying you can't think of anyone with a motive to kill Arne Breit, am I right?"

"No one," Pete said. "But I'd like to ask you another question about the robbery theory. Arne was killed by two shots to the head, I understand. That doesn't seem like something the garden variety robber would do if he were panicked."

"Not bad for a guy who's been away from this sort of thing for thirty years."

Pete suddenly felt like he was sitting in front of Special Agent Keegan Harris in just his skivvies. Her comment suggested she even knew about his years working for Major Baumann. "Do you know my mother's maiden name, too?" he asked.

She smiled and said, "Not yet. But you're not the only one who thinks that the way Mr. Breit was killed doesn't look like a robbery. To be fair, even your sheriff is starting to look beyond that theory."

"You have an idea of who might be behind the killing, don't you?" Pete asked slowly.

"Nothing I'm going to share with you."

"What a surprise," Pete said.

Harris didn't respond to his sarcasm, but instead went on to her next question. "I realize it's a little out of your bailiwick, but do you know a man named Hank Sims? He runs charter boats out of a marina in Traverse City."

Pete thought for a minute. Then he shook his head and said, "I don't think so."

"Arne Breit never mentioned him?"

"Not to me." Then Pete remembered something possibly relevant to what she'd asked before. "Going back to your previous question, there's a guy who used to work for Arne. I understand there was friction between them now and then."

"You're referring to Kurt Romer, I assume."

Pete laughed and said, "Yes, I'm referring to Kurt Romer. Two years ago, I was looking into a drowned woman's death for a client and asked Arne about him. He gave me some background on Romer and told me about a disagreements he'd had with him over his tardiness for work in the mornings."

"But he wasn't involved in your case."

"Not as it turned out, but Romer's drug activities surfaced during the course of things and he was sent off on a holiday for a couple of years courtesy of the federal government. I think he's still in prison."

"He's been out for two months."

Pete tightened his lips and nodded. That he wasn't aware of. "Okay, well Arne didn't have anything to do with his drug conviction anyway and the other stuff seems minor."

"Last question," Keegan Harris said. "Did Mr. Breit ever consult you about visa and immigration matters?"

"No," Pete said. "That I'd remember. Why do you ask?"

"Just wondering. On his longer charter fishing trips, I understand he'd sometimes cross into Canadian waters and stay overnight in a Canadian port. I thought he might have consulted you on procedure, the need for passports, things like that."

"It never came up. I could have helped him with that, too. We did a fair amount of visa and immigration law at my old firm in Chicago."

"But he never consulted you on those matters?"

"Never."

Keegan set her coffee mug on the desk and rose to her feet. She handed him a card with the telephone number scratched out and a 231 number written in. "You can reach me at this number if you think of anything you believe may be relevant to our conversation. Feel free to call or leave a message any time."

He followed her to the outer office and waited as she donned her parka and wrapped the bulky scarf around her neck. She thanked him for his time and stepped into the wind and disappeared down the street. Pete stood there a few minutes, wondering. He didn't have the same personal stake in Breit's killing that he did in unraveling what happened to Lynn Hawke, but Keegan Harris' questions had ratcheted his curiosity up a notch.

THIRTEEN

Pete missed Sheriff Emory Bond's call because he was in the shower. When Pete called back, Bond told him that he'd made a final decision to classify Lynn Hawke's death as an accident.

"Will there be announcement?" Pete asked.

"It's up to the press. They reported our preliminary conclusion in the story that ran originally. It's up to them whether they want to do a follow-up saying we've confirmed that conclusion."

"How about the car?"

"It was totaled and might not be worth repairing given the age and all. We'll follow our usual procedure. We'll keep it in our yard for ninety days, and if a member of the family doesn't claim it, we'll dispose of it for parts and scrap. You might pass this information on to the family if you locate any of them. We'll also send written notices to the insurance company and to the address shown on Ms. Hawke's Michigan driver's license."

"Okay, thanks for keeping me informed."

"One more thing, Mr. Thorsen. When we were inspecting the vehicle, we found the vic's cell phone under the seat and some things in the glove box. Proof of insurance and other papers, a couple of small tools, that kind of thing. We'd like to turn this stuff over to someone in case we wind up junking the car."

Pete thought about it for a moment and said, "I have to be in Traverse City day after tomorrow. I'll swing by your office and pick it up. Leave everything in a box with my name on it."

■ ■ ■

Pete mulled over his final session with Dr. Jennifer Cui as he headed north on M-22. She didn't seem pleased when he told her, but the choice was his. It wasn't in his makeup to have a therapist as a permanent part of his life, and besides, the nightmares and binge drinking that had started after that night at the Colonel's house had subsided.

Dr. Cui implied in not-so-subtle terms that he was practicing denial and maybe he was, but it had worked pretty damn well for him up to this point. Understand the root causes of a problem and then map out a plan to control the consequences. That's the way he'd gotten through his unhappy childhood and the rough stretches of his life since then. What he was going through now was no different.

As he drove north toward Suttons Bay, he imagined what the roads must have been like the night of the ice storm. It was hard to believe that a driver, no matter how exhausted, could fall asleep at the wheel in those circumstances. More likely, her adrenaline would be pumping and her eyes would be glued to the road and she'd be clutching the steering wheel and creeping along because of the conditions. If she was on the roads at all, which he still couldn't understand.

Pete located the Sheriff's Office. Bond wasn't there, but a deputy found the box with his name scrawled on it. He signed for the box and was back on the highway in minutes, clutching his coat around his neck for warmth.

■ ■ ■

An e-mail from Kjersti was waiting for him when he got back to his office. It laid out the editorial schedule for the articles he was writing for *The Fjord Herald*. The needling last sentence asked how he enjoyed his lunch at the Copper Gate. He grinned and shot a response back saying that the food was good, but the décor was more sedate than he'd been led to believe.

Pete looked through the box he'd picked up at the sheriff's office. Lynn's cell phone was a flip model that was about five product generations behind. Like his, he thought approvingly. He knew he wouldn't find anything, but he checked the directory feature of the phone just in case. He found nothing under H for Melissa Hawke or Richard Hawke. He also found nothing under the Ms for Melissa or the Rs for Richard.

The phone had an AT&T logo. That didn't mean that AT&T was the service provider, but it was a reasonable bet. He wondered if Lynn had made any calls the night of her accident. The cell had a low battery. His charger fit the phone, and while he was waiting for it to work, he looked up the AT&T number.

A half-hour later, he called AT&T on Lynn's cell, and after following several prompts, was pleased to get a live person. He explained what he wanted and spent another ten minutes being bounced from one department to another until he finally got hooked up with someone who could think for herself. He explained that Lynn Hawke had died in a car accident, that he was the attorney for the Hawke family, and that he wanted to settle her account with AT&T, but needed a final bill with a list of the calls Lynn had made since her last statement. He gave the woman Lynn's cell phone number and her Beulah address. As a back-up, he gave her the Seattle address.

He was in luck. The woman found the account and pointed out that since Lynn had a call package, he really didn't need the list of numbers she'd called in order to settle the account. She said she'd cancel service as of the current date and send a final statement. Pete had to shift gears and say that when he probated Lynn's estate, he'd have to file detailed disclosures with the probate court. Anticipating what some petty court clerk might require would save both of them time and energy in the long run.

They made common bond and the woman told Pete in elaborate detail what her family went through when her mother died. He professed sympathy. While talking, she was obviously working the system. She said she'd cancelled the account and would send a final statement with the call information to the mailing address they had on file for Lynn. That probably was Bartholome's apartment in Seattle. Pete had to persuade the woman that sending the statement there might delay matters for weeks as it bounced around in the mail. Finally, she agreed to fax the statement to him if he would furnish proof that he was the attorney for Lynn's estate.

Pete spent the next half-hour drafting a letter on his Michigan lawyer's letterhead summarizing what he'd told the woman. He attached a copy of a news story about Lynn's death and a photocopy of his business card. It was a self-serving package, but he hoped it would do the trick. He then faxed everything to the woman at AT&T.

Pete looked through the rest of the items in the box. He found nothing else of interest unless you were into needle-nosed pliers or felt you could talk Culver's into accepting a half-off certificate that was two years past its expiration date.

FOURTEEN

Angie DeMarco called the next morning. After needling him again about his sleazy female friends and reminding him for the twelfth time that she'd about used up her chits with her law enforcement contacts, she told him what the check of Gilbert Bartholome's fingerprints revealed.

"Your rival's birth name is Gilbert Luna, but he now goes by Gilbert Bartholome. I'm not sure when or why he changed his name. About twelve years ago, he was charged with forgery, but got off on a technicality. Three years later, he had new forgery charges against him that were dropped for lack of evidence. Lucky guy, huh? We couldn't find anything since that time."

"What was Bartholome charged with forging?"

"Financial instruments. He allegedly preyed on rich old spinsters."

"A con artist."

"This makes your day, huh? You knew he was a felon all along, didn't you?"

He laughed.

"Does your hussy girlfriend know about this?"

"She's dead, remember?"

"Oh, that's right. It's hard to keep your tangled relationships straight. You said you're not a suspect in this woman's death if I remember correctly."

"I'm not a suspect."

"If the woman's dead, why do you care about Bartholome's background?"

"To satisfy my curiosity." Pete knew if he volunteered any details, such as how Lynn had gone to lengths to conceal her relationship with him, he'd just be inviting another hour of interrogation.

"You really should stay out of these things," she said. "Have you ever considered moving back to Chicago and practicing law again? There are a lot of people around the firm who'd love to have you back."

"No, dear, that chapter of my life is behind me. I've proven I can do the big firm thing and make money. I've turned the page. I'm happy with where I am right now."

"Will you at least give me a chance to change your mind?"

With Angie, he could never tell what was innuendo and what was a sincere proposition. He'd long ago decided not to become romantically involved with her, but at the same time, valued her friendship. He said, "Sure, we'll discuss it at Gibson's as soon as The Hawk returns to its nest. Maybe sometime in April? I have to come down for my final meeting with the Executive Committee around that time."

They agreed on a date.

"That's chiseled in stone, right?"

"Chiseled in stone."

"If you fink out on me, I'm going to send Guido up to visit you."

When Pete was off the phone with Angie, he walked down to the beach and gazed out. It wasn't exactly beach weather, but the temperature was supposed to climb into the upper fifties in the afternoon. That was positively balmy compared to what they'd experienced in the past few weeks.

Pete wondered what Lynn saw in a guy like Bartholome. Or whether she knew about his past record as a forger. It seemed implausible that she wouldn't have known something after five years. That was a long time to conceal the past from a person you were involved with.

Two of his army surplus silhouette targets had fallen over during the winter. After repositioning them, he went inside to get his longbow. The bow had been made for him by an old craftsman in Norway named Ulf and he loved the feel and look of the smooth yew wood. He didn't hunt game, and in fact hadn't done any kind of hunting since he enlisted in the army, but in decent weather he liked to practice with the bow to stay in touch with his ancestors.

He drew the bowstring back to his right cheek several times to get the feel back after a winter off. When he felt ready, he nocked an arrow, drew the string back while he sighted along the arrow, and released. The arrow whistled through the air and grazed the closest silhouette and rattled into the trees. Winter rust, he told himself. He tried another arrow and this time it tore into the edge of the silhouette's shoulder. Better. He reloaded and drilled the silhouette more toward the center this time. He nodded in satisfaction and shifted his aim to the intermediate silhouette. A clean miss with his first arrow. He nocked another arrow and tried again. It landed with a satisfying *Thunk!* He kept firing until he was out of arrows.

As he retrieved his arrows, he thought about Lynn Hawke and how everything about her was a lie except her prowess with a bow. One of the first things Harry had mentioned after he introduced them was that Lynn was a world-class archer who had been an alternate on the U.S. Olympic team. Pete witnessed her skill first hand when they practiced together. She plunked the silhouettes dead center virtually every time, including when she tried his longbow. She used a modern compound bow herself, but clearly admired Pete's bow which was the same as archers had used centuries earlier.

To spice up his practice sessions, Pete often visualized the faces of adversaries on the silhouettes. His former law partner, Marty Kral, had occupied that spot for years. Now Gilbert Bartholome replaced him. He'd never met Bartholome and had no idea what he looked like. He just knew he didn't like him and imagined a sinister face with the word "felon" below it.

He zeroed in on Bartholome. *"Thunk!"* A center hit. He grinned and nocked another arrow and let it fly. *"Thunk!"* Another solid hit. He shifted his aim to the intermediate silhouette. *"Thunk!"* The silhouette quivered when the arrow hit. He kept launching arrows until his supply was exhausted.

He once told Harry about his motivational practice technique. Harry was appalled and preached endlessly about how bloodthirsty the Vikings were and how they were never reliably civilized. Pete chuckled at the thought and wondered what he'd say if he knew Pete were using Lynn Hawke's boyfriend as his new motivational gimmick.

After three rounds, he'd had enough. He rubbed his hands together to restore some warmth, collected his arrows, and headed back to his cottage.

FIFTEEN

Pete was pleasantly surprised to find a fax from AT&T when he got to his office that afternoon. He had visions of the woman he'd talked to finding it necessary to go through twelve layers of bureaucracy and then being told that the company couldn't give out the requested information without DNA confirmation that Pete was related to the deceased and was on Lynn Hawke's account. The lure of immediate payment of the $76.95 monthly charge must have been too great for management to resist.

He sorted through the fax pages until he found the call list. It covered three pages. Most of the numbers were in the Seattle area, but on the day of her accident, it showed Lynn had made three calls to a number with a 231 area code. He checked the number against the one he'd taken from the corkboard in Bartholome's apartment. They were different.

Pete knew he could either go through a data broker to find the name of the person Lynn had called that night or he could call directly as he had with the other number. Pete opted for the direct approach again. If he struck out, he could always go back to a data broker.

He was about to dial the number on the AT&T call list and then stopped. His name would show up as the caller if the person at the other end had caller ID. That had also been his concern when he called the other number. He decided to call from Harry's office. Reporters called people and establishments all the time and it wouldn't raise questions.

Harry was hunched over his desktop computer pecking away at the keyboard when Pete walked in. Harry peered over his rimless half-glasses at him and his bushy eyebrows knit together. He said, "I was about to call you. I have a taste for a pulled-pork sandwich and thought we could go next door for lunch."

Pete glanced at the clock on the wall and said, "Its only 10:30 a.m."

"I didn't say right now. I thought we could go in a half-hour or so and beat the noon rush."

"Noon rush in March is seven people."

"Hey, I've seen a lot more than seven people in that place at lunch-time. A lot of the tradesmen come in and they plan ahead just like me. They like to come early to avoid the noon crowd too."

Pete resisted the temptation to say that all of the tradesmen in the county could show up at once and there'd still be ten tables open, but instead he said, "Okay, but first I have to make some calls. Do you mind if I use that phone?" He pointed toward the telephone on a desk in a vacant cubicle.

"What's the matter? Is your service out?"

"No, but with everyone having caller ID these days, I'd like to be able to hang up if I have to without disclosing my identity."

"Caller ID will show that the call came from my paper."

"I don't care about that."

Harry looked at Pete with narrowed eyes and said, "Oh, you don't care if a hang up call comes from my office? Why don't you want your own name to show up?"

Pete sighed and told Harry how he'd come into possession of Lynn Hawke's cell phone and that she'd made several calls to a 231 number shortly before her accident. He wanted to find out who she called.

Harry grunted. "Thorsen Investigations again, huh?"

"It's not an investigation. I'm just curious."

Harry shot him a look and waved toward the open desk and said, "Make yourself comfortable. Just don't bother me until it's time to leave for lunch. I have a newspaper to get out. And don't do anything to tarnish my paper's fine reputation."

Pete moved to the cubicle and dialed the 231 number. After three rings, an automated response came on with a message that said, "You've reached Conti Vineyards. If you know the number of the person you're calling, please enter the extension now. Otherwise, stay on the line and someone will assist you." This was working better than expected, he thought. No need to pay a data broker. In a few moments, a woman identified herself as Loretta and asked if she could help him.

"Harry McTigue," he said, "from *The Northern Sentinel.*" Pete was doodling on a note pad while he talked, but out of the corner of his eye he saw Harry's head snap up at the mention of his name. Pete raised his hand and signaled for him to remain quiet. "We're planning to run a series of articles on local wineries this summer," he continued, "and I was wondering if someone from Conti Vineyards would be interested in sitting for an interview with one of our reporters. We'd like to develop a profile of your place, maybe shoot some photographs, that kind of thing."

Harry had walked over and now stood within two feet of Pete. His ample belly was even closer. Judging from his pantomime, he was frantically trying to figure out what Pete was doing. Pete hushed Harry with another hand signal and swiveled his chair so his back was to him.

"Gee, that sounds exciting," Loretta said. "You'll have to talk to Mr. Conti, though. Should I see if he's available?"

"Thanks, but not right now," Pete intoned. "We're just trying to get an expression of preliminary interest from several vineyards. If you think Mr. Conti would be interested, one of our reporters will call him back in a few days. Does he have a direct extension?"

"Yes," Loretta said breathlessly, "he's on number one. Number one for the boss, get it?"

"Very clever," Pete said, trying to be serious. "I'd appreciate it if you would tell him *The Northern Sentinel* called and we'll call back."

"I will," Loretta gushed. "Do you think you might want some of our employees in your photographs?"

"Almost certainly," Pete said. "I have to run, Loretta. I have another call coming in. Please tell Mr. Conti we'll be in touch with him."

"What are you doing?" Harry sputtered as Pete put the phone down. "I'm not planning any articles about local wineries!"

"Calm down," Pete said. "I'll explain everything over lunch. I'll even buy to make it up to you. But first, I have to make another call."

"You aren't going to make any other promises about the *Sentinel's* editorial content, are you?" he asked, looking at Pete suspiciously.

"No, that was a one-shot thing," Pete assured him.

Harry continued to hover close as Pete dialed the second number with a 231 area code. The phone rang and rang with no answer from a machine or a live human being. Well, one for two wasn't bad.

Pete showed Harry the scrap of paper with the telephone number written on it. "Would you say that's a man's handwriting or a woman's?"

Harry studied the number for a while and said, "A man's. Women have better handwriting than this. Where did you get this?"

"I found it in Bartholome's apartment in Seattle. I'm trying to find out whose number it is."

■ ■ ■

Dinghy's was at most a quarter full when they walked in. They opted for a booth and both ordered the pulled pork sandwich. Harry added a large bag of barbecue chips, making a big to-do about how he would share with Pete.

"So Lynn called Conti Vineyards three times that night?" Harry asked.

"Yes, three times. Then she drove, what, forty plus miles in the worst ice storm this area has experienced in years? It seems clear she was headed for Conti's place in view of the calls and where she was when the accident occurred."

Harry furled his brow and after a moment said, "If she was headed for Conti Vineyards, wouldn't it have been shorter to take M-22?"

"Maybe," Pete answered. "But if she was coming from her house, which I think she was, she was already close to U.S. 31. Maybe she also thought the driving conditions would be better if she went through Traverse City and then drove north. The way M-22 winds around, it can be bad enough even in good weather if you go the other way."

"I see what you mean," Harry said. "But I can't understand why Lynn would be going to Conti Vineyards late at night. Even if the place was open during the day, it would have been long closed by then."

"She had to be meeting with someone who works there, don't you think?"

"Like who?"

Pete shrugged. "It could just be a coincidence with calls and the direction she was traveling."

"No, no. I agree that Conti was the likely destination based on everything you've said."

They sat quietly and ate their pulled-pork sandwiches. Harry offered the chips to Pete when he ripped the top open and then kept the bag on his side of the table with the opening pointed toward him. He alternated between taking a bite of his sandwich and devouring a handful of chips.

He gestured at Pete with his half-eaten sandwich and said, "I still don't understand why you had to tell that woman we plan to run feature articles on the vineyards. We sometimes run that kind of stuff in the summer months when the tourists are here because they've come to expect coverage from my paper that gives them ideas for fun outings. But I haven't decided what to run this year. Now you've boxed me in. And you could have made up the name of some fictitious reporter rather than passing yourself off as me."

"Sorry, I had to think fast when the woman answered. I didn't know I'd get a vineyard when I called that number. What else could I say, that I was calling to check on whose phone number Lynn called the night of her accident? Besides, what better way to find out about Conti Vineyards than to interview the boss?"

Harry finished off the rest of the chips, and when he was done chewing, he asked, "Who's at the other number we were just looking at?"

"I don't know. That's why I was calling."

Harry gave Pete a look and said, "You can't drop this, can you? I thought you told me the sheriff concluded that Lynn's death was an accident."

"Correction. He said they found no evidence that it was anything other than an accident."

"Same thing," Harry replied dismissively.

"No it's not. Aren't you the guy who preached to me a while back about the great inquiring mind you have? Don't you wonder why Lynn lied to all of us, why she moved to Seattle, why her live-in boyfriend split when he found out she was dead, why she was back here driving around in an ice storm in the middle of the night, and what connection Conti Vineyards has to this whole affair?"

Harry waved a hand and said, "You can call it anything you want, but you're investigating. Why don't you get back to your writing and let this stuff go?"

"I am writing. I'm just able to do more than one thing at the same time."

Pete was signing the credit card statement to pay for their lunch when Harry added, "I can understand your investigations in the past, but this one? Are you sure it's not your Scandinavian pride boiling over because Lynn crapped on you?"

Pete watched the ski race rerun on the flat-screen television over the bar for a minute and said quietly, "She didn't crap on me."

"I'm using the same expression you used when you told Rona and me about the conversation you had with your daughter."

"I didn't say 'crapped.' I said 'dumped.'"

"Same thing."

"No it isn't. 'Crapped' sounds worse."

Harry rolled his eyes.

Pete looked at the television again for a while and then said, "Did I tell you Bartholome has a criminal record?"

Harry's eyes widened. "How did you find that out?"

Pete told him how Angie had had one of her police department contacts lift Bartholome's fingerprints from the can of shave gel and run them through the national crime data base.

"Do you think Lynn knew this?"

"No idea."

"Hmm," Harry murmured.

"Your next edition comes out in two days, doesn't it?" Pete asked.

Harry nodded.

"How would you like to start listing me as a contributing editor — unpaid of course — and show my name in that little box where you list the publisher, the editor and other people associated with the paper? You wouldn't be fabricating anything because I've already written a couple of pieces for your rag."

"Now you've got me confused."

"I'm going to try to interview this Mr. Conti for the article you're going to run on his vineyard. If he checks the editorial information, I'd like to be listed as a contributing editor."

Harry's face brightened. "That's a great idea," he said. "It helps me, too, because it makes my staff look bigger. *And,* it solves another problem I have. You know the busybody who contributed a couple of crappy pieces on that Archibald Jones guy who was behind the debacle that drained half the lake? He's been pestering me to name him a contributing editor, too. I could list both of you."

"My name would appear first, though, right?"

Harry grunted. "No doubt about that. Maybe I could list the cleaning lady second and the Archie Jones freak last."

After lunch, Pete continued his efforts to find the name of the person behind the telephone number he'd found at Bartholome's apartment. He used his office phone to call because he'd cancelled Lynn's cell service.

For the third time, no one answered and the call didn't bounce to an answering machine.

He checked the website of the firm he'd used to try to find the cell phone numbers of Lynn's nonexistent children and found they provided telephone break services as well. He spent ten minutes figuring out how to use that aspect of the site and plugged in the number.

Then he forgot about Lynn Hawke for the afternoon and turned to his research for the articles for *The Fjord Herald*. At 5:00 p.m., he checked his e-mail and saw the response. The phone number was registered to a place called The Peg at a Maple City, Michigan address. Maple City was a wide spot in the road on the Leelanau Peninsula and he hadn't been through there in years.

SIXTEEN

He was late getting to his office the next morning, and when he arrived, he found a note from Brenda Lyons asking him to see her. She looked up from her computer screen when he knocked and waved him in.

"Just a minute, Pete. I'm finishing the copy for a new listing." She pecked away at her keyboard for a while longer and then hit the print button.

"There," she said, handing him a sheet of paper. "How does this look?"

He scanned the sheet. It was filled with superlatives in typical real estate-speak. "Very nice," he said. "I'd buy the place if I were in the market for a new house. I particularly like the part about the house having been designed with gracious entertaining in mind yet perfect for retired couples with grandchildren as well."

Brenda smiled. "You didn't know a house can serve multiple functions, did you?"

"Not until I read your listing sheet."

"Guess what?" she said, holding up both arms and clinching her fists in triumph. "I think I have a buyer for Lynn's house. This couple from

Detroit has been renting up here for years. They saw the house yesterday and loved it."

"It's a nice place."

"They're going to let me know this afternoon. I told them about Lynn's accident. They feel terrible, of course, but I guess it makes it easier for them. They don't have to deal with a seller who needs ninety days to get out."

"When would they like to close?"

"Would you believe the end of this month? They have cash and don't need to jump through the mortgage hoops."

"Wow," Pete said.

"That raises the thing I want to talk to you about. I have two men who can move Lynn's furniture into a storage unit, but I don't want to do that with her paintings and personal papers." Brenda looked at him hopefully and asked, "Could you store those things at your house? Temporarily, I mean?"

"I can't take them," he said without equivocation. "I bet Rona Martin has room at her house, though. She has that big Victorian and only two people live there."

"Do you think she'd do it?"

"Let's ask her."

Pete turned Brenda's phone around and dialed the number for Rona's restaurant, thinking that's where she was likely to be.

"Rona, it's Pete. I'm here with Brenda Lyons. Can I put you on the speaker?"

When they could all hear each other, Brenda explained that she had a hot potential buyer for Lynn Hawke's house and a very tight closing timetable if an offer came through as expected. She asked whether Rona could temporarily store Lynn's paintings and personal papers while they figured out what to do with them in the long term.

Rona didn't respond at first, then she said, "Pete, do you have room at your cottage?"

"I already told Brenda that I can't take the stuff."

Rona was quiet again and then said, "I guess I can take them. Pete, could you help with the papers, though? I trust your judgment more than mine about what to keep and what to throw out."

"I'll help," Pete said.

"When do we have to have the things out?"

"Soon," Brenda said. "Assuming we get a contract. I'll know this afternoon."

■ ■ ■

Pete followed the walk along the bay until he came to the park. To avoid the mud, he cut over to Main Street and continued on until it intersected with M-22. He turned right on M-22 and walked along the shoulder. A dirty pickup with a snow blade still attached approached and as a courtesy moved into the opposite lane to avoid crowding Pete. The driver waved as he passed.

The walk had produced body heat and Pete lowered his jacket zipper half-way. Tight bundles of white dotted many of the bushes along the road and bided their time until the first truly warm day. Then they'd break free from nature's restraints and decorate the bushes with white blossoms and pink blossoms to announce the arrival of spring.

He stopped when he came to the Port City Marina. A late-model Toyota Tundra with the marina logo painted on its side was parked in front of the office. It was the only vehicle in the lot. He didn't see anyone outside and there was no police tape cordoning off the area where they'd found Arne Breit's body.

Pete knocked on the office door. A paunchy middle-aged man with a neatly-trimmed beard that wrapped around his fleshy face opened the door. He pushed his grease-smudged yellow Arctic Cat cap back on his head and said with a friendly smile, "Howdy stranger. Can I help you?"

"I was passing by," Pete said, "and thought I'd stop and ask what your schedule is for the spring."

"Well don't stand there in the cold. C'mon in and I'll check the calendar."

The man hooked his thumbs in his red suspenders and stared at the Bass-O-Rama calendar behind his desk. Then he gazed at the ceiling as though seeking help from above. "I reckon we'll open about the middle of April," he said. "I'll have to verify that with the rest of management, of course. You have a boat here?"

"Not yet, but I was told that Arne Breit's boats are going to be put up for sale. I might bid on one of them."

"Umm," the man murmured, "I haven't heard about no auction. Did you know Arne?"

"Not well, but I knew him. His death came as a real shocker."

"I'm with you, friend. Who in hell would want to do Arne in? He was friends with everybody."

"Yeah," Pete said, "a good guy. I represented him a few years back when he had a problem with a guy in one of his charter groups."

"Are you an attorney-at-law?" the man asked, peering at him with fresh interest.

"I am," Pete replied.

"Well, I shore am glad to meet you," the man said, extending his right hand. "Yancy McGee here. My friends call me Chubs. I'm the assistant manager of this here marina." His chest puffed out a little more.

Pete accepted his hand and said, "Pete Thorsen."

Chubs stood looking at Pete with a grin that threatened to leave fresh creases in his weathered skin. "You didn't ask me about my nickname. Most folks do."

"I assumed it was from your childhood or something," Pete said. "A lot of people have catchy nicknames."

Chubs continued to grin. "You know what a chub is?"

"It's a fish, isn't it?"

"You must be a country boy yourself. Yeah, it's a fish. Rivers mostly. Dang good eating, too, if you catch 'em in the spring when the water's still cold. When I was a boy, the Elks Club had a fishing contest for all the kids in town. I caught fourteen chubs that day. No one else was even close. I think the next highest kid caught eight and he was three years older than me. That's something, huh? People have called me Chubs ever since."

"That's a good story. You're from this area then?"

"Bred, born and raised. How about you? I don't recall seeing you around. Course Frankfort has gotten so big I don't know all the folks like I once did."

"I have a place on Crystal Lake," Pete said. "I moved up here full-time after I hung things up at my old law firm in Chicago. My office is on Main Street." He found one of his business cards and handed it to Chubs.

Chubs studied the card for a long time, then looked up at Pete and said, "I been thinking about going to law school myself. I tried to talk to that old attorney-at-law who has an office in Beulah, but he don't give me the time of day. It's nice to make the acquaintance of a man I can finally talk to about these things."

Pete nodded. "What law school are you considering?"

A crafty look crept over Chub's face. "Oh, I ain't thinking about one of them places with a fancy building and all. I been in touch with this school that will let me take all of my courses by mail, or if you're really up-to-date, by e-mail. They call them places correspondence schools," he said with the aura of a man who possessed a carefully-guarded secret. "And," he added, "here's the best part." He leaned closer to Pete and said in a voice that was obviously intended to be heard only by a fellow man of the law, "They don't care if a person has one of them college degrees. I wouldn't have to quit my day job, neither."

"That sounds like the best of all worlds. But getting back to Arne Breit for a minute, did you know him well?"

"Shoot, I knew Arne for years. Ever since he started keeping his boats here. Good man, good man."

Pete nodded and was thinking about what else to ask Chubs when the assistant manager helped him out.

"We was both in the Car Ferry the night he was killed. Having a couple of beers, shooting the breeze. Then we spotted this hot babe. We moved in on her, you know, in kind of a pincer movement? Ol' Arne on one side and Chubs on the other, both giving her our best stuff. After a while, it was clear she was taking a real shine to me so Arne, being the gentleman he was, kind of faded from the picture. I tell you, if that babe had gone for him rather than me, Arne would still be alive this very day. Course, I had a leg up with her because of my executive position and all."

"Did you tell the sheriff this?"

Chubs looked put out. "They never asked."

"You could have volunteered the information."

"I thought of that, but shoot, then I would have had to involve the babe and everything. Besides, what could I tell the sheriff? I wasn't there when Arne caught it. I was planning my next move with Cora Lou."

"Cora Lou is the woman you were both talking to?"

"Yeah, I'll tell you Pete, ladies like her don't come along every day. She's got a way with herself, you know? Real looker, too. What them young folks call a full package."

"What kind of man was Arne?" Pete asked.

"Oh, real fine gentleman. He didn't have my gift of gab, but that don't mean he wasn't a good man. Recently, Arne started to worry me a little, though. He was different. Suspicious of everyone and all. What's that word, paranormal?"

"Paranoid."

"That's the word I was thinking about. Paranoid."

"In what way had he become paranoid?"

Chubs lowered his voice again. "He didn't like to talk about things anymore. Like he was afraid someone might overhear him. In fact, one night he told me he was concerned that the police had put some of them listening things in his house. He hardly ever used the telephone anymore, he told me, and he couldn't sleep because he was worried about what might be in his house. I guess he was afraid he might talk in his sleep or something."

"You're around here on a regular basis during the season, aren't you?"

"I'm here 24/7, Pete. That's why Port City has been taking business away from them other marinas. I like to think ol' Chubs is responsible for a lot of that. Service, service, service, that's my motto. Course this year, I might have to take a little more time off seeing as how Cora Lou's in the picture and all."

"If you've been around 24/7, as you say, you must know which boats are out on the water and which are in dock."

"I'll tell you Pete, I'm able to keep track of them things because I've got what they call a photograph memory. Once something is up here," he said, tapping his temple with a forefinger, "it don't leave. That's why I believe I'll make a crackerjack attorney-at-law."

"Arne made some longer trips in addition to his day-trips, didn't he?" picking up on Keegan Harris' line of questioning.

"He didn't used to. Until a couple of years ago, he ran short trips just like the rest of them charter boat guys. Then he started mixing in a few longer trips. A new strategy, he called it." Chubs' voice sank to a whisper again and he added, "He said he couldn't make enough money by just doing day trips and he had a lot of expenses with his boats and everything."

"I understand Arne liked to hit the casinos now and again."

"Shucks yes. He was a fun-loving guy. Plus he didn't have to worry about them listening things when he was at the casino. I taught him everything I know about blackjack. Let him in on my foolproof system and everything. You a gaming man, Pete?"

"Occasionally."

"I could teach you my system, too. If you want to go down to Little River or one of them other places some night, you just let me know. I tell you, my system can't fail. Casinos don't like to see me coming."

"That would be fun," Pete said. "Well, I've taken up enough of your time. It was really nice to meet you."

As he rose to leave, Chubs grabbed his arm and said, "Do you suppose I could buy you a couple of beers some night so you could tell me what an attorney-at-law does from day-to-day? That'll give me a leg up on those other yahoos I'll be competing with."

"Sure," Pete said, "let's see if we can find a time. Maybe in a month or two when my schedule settles down."

Chubs winked at him. "I'll ask Cora Lou to join us when our business talk is over. I'll tell you, Pete, she's fallen for me like a shit tumbles down an outhouse hole. I think you'll see why I'm so smitten with her." He winked again and cupped his hands in front of his chest. "She's got bazooms out to here, too."

On the way back to his office, Pete thought about what Chubs had told him about Arne Breit and how he'd become paranoid. His gambling activities were consistent with what Keegan Harris had told him, too, although with Chubs' knowledge of the gaming tables, Arne could only have been a big winner night after night.

He turned to finding out more about The Peg and was pleasantly surprised that the bar had its own website. The welcome page showed a rambling, low-slung structure with a purple exterior. Or maybe it was blue, he couldn't tell. The sign in front claimed that the establishment served the best food in the north and every beer and malt liquor ever brewed, and was decorated with a replica of a shoe peg.

Mexican food seemed to dominate the menu. Various kinds of tacos were featured along with enchiladas, tamales, and chicken and other quesadillas. A small section near the bottom listed an assortment of burgers.

The Peg took its name from the shoe peg factory that dominated the Maple City area in the late nineteenth century. Before it was renamed, the community was called Peg Town. Shoe pegs, Pete learned, were small wooden devices that were once used to attach soles to the upper parts of shoes.

The place was either a dive or a hidden gem. He had no dinner plans, and while he didn't relish a drive to Maple City, he convinced himself that it wasn't the worst idea to branch out now and then. Maybe Harry would join him if he talked up the food. He pulled out a Michigan map and plotted the shortest route to Maple City.

SEVENTEEN

"There are a lot of restaurants in the area better than this place," Harry groused as they sped north on M-22.

"How do you know?" Pete asked.

"Some things a man just knows."

Pete turned away from Harry and smiled. Enduring Harry's complaints was a small price to pay for the cozy warmth of his Ford Explorer.

"Jeez," Harry said as they neared Maple City, "maybe this area is nice in the summer, but at this time of the year, it's like the country God forgot."

"Out of season, every place in the north looks like God forgot about it," Pete said. He clicked on the overhead light so he could read the map. "Turn left at the stop sign coming up. That road should take us into Maple City."

"How far?" Harry said irritably. "A hundred miles?"

"One mile, Sunshine. We're almost there."

When they reached Maple City, Pete guided Harry to where he thought The Peg should be located.

"Now we're headed out of town," Harry grumbled. "You sure you have the directions right? Of course, in this metropolis, you're out of town after you've gone two blocks."

"Keep going," Pete said with a straight face. He scanned the roadside for a building that looked like the structure pictured on the website. He saw a sign illuminated with a weak spotlight coming up on the left and said, "Slow down. I think that's it just ahead."

The Peg's unpaved parking lot was dark except for the light reflecting off the sign and the soft yellow glow that filtered through the bar's windows. Harry navigated through the rows of irregularly parked vehicles, looking for an open slot.

"This place is a dump," Harry said. "Do you see some of these pickups? I've seen better vehicles in a junk yard. And do you see that junk piled along the side of the building? They should clean this place up."

Pete looked where Harry was pointing and said, "That's not junk. That's a snow blade. It looks pretty new to me."

"Well it shouldn't be stored in a public area," Harry groused. "They should put it in a shed or something."

"This area gets snow in the winter, remember? How do you keep a parking lot clear without snowplow equipment?"

Harry forgot his gripes when he saw a pickup back out of a slot twenty feet from the door. Pete heard gravel ping against a pickup as Harry accelerated to beat an incoming vehicle to the spot. Harry pulled in ahead of his adversary and crowded the clean SUV on his side while staying as far away as he could from the rusted out station wagon on his right. Even in the dim light, it looked like the last vehicle of its kind left on the planet.

"We're lucky we got a place up front," Harry grumbled as they exited his Explorer. "If we had to park by the road, we never would have found the door."

"Thanks to your superior eye sight and driving skills," Pete said. "This place doesn't look bad. If we don't like it, we'll cross it off our dine-around list."

"It's not *on* the list. At most, it's on probation."

The Peg was dominated by a long barroom that extended for most of the building. The bar itself was well-polished with a brass foot rail. Like an old-time saloon. A pool table with an overhead light dominated one end of the room. On the opposite end was a postage-stamp dining area that was separated from the bar by a broad arch doorway. It was standing room only at the bar; the eight tables in the dining area were all unoccupied. The smell of cigarette smoke mingled with the pungent odor of stale beer.

"Let's sit back there," Harry said, gesturing toward a far corner of the dining area. "Apparently this part of the state hasn't heard about the smoking ban yet."

A waitress with jet black hair and a toothy smile approached their table. Her black uniform dress had a shoe peg embroidered above her left breast, and her bosom and waistline tested the fabric's elasticity. She seemed delighted to finally have customers and stood with her order pad poised. "Have you two gentlemen dined with us before?" she asked.

Pete shook his head and replied, "First time." Harry sullenly buried his face in the menu.

"If you gentlemen don't care for Mexican food," she said, sizing them up, "we have some great burgers I think you'd like. Most of the gentlemen who order burgers like them well-done, but you can get them some other way if you like." She looked at them hopefully.

Harry looked up and said, "I was thinking about the quesadillas. Can we get a couple of beers while we decide?"

Her smile widened. "By all means. Do you gentlemen know what kind of beer you'd like?"

Pete ordered a Miller Lite. Harry turned his menu over, looking for a drink list, and seeing none, asked, "What do you have?"

The waitress ticked off several domestic beers.

"Do you have Dos Equis?" Harry asked.

"Yes," she gushed, obviously pleased with his taste. "That's one of our premium brands. Most of our gentlemen prefer something less expensive."

Harry looked at Pete and said, "You want to switch and join me?"

"Why not," Pete said.

While the waitress was at the bar getting their beer, Harry said in a low voice, "This place looks like it caters to the Hispanic crowd judging from the food and the people in the bar. A lot of them probably work in the vineyards around here."

"It's early for the vineyard workers to be here, isn't it? The picking season is months off."

Harry donned his knowledgeable newspaperman hat and said, "Some of the workers stay year around these days. They pick up odd jobs in the winter. And of course, if any of them are undocumented, they don't want to chance crossing back and forth over the border."

The waitress brought their Dos Equis and Harry immediately sampled his. "Umm," he said. "That's good." He looked at the waitress and said, "I was thinking of something to start. Do you have wings?"

"We have nachos that everyone just loves."

"Nachos would be great," Harry said, giving her a coy smile that would have Rona reaching for a sharp implement if she saw it.

While the waitress scurried off to get their nachos, Harry turned to Pete and said, "Tell me again why you wanted to come to this place?"

"I already told you twice. I found a telephone number in the apartment in Seattle and traced it to this bar. I wanted to see the place and try to figure out how why Lynn or her boyfriend kept the number pinned to their bulletin board."

"I'd say her boyfriend. That was the piece of paper you showed me, right?"

"Yes."

"It looks like just a bar to me."

Pete shrugged.

While they were waiting for their nachos, Harry said in a low voice, "I don't think this place gets too many strangers. Do you see those looks we're getting from the crowd?"

"You're imagining things. People are probably just curious about why we would come here to eat."

"I don't think you're very observant. Those are hostile looks we're getting."

Harry roared through the nachos, and when the waitress brought their main courses, he attacked his quesadillas like it was the last night Mexican food could be legally purchased in the state. Pete ate his burger quietly; his mind was on other things.

The waitress appeared at the table again and asked, "Did you two gentlemen save room for desert?"

Pete was about to say no thanks when Harry jumped in and with a wink and an ear-to-ear smile asked, "What do you have, Sweetheart?"

The waitress giggled and ticked off several deserts, most of which sounded like they came from northern Michigan rather than northern Mexico. Harry finally settled on the flan. It took fifteen minutes to arrive, and when it did, Harry had his fork poised like he hadn't polished off two courses already. "Mmm," he said. "That's good." He lowered his voice and said out of the corner of his mouth, "It's a little stale, like it was shipped here by truck from Chihuahua state, but it's still pretty damn good."

When they were finished, Harry grabbed the bill and thanked the waitress with great fanfare. He showed Pete the amount of the tip he'd written on the credit card slip and winked again. "Rosa is really good," he confided with obvious enthusiasm.

On the way out, Pete said, "I need a few minutes."

He approached the bar and ran his hand over the wood. Maple, he'd guess, which made sense given the area. He asked the bartender if the manager was around. The patrons in the vicinity toned down their conversation and seemed to be paying attention to what he said.

The bartender said, "He's out of town." He didn't volunteer further information and continued to wipe glasses with a tattered towel.

"Okay," Pete said. "Does he have a card? I'd like to talk to him when he gets back."

The bartender took a card from a holder near the cash register and slid it across the bar to him without saying anything. The name on the card read Alfred "Sandy" Sandoval.

"He goes by Sandy I take it?" Pete asked.

The bartender nodded and plucked more glasses from the dish rack and continued with his wiping chores.

"A friend of mine used to come in here once in a while. Lynn Hawke, do you know her?"

The bartender paused and stared at him for a moment. He said, "Doesn't ring my memory bell, as they say." He resumed wiping.

"That's funny, she mentioned this place several times."

The bartender held a glass up to the light and said, "How many women do you see in here? This isn't a fern bar. If she came in here, I'd remember."

"She's about five-seven, long light brown hair, good figure. Does that help?"

"Sounds like a babe," the bartender said. For the first time, an expression other than a stony look appeared on his face.

"I don't know if I'd call her a babe," Pete said, "but she's attractive."

"Sorry, pal. I can't help you with your friend. Don't know her and haven't seen her."

"Well," Pete said, "I get up to this area every now and again. I'll stop in the next time I'm here and meet Sandy. Maybe he has a better memory."

The bartender shrugged and held another glass up to the light. "Maybe," he said.

After they got in the Explorer, Harry said, "What were you talking to the bartender about? I couldn't hear a lot of the conversation."

"I was trying to find out if he knew Lynn or had ever seen her in the bar."

"And?"

"He said The Peg's a man's place and if a babe like her had ever been in there, he'd remember."

Harry found the road out of town and turned to Pete and said, "You don't think a lot of people in that place looked hostile?"

"You're too suspicious. I grew up outside a town that was even smaller than Maple City. We had thirteen taverns within the village limits or just outside and a U.S. Census population of fewer than two hundred people. If someone the locals didn't know stopped in one of the bars, they always wondered why he was there, too. It's the nature of small towns."

"Okay," Harry said skeptically. "But I'm telling you, those guys looked hostile to me."

EIGHTEEN

Pete was crossing the street to go to the drug store when someone in a dark sedan honked at him from a half-block away. He waved and quickened his pace to get across the street. The car pulled over to the curb and the passenger-side window slid down. Pete bent over and peered in the car. It was Joe Tessler, the plainclothes detective who worked for Sheriff Franklin Richter.

"What's the problem, Joe? Did I violate an ordinance that prohibits crossing the busy streets of Frankfort in the middle of the block?"

Tessler's black hair always reminded Pete of a raven's wing the way it swept across his forehead. Tessler brushed his hair to one side and laughed. "No ordinance violation, counselor," he said. "I just wanted to say hello. Haven't seen you for a while."

"That must mean I'm not on Sheriff Richter's suspect list for any heinous crime."

Tessler grinned at the reference to Richter. "Not at the moment anyway. I've had you on my list of people to call. Harry McTigue tells me you have some thoughts on the Arne Breit shooting and I thought I should hear them first hand."

"In the middle of the street?"

"Not here," he said, "but if you're not in a rush, I could give you a motor tour of Frankfort and we can talk."

Pete gave him a deadpan look. "This sounds like a ruse to get a person of interest in your vehicle to hot box him."

Tessler laughed again. "No ruse," he said. "Just a conversation between gentlemen."

"Aren't you concerned that Sheriff Richter might see us together? You'd be looking for a new job."

"Are you going to tell him?"

It was Pete's turn to laugh. "Okay," he said. "You caught me on a day when I happen to have a hole in my busy schedule." He slid into the passenger seat and immediately smelled stale cigarette smoke. His first impulse was to lower the window, but in view of the raw weather, opted for warmth instead.

"Where should we go?" Pete asked. "The corn fields of Indiana are a bit far to drive." He knew Tessler had spent several years with the Chicago PD and would know about one of the mob's preferred sites for dumping bodies.

"Indiana is a little far," Tessler agreed, looking amused, "although if we went down there, I could show you some lovely sites where made guys reportedly buried a few of their own. Let's just drive around town. My glass is tinted so you don't have to worry about being seen with me."

"Or you with me."

Tessler shot him another grin and continued on to the lake. He turned around and headed back down Main Street. When they came to the Car Ferry, Tessler slowed to a crawl and said, "Arne was here on the night he was killed. He left alone about 10:00 p.m. based on statements from witnesses." Tessler speeded up again and proceeded until he reached the M-22 intersection where he turned right. He slowed to another crawl as they approached the Port City Marina and pulled over on the edge of the parking lot. "He was killed right over there. We're not sure whether he came directly to the marina or whether he went someplace first and then came back."

"You can't tell by the time of death?"

"They can only estimate time of death within a few hours so we have no way of knowing exactly what his movements were."

"I assume no one saw him around town after he left the Car Ferry."

"Not that we've been able to determine." Tessler stared at the marina parking lot for a long moment and said, "I'm still trying to figure out why it all went down here late at night."

"A lot of us are. But I heard you guys figure it was a robbery."

"That's Frank's theory," Tessler said dismissively.

Pete picked up on his tone and said, "Don't tell me there's a disagreement within the ranks?"

"No disagreement. I haven't totally discounted the robbery theory. I was just trained to explore all the angles."

They sat silently for a couple of minutes. Then Tessler looked Pete's way and asked, "How do you see it?"

Pete took his time responding. "One possibility," he said, "is that someone saw Arne leave the bar and followed him."

"I thought of that, too, but it makes no sense that Arne would pull into the Port City Marina and wait for his assailant to arrive. I can see it if what went down had occurred at Arne's house."

"True," Pete said. "The other possibility is that Arne was meeting someone he knew and wanted it to occur at an out of the way place for some reason."

"Possible," Tessler said, looking thoughtful. "Any idea who he'd be meeting and why they'd picked a place like this?"

"Not really."

Tessler began to roll again. They passed through Elberta and proceeded up the hill to the overlook. The parking area was completely deserted, which wasn't unusual for the off-season. Tessler pulled up to the thick cable that separated the parking lot from the edge of the steep bluff. The bluff dropped off to the beach area, and the gray waters of Lake Michigan slapped against the sand in relentless waves. Away from the water, patches of crusted snow were visible among the rolling dunes and the dead grass and the scrub trees.

"Pretty, huh?" Tessler said.

"Pretty is half of it. Desolate is the other half."

"This is one of my favorite places even in the winter," Tessler said. "Good spot to think."

Pete just nodded.

"Do you mind if I smoke?" Tessler asked.

"I'd prefer you didn't," Pete said. "It smells like your car could use a good airing out as it is."

"No problem," Tessler said, tapping his unlit cigarette against the console. "I should quit anyway. We can lower a window if the smell bothers you."

"Leave the windows up. Mentally, I've already opted for dying of second-hand smoke rather than suffering frost bite."

"Sorry," Tessler said. He sat silently gazing out at the dreary lake.

When Tessler didn't speak for a couple of minutes, Pete asked a leading question to get the conversation rolling again. "I take it you have no suspects."

"None. This is the first homicide I've worked that we don't even have a person of interest. We've been completely shut out up to this point."

"What do you know of Arnie's time in the Car Ferry?"

"He arrived between 7:30 p.m. and 8:00 p.m. from what people tell us. He had a few beers, shot the shit with various people for a couple of hours, then left. He didn't have words with anyone. Typical affable Arne. No one noticed anything different about him. Three people told us he left alone."

"Did you talk to Chubs?"

"The marina guy?"

"Yes."

"In case you don't know Chubs, he's something of a local blowhard and we don't think you can rely on much of what he tells you. He says stuff to inflate his importance. According to witnesses, he and Arne were after the same slut. A regular at the Car Ferry who lives near Thompsonville. We don't see any connection there. Chubs and the woman didn't leave with Arne, and in fact, they were still in the Car Ferry at midnight according to the bartender."

"That squares with what Chubs told me."

Tessler lifted his eyebrows. "You talked to him?"

"By accident. I was out for a walk one day and passed by the marina. His SUV was there and I stopped to ask what they intended to do with Arne's boats," telling Tessler a slightly different fib than he told Chubs. "Chubs was in a talkative mood."

"He usually is," Tessler said.

"One thing he said sticks in my mind. He said Arne had become paranoid recently. According to Chubs, he fantasized that his phone and house were bugged. I guess it was really bothering him."

Tessler stared at the lake. "That might explain why Arne met this unknown person in a deserted marina."

"It might."

"Do you believe Chubs?"

Pete shrugged. "I have no reason not to. That isn't something he'd exaggerate just to hear himself talk."

Tessler stared at the lake some more before he said, "That still leaves the questions of who Arne met and why."

"It does and I can't help you there because I have absolutely no idea. I think what you have to do is poke around and see if you can find anything in Arne's personal or business life that might shed light on it. His associations, what he might have been involved in in the past, that sort of thing."

"Harry was right. You do have pretty good instincts for this type of thing. Were you a criminal lawyer in Chicago?"

Pete laughed. "The farthest thing from it. I learned early on that I wasn't cut out to handle criminal matters."

"Why's that?"

"When I was a second year associate, our firm was on retainer from a foundation to provide *pro bono* defense services to members of Chicago's street gangs. The theory was that members of the Black P. Stone Nation and other gangs weren't getting good representation from the local criminal defense bar. I was assigned to the team handling the appeal of a conviction of a prominent gang member for blowing away this guy on the street in front of about seventeen eyewitnesses.

"I took the train to the prison in Joliet to interview him, and all the way down there I kept thinking of questions I should ask. I might as well have slept. From the time I walked into the interview room, all the guy did was tell me that when *I* got him out, *he* was going to go after the lawyer who represented him at the trial because the lawyer had no excuse for not getting him off. That cured me of wanting to do criminal work."

Tessler laughed. "Sounds typical of those guys. Nothing is ever their fault. So what did you wind up doing?"

"Corporate. Deal work. I had a lot of opposing counsel scream at me across the table, but I never had to worry about what they might do at night."

"Somewhere along the line, you developed an instinct for criminal investigations."

"I think it comes from watching my old boss at the CID when I was in the army."

"You were with the CID?"

"Not exactly," Pete said. "I was in an armored artillery unit, but after the first month I was assigned to drive a Jeep for a major who was in the CID. The temporary assignment became permanent until I left the service."

"When I was with the Chicago PD, we had a guy in homicide who'd been with the CID. That's the army's version of the detective department, isn't it?

"Sort of. Joe, does the manner in which Arne was killed tell you anything?"

"Yes, it doesn't look like an ordinary robbery."

"No it doesn't. When's the last time you saw a panicked robber shoot a victim twice in the head?"

"Never," Tessler said. "It looks more like an execution by a professional."

"Or a gangland killing."

"Up here? That doesn't make sense, either. "

"There must be something behind this that has the feds interested. As you know, Keegan Harris came to see me the other day. She knew a lot about the case, but was completely closed-mouth about what the government's interest is."

"Join the club. She wouldn't tell me anything either."

"That's why I mentioned organized crime. It has to be something like that."

"If it was the FBI, that might make sense. But Homeland Security doesn't get involved in organized crime investigations unless they're linked to something within their jurisdiction. Like terrorism."

"The closest Arne came to terrorism is when he went after the guy on his boat who refused to release an undersized fish."

Tessler chuckled.

Pete hit the button to crack the window. The cold air began to creep in, but he needed relief from the cigarette smoke.

"Okay," Tessler said, "this conversation has been useful. I'll drop you back at your office."

"The drugstore."

"Oh, right, the drugstore."

On the way back, they both glanced at the marina again as they passed. Tessler turned left on Main Street and a few blocks up, pulled to the side in front of the drugstore. Before Pete got out, he said, "You know what I'd do? I'd check Arne Breit's house and see if there are any taps. The phones should be easiest to check. Do you have someone in your office who knows wiretaps?"

"We don't, but I know a little. I can't install a bug, but I'm pretty sure I can tell if one is on a phone."

"Would you let me know? Off the record of course."

"I will. And I'd like to say one thing more before you go. I can't tell you this officially, but I know we treated you like shit in the Cara Lane case."

"Is that an apology?"

"Not officially, as I said. If I'm asked, I'll deny our conversation. But off the record, there's no reason why the two of us have to be at odds."

"If Frank's not around anyway."

"Right. If Frank's not around."

■ ■ ■

Pete was on the Internet researching the Vikings' influence on what is now modern Russia when his telephone rang.

"You were right," Joe Tessler said. "There's at least one listening device in Arne Breit's house. On his phone."

"You went over there already?"

"Stopped at the office to get a key and went right over."

"What did you do with the tap?" Pete asked.

"Left it. I thought it might lead us to something. I'm having one of our deputies watch Arne's house in case someone comes to remove it."

Pete thought some more. "You have any idea who might have put the tap on?"

"The same idea I'm sure you have."

"The feds."

"Right."

"I think your case may be bigger than a killing during a robbery that turned bad, Joe. Keep me posted, will you?"

"I will, and now that we have a truce, I'd like to continue to bounce things off you once in a while if it's alright."

"Feel free."

"Maybe I'll even work on Frank. Get him to appoint you an honorary deputy or something."

"Wouldn't *that* be fun."

NINETEEN

Conti Vineyards wasn't the largest winemaker on the Leelanau Peninsula, but it had a reputation for being one of the best. Their Pinot Noirs and Pinot Grigios were particularly well regarded and had won several regional awards.

As Pete drove to his appointment with Alain Conti, he thought back to the gymnastics he had to go through to remain consistent with his original inquiry and confirm the interview. Most importantly, he had to make the calls from Harry's office and then wait around to be called back. Harry watched with amusement. All parts of Pete's story apparently hung together, including his status as a contributing editor of *The Northern Sentinel*, because he finally got an appointment with Conti four days after his initial call. After that, he felt comfortable making and receiving calls on his cell phone since, as he told Loretta, he was frequently "out on assignment."

Conti Vineyards was located ten miles north of Suttons Bay and approximately two miles west. Pete's portable GPS unit guided him on the right route and periodically spoke to him in its robotic voice. To his right, the bay glistened in the mid-afternoon sunlight and the brisk wind whipped the surface into frothy whitecaps on the blue-green water.

It was warmer, but not quite warm enough. He pulled his coat tighter around his neck.

He heeded the GPS unit's command and exited left off M-22 and followed the road west until he came to a prominent wooden sign that announced Conti Vineyards. The sign had colorful grape clusters painted on a large slab of wood that was suspended between upright posts. Not exactly unique, but it was eye-catching and certainly conveyed an image of what the place was about.

The entrance road was impressive even with the dormant brown countryside. Stately trees lined the road like welcoming sentries and guided visitors to the buildings on the crest of a low hill. The scene reminded him of the tree-lined roads in many European landscape paintings. The drive must be beautiful in the summer when lush green leaves knit together to form a green canopy overhead.

As he ascended the hill, the features of the massive gray stone house became more visible. It was designed in the French chateau style, and judging from its position, must provide an impressive view of the surrounding countryside. The tasting room was in a smaller stone building of similar design that occupied the opposite side of the paved brick courtyard. A gargoyle fountain, shut down for the winter, gave the place an Old World look.

An egg yolk yellow Volkswagen Beetle was parked in front of the smaller building. He pulled in alongside the Beetle. The wind whipped at his face as he walked to the entrance. He pushed open the door and found himself in a large room that reeked of the wine culture. A thirty-something woman in jeans and a green apron fussed with the stemware that dominated the shelves behind the bar. She looked up when the chimes jangled.

She flipped the towel over one shoulder and came over to greet him. She asked in a friendly voice, "Are you the reporter?"

"Yes, Pete Thorsen. From *The Northern Sentinel.*"

"I'm Loretta Mann. We spoke on the phone. Welcome to Conti Vineyards."

He nodded and looked around at the timber and stone room. Wine bottles filled the racks along the walls and old wine casks and other artifacts added a nice touch. "Very nice," he said.

"Thank you," Loretta said with more than a touch of pride. "We're excited to be included in your series on Leelanau vineyards. When will the feature run?"

"I'm not in charge of scheduling, but I expect it to be sometime in early summer. That's when the tourists start arriving. We publish a special section in the summer months that highlights area attractions. The Leelanau wine country supplement should be a big hit. It should be good for sales, too."

Loretta glanced at the clock on the wall and said, "I better get you over to the Manor House. Mr. Conti doesn't like to be kept waiting."

They walked across the courtyard to what Loretta referred to as the Manor House. He followed her in, and almost immediately an ear-piercing buzz filled the quiet air. A man in a green chef's jacket and cap appeared out of nowhere and stood poised like an oversized cat looking at them.

"Oh, my," Loretta said. "Do you have car keys or other metal objects in your pockets? I forgot we had this new alarm system put in."

Pete fished his keys and some change from his pockets and laid them on a hall table. Then he stepped back, and just like at an airport, passed through the security area again. This time, the alarm remained silent. The chef who'd been watching them intently disappeared.

Pete heard a rustling sound in the hallway. A silver-haired man powering a wheelchair with his hands appeared. He was heavyset and wore a gray tweed sports coat with patches on the elbows and a black turtleneck sweater. The epitome of a country gentleman.

"I'm sorry we set off the alarm, Mr. Conti," Loretta said. "I forgot to tell him to take his keys out of his pocket."

Alain Conti smiled and waved a hand. "These things can be such a nuisance, but unfortunately they're necessary in the world in which we live." He ignored Loretta's attempt to assist him and hoisted himself shakily to his feet. The pain was obvious from his expression. He steadied himself and extended a hand. "Alain Conti, Mr. Thorsen," he said. "Welcome to Conti Vineyards. A pity that you couldn't come on a nicer day when we could sit outside and enjoy the view."

"Nice of you to have me," Pete replied. He handed Conti the press credentials Harry had made up for him. Conti looked at them briefly and handed them back.

"What does a contributing editor do?"

"Essentially, I'm a freelancer. Now that I live in this area fulltime, I devote my time to things that interest me."

"You weren't a journalist in Chicago?"

"No," Pete said, having a feeling that Conti already had him checked out, "I practiced law. But writing has always been my passion and now I can devote all of my time to it."

"I see," Conti said. "A man should always pursue his passion."

Pete glanced around and said, "This is quite a house you have."

"It's modeled after the manor house our family used to have in Burgundy."

"Conti sounds Italian. But you're of French descent?"

"Yes. My father's family was originally from Tuscany, which explains the name. Actually, Conti is quite a common name in France. There was a lot of cross-border movement over the centuries. Can I show you around before we sit down to talk?"

"I'd enjoy that."

"You don't mind if I use my wheelchair, do you? My legs are a little shaky these days."

"Please," Pete said, "whatever you find most comfortable."

Alain Conti eased his bulk into the wheelchair again and waved off another attempt by Loretta to help him. Pete followed as he powered the chair out of the spacious foyer and down a hall to the right. For the next half-hour, Conti gave him a tour of the house, commenting on each room. They took an elevator to the second floor to continue the tour. It was slow, but moved soundlessly. When they were finished, they took the elevator to the first floor again and Pete followed Conti to the pecan-paneled study.

"How long have you owned this vineyard?" Pete asked.

"Nearly seven years," Conti said. "It's not France, but it has a special place in my heart."

Pete pulled a spiral notebook from his coat pocket and began to take notes.

"To begin, would tell me more about your family background?"

Alain Conti repeated how his family had left Tuscany and come to France twenty years after the French Revolution. Eventually they acquired a prominent vineyard in Burgundy, but lost it during the tough times that followed World War I. Conti's grandfather came to America shortly after that to work in Napa Valley, but he was never was able to fulfill his dream of owning a vineyard to rival the one in Burgundy.

"This is off the record and not for inclusion in your article," Conti said, establishing that he knew something about the protocol of dealing with the press, "but my father was a bit of a dreamer and a drifter. He paid lip service to my grandfather's dream of replicating our family's wine operations in Burgundy, but he did nothing to further the dream. Then I discovered the Leelanau Peninsula and this place when it was put up for sale by an estate."

Pete was anxious to ask Conti about his personal background, but remained patient and asked, "How many acres do you have?"

"Let me show you." He asked Loretta to bring the schematic of the vineyard. In a few minutes, she returned lugging an artist's sketch and a mahogany easel. She set them up between Pete and Alain Conti.

"I don't think it's necessary for you to hang around," Conti said to her. "Mr. Thorsen, can Loretta get you anything before she leaves?"

"I'm fine, thanks."

Conti explained his estate's wine operations. It was divided into three vineyards, he said, pointing to the schematic and tracing the boundaries of each. A total of seventy-two varieties of grapes were grown on the estate. All grape varieties were carefully selected to match the Leelanau

Peninsula's climate and soils. Pinot Grigio and Pinot Noir were among the most popular vinifera varieties, he said. He lectured for ten minutes on the importance of pruning to restrict yields, the intricacies of crop thinning, and the summer de-leafing process. Then he got into wine-making, explaining that all of their wines were made using traditional methods. The fruit was handpicked and sorted and the wine was fermented in stainless steel vats and aged in American Oak casks.

Pete took copious notes as Conti spoke and periodically asked questions. When Conti was finished with his tutorial, Pete shook his head and said, "Boy, the average person who enjoys a glass of wine now and then probably has no idea what goes into making it."

"We offer seminars in the summer for people who are truly interested. And of course, connoisseurs know the difference between wine that's been produced the correct way and the grape juice some places turn out just to make money. We like to think we use the best methods developed in France over the centuries."

Pete used a lull in the conversation to ease into the personal questions that were festering in his mind. "This won't get into our story, obviously, but for background purposes, I'm curious about the burglary Loretta mentioned. It must have been serious for you to put in a metal detector."

Conti looked at him and for just a moment, there was a change in his expression. "Yes, they took a number of things, including a lot of silver and some old journals that had been in my family for more than a century. That's something insurance can never compensate you for."

"I'm sorry to hear that," Pete said sympathetically. "It must have been hard to lose a part of your family's history." He scanned his notes and said, "I wonder if we could go back to the winemaking process for just a minute. I want to make sure everything I took down is correct." For the next half-hour, they retraced ground they'd covered earlier and Pete probed for details. When they were finished, they discussed photographs Conti had of the interior and exterior operations and what *The Northern Sentinel's* photographer might want to shoot to supplement them.

Pete rose to his feet and said, "Thanks for spending so much time with me. You have a terrific operation here. I'll have to talk about it with my managing editor, but I can easily see featuring Conti Vineyards as the lead in our series."

"That would be nice," Conti said.

Conti followed in his wheelchair as Pete headed for the foyer. Pete took a last look around and nodded approvingly. Then he said to Conti, "I knew a woman a couple of years back before she moved to the West Coast. She was a small business accountant and her clients included several vineyards in the area. She used to tell me that wine clients were the most enjoyable segment of her practice. Lynn Hawke, do you know her?"

Conti looked at him impassively and shook his head. "I don't think so. Maybe my business manager does. I'm afraid winemaking is like religion to me. I concentrate on producing great wine and leave the business side to others."

"Well, no difference. She's gone now anyway. Mr. Conti, I'm grateful for how generous you've been with your time. I'll be in touch with any follow-up questions I have and about the photography."

Outside, he gazed at the surrounding countryside from his hilltop vantage-point and marveled at the sight. Even with the brown from the northern winter kill, the scene was magnificent.

He was disappointed that he could only find one opportunity to ask about Lynn Hawke and had no opening to gracefully ask about the telephone calls she'd made to Conti Vineyards the night of her accident. He needed to find out more about Alain Conti.

TWENTY

Pete had two hours before he was supposed to meet Rona Martin at Lynn's house to collect her paintings and personal papers. He logged onto his computer and Googled Alain Conti to see what more he could find out about him. He got literally hundreds of hits.

Eventually, he narrowed the search to the right Alain Conti. *Wine Spectator* had interviewed him a year after he bought what was now Conti Vineyards. The piece included much of the same information that had come out in Pete's interview, but went into more detail about Conti's ancestors when they were in the wine-making business in Europe. The piece also included several references to his father, not all of which were complimentary, but almost nothing about Conti himself. Buried in one article was a single reference to Conti having been "with the government." No information about which branch of government or how long or when he left.

Pete spent the next hour surfing through articles about Alain Conti in *Traverse Magazine* and other regional publications. He found two pieces written by Conti for publications of lesser note than *Wine Spectator*, but both dealt with the technical aspects of the wine business. The other hits that related to the Alain Conti he was interested in all pertained strictly to wine and food matters as well.

He considered asking Angie DeMarco to have one of her law enforcement friends check out Conti, but abandoned that idea for practical reasons. He had almost nothing to go on. No water bottles or shave gel cans from which to lift his fingerprints, no specifics to provide a background trail as a starting point. More importantly, he preferred to avoid the flak he'd have to take if he asked her for another favor on the heels of his request for background on Gilbert Bartholome.

Since he lacked the knowhow to dig up background on Conti himself, his only realistic option was to hire a private investigator. He knew two. One was Adam Rose who'd helped him on a case the year before. At the time, Rose lived in Traverse City so he could be close to his ailing mother. She died soon after the case was over and Rose moved to Chicago to ply his occupation in a larger arena. The other was Halvor Nilson who was also in Chicago and forever hounding him for business, playing on their common Norwegian-American heritage. He decided to try Rose first.

He got him on the first try which wasn't a good sign as far as his business was concerned. "Adam, Pete Thorsen. We haven't talk in a while."

"That's right," he said. "I was probably out when you called. Been working all these cases."

"Things slow?"

"I've been busier. How's life in the north country?"

"Cold and quiet."

They spent a few minutes catching up and then Pete said, "I could use your talents on a minor job if you're interested."

"Does minor mean I won't need my piece?"

Pete laughed. "Not at the beginning, anyway." He told Rose about Lynn Hawke's fatal car crash and what he'd learned since that time. He mentioned that Lynn had made three telephone calls to Alain Conti the night of her accident and said he wanted to find out more about him.

"I thought you were out of things like this after our experience last year," Rose said.

"This is different," he said without elaborating.

"What do you want to know about Conti?"

"Anything and everything you can dig up. Who he is, what he did before he bought Conti Vineyards, that kind of thing. You're a whiz at information searches as I recall. Think you can help?"

"Well, I'll have to clear my not-too-busy schedule, but I believe I can fit it in. Do you have anything more to go on with this guy Conti?"

"Just what I told you. I'll send you the citations to some magazine articles he either wrote or where he's mentioned."

"I've seen how patient you are with these things," Rose said. "When do you need this?"

"I'm like your attorney pal, Ira Manning. Yesterday."

■ ■ ■

Rona was sitting in her car waiting for him when he arrived at Lynn Hawke's house. She followed him inside and they spent a few minutes discussing what needed to be done. Then they separated to tackle their respective tasks.

Pete lugged a stack of flat banker's boxes into the room that had served as Lynn's office and assembled and taped five of them. He had a good idea of the contents of the desk drawers and file cabinets from when he was at the house before. The upper desk drawer contained a potpourri of pens, paper clips, and sundry other office supplies. There was no way he was going to try to organize all of that so he removed the drawer and dumped everything into one of the boxes. He moved on to the other drawers and did the same. His emphasis was on getting the material boxed up rather than on organization. He followed the same approach with the credenza.

Most of the documents in the file cabinets related to Lynn's accounting practice. Billing records and correspondence and copies of financial statements and marketing materials. Again, he'd be there for two days if he sorted through every piece of paper. He took a save-everything approach and began to fill more banker's boxes.

He came to a folder labeled "Agreement with B. Rodes" and paused to look through it. Barbara Rodes was the woman Lynn had left in charge of her accounting practice when she moved to Seattle. He thumbed through the folder and found a three-page handwritten agreement between Lynn and Barbara. He smiled as he read through it. It was a typical document crafted by lay people and was filled with the whereas clauses and the recitals they thought a lawyer would use. The recitals covered such things as the time and effort Lynn had devoted to building the practice, that she retained all rights to the client base, and recounted Barbara's expertise in accounting and financial matters.

The heart of the business relationship between the two women was memorialized on the second page. It repeated some of what they'd covered on the first page and then provided that Barbara would use her "best efforts" to serve Lynn's clients, and in return, was entitled to half of the net profits. The other half would be deposited in a bank account designated by Lynn. At the end of the year, they would reconcile the accounts. The agreement would continue from year-to-year, except Lynn retained the option to terminate it immediately if Barbara breached any of her obligations or, at Lynn's discretion, upon ninety days written notice. The third page contained more "whereas" clauses and the signatures of Lynn and of Barbara on behalf of her limited liability company.

As he was reading through the agreement, he felt someone's presence and looked up to see Rona standing in the doorway.

"Find anything interesting?" she asked.

"I was reading the agreement between Lynn and Barbara Rodes. Rodes is the woman Lynn left her accounting practice with."

Rona smiled. "When you have a good breaking point," she said, "could you help me carry some of the larger canvases to the car?"

Pete helped Rona and returned to the office to complete boxing up the files. All of the boxes wouldn't fit in his Range Rover and they agreed that Rona would have Brenda's crew pick up the rest when they moved the furniture. It was almost 5:00 p.m. when they finished. Pete told Rona he would meet her at her house with the files after he made a stop.

TWENTY-ONE

Barbara Rodes' name was stenciled across the plate glass window of her storefront office in gaudy gold letters. The inside lights were on and Pete could see a woman hunched over a stack of papers.

A sweet artificial bouquet greeted him when he opened the door. It made his eyes water and triggered an impulse to cough. He spotted the source. Five green cans of air freshener, all of the Mountain Breeze scent, stood on the credenza behind Barbara's desk. She'd obviously given her office a fresh burst just before he arrived.

He said, "Barbara?"

The bird-like woman behind the desk squinted at him as though she were trying to remember whether she knew him. She finally said in a high-octave voice, "May I help you, sir?"

"I'm Pete Thorsen, the attorney for Lynn Hawke's estate," using the line that had worked for him so far. He handed her one of his business cards. Barbara Rodes studied it for a long time.

"You probably heard about Lynn's fatal automobile accident," he added.

"Yes," she said, looking up from the card. "I was shocked." She brushed her ragged bangs away from her eyes. "When your business partner and an old friend dies suddenly like that ..." She shook her head and her voice trailed off. "I didn't know what to do about the practice. I tried to call the phone number I had for Lynn, but no one answered."

Pete didn't tell her that Lynn's cell phone was under the front seat of her totaled twelve year-old Volvo and the Leelanau County Sheriff had possession of the vehicle after the accident. The cell also had a very low battery. He just said, "I had the same problem," and didn't offer any details.

"Maybe you can tell me what I should do with the clients," she said hopefully. "Do you think I should send out a memorandum notifying them of Lynn's death?"

"Hold that for a moment," Pete said. "First get me up to speed. I'm familiar with the terms of your agreement with Lynn, but maybe you can tell me how she happened to tap you to oversee her accounting practice while she was away. Did you have a previous professional relationship with her?"

Barbara continued to fuss with her stringy hair and replied, "We knew each other from Chicago. She was at Ernst & Young and I was with a small accounting firm. I hadn't talked to her in years, but then she called one day and asked me to help with her practice."

Pete nodded. "Were you still in Chicago at that time?"

"I'm from Muskegon and was living there. I moved up here after Lynn and I signed our agreement."

"That seems clear enough. Okay, the agreement …"

Barbara interrupted. "Does the air in here seem stale to you?" she asked. She fanned her face with a hand.

"A little," he lied just to be polite.

Barbara reached for one of the aerosol cans. She aimed the nozzle to Pete's left and fired a long burst of Mountain Breeze. Then she aimed to his right and let loose another burst.

"I hope I didn't get any spray on you," she said apologetically. "I like to keep the office smelling fresh."

Pete was thankful for her good aim and resisted the temptation to run to the door to gulp some fresh air. He said, "About your agreement with Lynn."

"Oh yes," Barbara said, "I'm sorry. We didn't use a lawyer, but I think it's binding. We tried to write it up just the way a lawyer would."

"An agreement doesn't have to be drafted by a lawyer and be tied up with a lot of ribbons and bows to be binding."

"I think I've lived up to my obligations and used my best efforts to serve the clients, too," she volunteered. "Just as the agreement says."

"I'm sure you have."

"Since I heard about Lynn's death, I've continued to serve the clients the same as before. That's what a professional person does."

"It sounds like you did the right thing."

She seemed to feel a compulsion to talk and said in her squeaky voice, "Our agreement doesn't say anything about the death of one of the partners. Maybe we should have covered that possibility. Do you think that's a problem?"

"Depends," Pete said. "Going forward, my goal is to be sure we give effect to Lynn's intentions. Did you have any conversations with her in the past few months?"

Barbara Rodes peered at him through her glasses and hesitated for a long moment. "I talked to her," she said. "But I don't know if I should share confidential conversations I had with a business partner."

"She's dead," Pete reminded her.

"Still …"

He tried a different approach. "Look, Barbara, as the attorney for Lynn's estate, I have to decide what to do. The probate estate succeeded to all of Lynn's rights, including your agreement with her. As the attorney for the estate, I can either leave the business with you or I can give you notice of termination as the agreement allows and get someone else to take over the practice. I have to know the facts to make the right decision."

Barbara looked alarmed and tugged at her hair again. She said timidly, "It wouldn't be fair to terminate the agreement. I've worked hard for almost two years to keep the clients happy. I also moved up here specially to take over the practice. I had expenses and I'm away from my family."

Pete shrugged. "The law's the law whether you think it's fair or not." As he sat there looking at her, he remembered how Lynn had to come back the previous summer to put out fires caused by Barbara's less than stellar client relations skills, but didn't raise that fact. He sensed, however, that hand-holding wasn't her strong suit.

She straightened some papers on her desk and said without looking at him, "What would you like to know?"

"For starters, did Lynn ever mention wanting to come back here?"

"Once," Barbara said nervously. "We talked about how we could work together if she came back. She didn't say she definitely was coming back, but she seemed to be thinking about it."

"Did she say why?"

"I think it had something to do with her boyfriend," Barbara said haltingly.

Pete tried not to appear too interested and said as casually as he could, "Were they having problems?"

"I think it was her boyfriend's disagreement with his business partner. She said it was affecting their relationship."

"Did Lynn tell you anything about the disagreement?"

Barbara gave the air a couple more bursts of Mountain Breeze. Pete ducked reflexively as the spray came closer this time. She appeared flustered and said, "Mr. Thorsen, are you sure this is important to my agreement with Lynn? That was more her personal life. Maybe we can talk about how I can take over Lynn's practice. I developed this Client Retention Plan." She held up a document. "Would you like to see it? I'd be willing to change anything you think isn't right."

He didn't reach for the document, but instead said, "I do want to look at it, but I'd like to do it justice and I don't have the time right now. But getting back to your concern, I can see why you'd think my questions might not relate to the agreement directly, but all I'm doing is trying to make sure there are no collateral problems going forward. If Lynn intended to marry the guy she was living with but died first, I don't want to do something that would give him a claim against the estate."

Barbara's eyes widened and she asked, "Do you think he might make a claim?"

"It's hard to say," Pete said. "I've seen stranger things, and you know how those Pacific Coast states are. They have palimony and all sorts of legal theories that folks in the Midwest haven't even heard of. That's why I'm trying to learn the facts."

"Palimony. That's where two people are living together and one claims the property of the other, isn't it?"

"Essentially. But let's get back to something you mentioned earlier about the problem Lynn's boyfriend was having with his business partner. I know he's in the import-export business. Do you know who his business partner is?"

"I don't think the boyfriend's problems were with that business. I think Lynn meant his other business."

"You've got me confused. What other business?"

Barbara shook her head. "Lynn never told me. All she said was the problem related to her boyfriend's other business. I think she was getting tired of his arguments with his partner."

"When did she first mention that?"

"Lynn and I went to dinner to celebrate after we signed our agreement. She talked about it then. She said the arguments were over the direction of the business. She had too much wine and I think she told me things she didn't intend to."

"And?"

"The next day, she made me swear not to tell anyone about our conversation. She said I should treat it as a confidential conversation between two business partners. She said that if I told anyone about our conversation, it would be a breach of our agreement and she could terminate it."

Pete continued to probe. "Anything else you remember about the boyfriend's disagreement with his partner?"

She tugged nervously at her hair again and cleaned her glasses with a tissue. "Now that Lynn's dead, could I still get in trouble by talking about my conversations with her?"

"Absolutely not."

"You won't use anything I say as an excuse to terminate the agreement, will you?"

"No, you have my word. The only trouble you could get in is if you know something and hold it back and it has an adverse impact on Lynn's estate. Then you risk being sued by the estate for damages."

Barbara's eyes widened. "That wouldn't be fair. I haven't done anything."

Pete shrugged and said, "You can protect yourself by telling me everything you know."

Barbara sat there looking resigned. "What was your question again?" she asked.

"Whether Lynn said anything else about her boyfriend's disagreement with his business partner."

"I remember she said that one member of their group wanted to branch out and make more money and the boss was refusing. I also remember asking what the other business was. She said she couldn't tell me because it was too sensitive."

"Is that the word she used? 'Sensitive'?"

"I think so. That's what I remember anyway."

"What did she say the last time you talked to her?"

"She told me if the disagreement couldn't be resolved soon, she was going to leave Gil and move back here."

"How was her mood? Did she seem nervous?"

"Frustrated maybe, I don't know. I couldn't see her face because we were talking on the telephone."

"Okay, final question. Why did Lynn sign the agreement with you in July when she didn't leave until August?"

"She wasn't certain she was going to go to Seattle. She said she'd met a man up here and hadn't decided what to do. But she wanted everything to be ready in case she decided to leave suddenly."

"You've been very helpful, Barbara. And for your comfort, everything you've told me will stay between us."

"Thank you, Mr. Thorsen." She sounded relieved and then asked in a tentative voice, "And my agreement with Lynn will continue?"

"For the time being at least."

"What should I do with the money I've been paying Lynn?"

"Until we agree on a permanent arrangement, why don't you set up a separate bank account and deposit the money to that account. Then we'll decide how to handle things later."

"Do you think I'll be able to keep more than half? I'm having a hard time now."

"We'll see, Barbara. We'll try to be fair."

TWENTY-TWO

Pete was still feeling a little bad about misleading Barbara Rodes with half-truths when Rona came up and squeezed his arm. "Aren't they darling?" she gushed.

"They are that," Pete said. "I didn't realize there were that many shades of pink in the color wheel."

"I counted ten pink parkas," Harry said. "Out of twelve five and six year-old girls."

They followed the instructor down the slope without ski poles and with arms extended. They looked like they were about to give someone a hug. As the instructor turned, they turned behind her, executing perfect little snowplow turns. Weight over the inside of one ski, then weight over the inside of the other when they changed directions.

"I'll tell you," Harry said, "Rona's niece is going to be quite an athlete when she gets a little older. See how her skis carve the snow when she turns?"

To Pete, little Jennifer looked just like the other eleven girls. Accomplished for a five year-old, but nothing that would herald the second coming of Lindsey Vonn. "Did you ever ski?" he asked Harry.

"A lot when I was young. I probably could have skied in college except I wanted to go to a top journalism school and Northwestern didn't have a ski team."

"Just think, if you'd gone to college in Colorado or Vermont, you might have been right up there with Jean Claude Killy and Billy Kidd.

"I don't know if I would have been that good," Harry said thoughtfully, "but I'm sure I would have won my share of medals in college."

Pete turned his head to gaze at the landscape and smile. The entire area was brown except for the ski hill which had eighteen inches of hard pack courtesy of the best snow-making equipment a resort could buy. The cold weather must have cheered the management because it provided an opportunity to extend the winter sports season for an extra week.

"How about you?" Harry asked. "Did you ever ski?"

"Some."

"I'd probably still be skiing if I hadn't torn up my knee," Harry mused. "Bad?"

"It would have healed better if I'd had the benefit of today's sports medicine. But things weren't as advanced in those days. More like, see how it feels in a month and come back to see me if it still hurts."

Pete's mind returned to his conversation with Barbara Rodes. He had no intention of trying to interfere with her agreement with Lynn Hawke. The clients were hers now, win, lose or draw. He just needed to keep her on edge in order to pry loose the information he wanted. He didn't know how what she told him fit into the bigger picture, but taking a page from Major Baumann's playbook, he'd decide that later.

Harry must have noticed his distracted look because he said, "You look like you're a thousand miles away."

"Sorry, just thinking."

"I can't imagine about what," Harry said.

Pete shrugged. A few minutes later, he said, "Did you know Lynn was thinking about moving to Seattle as early as July that summer?"

"And your source for that is …?"

"Someone who knows."

Rona interrupted their conversation by saying, "You're a good sport to come today. It means a lot to my sister to have us here."

"Graduation day, huh?" Pete said and forced a grin.

"Let me introduce you to Carla." She walked over to where a group of moms were standing and grabbed a woman by the hand and led her back.

"Carla, this is our friend, Pete Thorsen."

Carla Neville was three inches shorter than Rona, but she had the same bottomless pools for eyes and dark hair pulled back in a ponytail. Her lime green parka contrasted with all of the pink on the hill, and the brisk air gave her a healthy look.

"You're the lawyer who abandoned the big city for the pleasures of living up north," Carla said.

"Yup, I'm like a boomerang. I started in the boonies of Wisconsin and now I'm back, only in a different state."

The four of them bantered for a while. Carla seemed as amused as Rona by the way Pete and Harry took obvious pleasure in getting on each other's case.

On top of the hill, the girls were queuing up for the last run of the ski season. The light was fading and each of them held green glow-sticks in their hands. The instructor pushed off and the girls followed her down the hill. The procession resembled a giant serpent from a fantasy movie. The head and twelve moving parts slithering around the small moguls and casting an otherworldly glow as they came down the hill. Pete had to admit it was quite a sight.

Carla drifted back to the group of moms who were giddy with excitement over the show put on by their little darlings.

"Seriously," Harry said, "who told you Lynn was thinking of leaving in July?"

"Barbara Rodes. She's the woman who handles Lynn's accounting practice. Plus I saw their agreement. It's dated July 14."

"Well, we know now that the story Lynn gave us about the emergency involving her suicidal daughter was a bunch of baloney."

Pete nodded. "Another thing I learned from Barbara is that Lynn's boyfriend," Pete said, simulating quote marks with his fingers, "was having problems with his business partner. I think Lynn knew that before she left."

"You said the boyfriend's in the export/import business, right?"

"Apparently he's in a second business, too, but Barbara couldn't tell me what it is. That's where the problem is. A disagreement over the direction of the business, whatever that means."

"Mmm," Harry murmured. "You're like a vacuum cleaner. You keep sucking up all of this information."

"You never know," Pete said, elbowing Harry in the side. "One of these days, I might come up with something that proves Lynn wasn't such a bad person after all."

Before Harry could come back at him, little Jennifer came over to Rona and took off her helmet that was covered with bright silver stars. She gave Rona a hug and said with a perky smile, "Did you see me come down the mountain, Aunt Rona?"

"I did. You were great!"

The wattage of Jennifer's smile increased. "Do you think they'll give out a trophy for the best skier?"

"I don't know, but if they do, we think you should win."

"Really? I'm going to tell my friends!" With that, she clomped off at an awkward gait to report to her pink-jacketed cohorts, proving once again that kids below the age of ten don't throttle back even when encumbered by ski boots.

"Cute," Harry said.

As Pete watched Jennifer, he thought of Julie and the exuberance she exhibited at that age. Still exhibited as a matter of fact. It was a reminder that he needed to be careful. Julie had one person she could count on to be there for her regardless of the circumstances and it was him.

Pete went off in search of the men's room, and when he returned, Harry grabbed him by the arm and said, "Do you remember last year when we talked about your running for sheriff?"

"No, I don't. I remember when *you* talked about it."

Harry gave him an earnest look and said, "Seriously, you're a natural for this stuff. My comment about you being a vacuum cleaner was meant as a compliment."

"Do you remember what my answer was when you raised this last year?"

"I know, I know," Harry said. "I was just thinking out loud."

"I have a self-help book at my cottage. It lays out a five-point plan for people to learn to keep their thoughts to themselves. I'd be happy to lend it to you."

"I get the message," Harry said. "I just thought you might have changed your mind since last year."

"Nope. You know how stubborn we Norwegians are. At least that's what you always tell me."

"Are you going to join us for dinner?"

"Thanks, but not tonight. Tonight, I'm going to go home, heat up that lobster bisque I bought in Traverse City the other day and bury my head in my Jo Nesbø thriller."

"That's the Norwegian crime writer, isn't it?"

"It is. Maybe I'll learn some new investigative techniques from reading about Harry Hole's exploits."

"The Scots were the real detectives, you know," Harry said.

"That's what I've been thinking. I think you'd make a great candidate for sheriff."

TWENTY-THREE

The following evening, Pete headed to Maple City for the second time in less than a week. Harry couldn't join him because of a prior commitment to attend a political event at the Eagles Club. Northern Michigan was buzzing about a young state senator who the party elders were eyeing as a candidate for higher office, and he was scheduled to attend a wild game dinner at the Eagles. Harry had finagled his way into sitting at the senator's table.

Pete remembered the route from the night he was at The Peg with Harry. The bar was packed again and he didn't have the same good fortune to arrive just as a vehicle parked near the front door was leaving. He wound up at the far end of the lot under a massive tree that was nearly indistinguishable from the night sky. As he was walking back, he repeatedly stepped in puddles of water he became aware of only after his foot plunked down.

All of the action was in the bar again and the restaurant section was vacant. Pete looked for Rosa, but didn't see her. Harry's favorite waitress was probably in the kitchen enjoying a break from her strenuous evening. He felt eyes on him as he made his way through the crowd. Just locals not used to strangers as he'd told Harry during their first visit.

The same bartender was on duty. He was assisted by a sturdy young woman with peroxide blonde hair piled up in a casually messy do. The leopards on her black sequined tee shirt fought for supremacy, and skin showed where the shirt didn't quite reach her black bar pants. When he approached the bar, the bartender's look telegraphed that he remembered Pete, but hadn't been waiting all day to see him.

"Pete Thorsen," he said. "Is Sandy here?"

The bartender jerked his head in the direction of the closed door near the end of the bar and mumbled, "He's with someone."

"Would you mind telling him I'm here and would like to talk to him for a few minutes when he's free?"

Pete ordered a beer and hooked a boot on the foot rail and tried to look casual. The bartender snapped the cap off a bottle of Miller Lite and slid it down to him. No coaster, no offer of a glass. He opened more bottles of sundry brands and loaded a tray for Leopard Girl.

Fully ten minutes after Pete asked him, the bartender walked down to the door and rapped twice. He said a few words to someone inside. A man eventually emerged, closing the door behind him, and the bartender pointed down the bar to where Pete was nursing his beer. The man said hello to several customers as he made his way to where Pete was standing.

"Sandy Sandoval," he said with an engaging smile. "I'm sorry I missed you when you were here before. Welcome back to The Peg."

Sandoval had a rectangular face with a fashionable 24/7 five o'clock shadow and dark hair that was slicked straight back. Even with his loose-fitting white shirt with the top buttons undone, it was easy to see that he worked at staying in shape. His light tan didn't look like it was a product of the northern Michigan winter.

Pete smiled back and said, "This place must be a gold mine. I've been here twice and it's been packed both times."

"It would be a gold mine if I could get my margins up. There's not that much profit in a bottle of Miller Lite." He continued to smile.

"That's why we have accountants," Pete said. "A woman like Lynn Hawke should be able to help with your bar economics. I heard about this place from her."

"Lynn used to be our accountant," Sandoval said.

"That's what I understand," Pete said. "Have you heard about her accident?"

"I did." Sandoval's brows knit together in an expression of concern and he added, "That was a real shock. A nice woman. What's your connection to Lynn?"

"I did some legal work for her a while back. Unfortunately, I'm now the lawyer for her estate."

"I see. Is your office around here, Pete?"

"Frankfort."

"Frankfort. This is a long way to come for a Miller Lite. You could have saved yourself some time and bother by calling."

"I thought about that, but I had to be over this way anyway to meet with a potential new client. Besides, I like neighborhood bars."

"Who's the client? Maybe I know him."

"I'd rather not say. He's also interviewing two other lawyers and I don't want word to get back to him that I've been blabbing about his affairs."

"Makes sense," Sandoval said. "What can I do to help you? I'm afraid I don't have a lot of time tonight. I have someone in my office and don't want to leave him alone too long."

"We found a telephone number for The Peg when we were sorting out the stuff in Lynn's house. I thought you probably were one of her clients, and you've confirmed that." He built a narrative that would hold water in case his name showed up on The Peg's caller ID, and he didn't want to tell Sandoval that he'd found his telephone number in Bartholome's Seattle apartment.

"We had a retainer agreement with Lynn before she left for Seattle," Sandoval said. "Four hundred a month I believe it calls for. Since she left, we've been dealing with a woman named Barbara Rodes on the same terms."

"I'll talk to Barbara and get a copy of the agreement. But getting back to Lynn for a moment, do you have any idea who she might have been coming to see in this area the night of her accident?"

"I really don't," Sandoval said. "I was as surprised as anyone that she'd be driving around the Leelanau Peninsula during an ice storm."

"All I can think of is that she had other clients in this area and was on her way to see one of them. Do you know if she did work for any of the vineyards?"

"I can't help you there," Sandoval said. "But even if she did, she wouldn't be visiting them late at night, would she?"

"I can't imagine why, particularly given the weather."

"Anything else, Pete? I'm afraid I have to get back to my guest."

"One last question. Are you going to continue to use Barbara Rodes going forward? Barbara and Lynn had an agreement and we need to know which clients plan to continue to use Barbara so we can calculate the financial settlement."

Sandoval looked thoughtful. "I haven't decided yet," he said. "Probably not. Lynn was an impressive woman and Barbara isn't quite in her class. Besides, we're getting too big for a one-woman show and probably need a firm with some depth."

"Do you own other bars?"

"This is the only bar, but I own three health clubs in the Traverse City area and I'm thinking about adding others. Possibly even one in your town."

"Really. Health clubs are good businesses these days. If you do stop using Barbara, I suppose we'll owe you a refund for any unused retainer."

"I hadn't thought of that. If we change, maybe we can time it to coincide with the end of the annual term of our agreement."

"That would simplify things," Pete said. "Let me know either way." He signaled for the bartender to bring his bill.

Sandy put a hand on his arm. "It's on the house, Pete. Maple City hospitality. You can reciprocate the next time I'm in Frankfort."

Pete thanked Sandoval, finished his beer, and left The Peg. He glanced at the black Chevy Silverado pickup with a bank of six auxiliary lights across the top of the cab. Since it was in a "reserved" slot, he assumed that it belonged to Sandoval. Pickups weren't Pete's choice of vehicles, but he had to admit it was a man's machine.

He tried to avoid the puddles a second time as he made his way to his Range Rover. The night seemed even darker than when he came in because his eyes hadn't fully adjusted from the inside light. As he approached his Range Rover, he heard the gravel crunch behind him. He heard it too late. A heavy object slammed into the back of his head and everything went blank. He fell to the gravel and lay there dazed. As he began to recover his senses, another blow struck. This time in the ribs. Pain shot through his body. He clutched his side and fought to catch his breath.

He rolled over on his back and could make out three hulking figures looming over him. One said something Pete couldn't understand. In the darkness, he could see one of the men prepare to kick him again. Pete mustered his strength and spun around and kicked in the direction of the shadowy figure's leg. He felt his boot strike flesh and heard the man grunt in pain as he dropped to the ground.

"Help!" Pete screamed, "Help!"

Pete rolled over again and started to get up. Another blow banged his ribs and slammed him back. He heard more unintelligible words and the men kicked at him from both sides. Each time a blow landed, pain shot through his body. He gasped for breath and covered his head with his hands as one of the men aimed a kick at his head. The boot crunched into his arm and a fiery sensation caused his fingers to go numb.

"Help!" he called again.

More blows landed. He fought to get to his feet, but was knocked back by more kicks. He flailed with his arms and tried to grab one of their legs. His fingers touched cloth, but the man pulled away.

He heard a voice in the distance say, "What's going on over there?"

The kicks stopped. The men who'd been pummeling him apparently heard the voice, too, and vanished into the darkness. Pete lay on the gravel, dazed and gasping for breath. He flexed his left hand in an effort to restore some feeling. His ribs were numb from the kicks. His vision began to clear, but he felt sick to his stomach, like he was going to puke.

A man Pete didn't know kneeled by him and placed a hand on his arm and said, "You okay, mister?" Pete flinched at the man's touch and shoved his hand aside. He gingerly touched the back of his head and then flexed his hand again. The feeling slowly returned, but the pain increased. Cold water soaked his jeans.

A second man with a flashlight knelt at his side and moved the first man back with his arm. When he got close, Pete could see it was Sandy Sandoval. "Christ, Pete, what happened?" he asked.

"I don't know," Pete gasped. "Some guys jumped me."

"Did you see who it was?"

"No," he said weakly.

"Let's get you inside."

Two men helped him hobble back to the bar. He sagged back in an arm chair near the pool table with his legs stretched out and breathed hard. Sandoval reappeared and said, "I called the sheriff's office. They're sending someone right over."

Pete nodded. His head was starting to ache and shooting pain replaced the numbness in his sides. Someone asked if he was okay, but he didn't feel like talking. He also found the stares of the men standing around him irritating. Slowly they went back to their drinking and talking, but periodically Pete could see them looking his way.

A young deputy burst in and Sandoval met him just inside the door. After talking for a moment, they came over to where Pete was sprawled in the chair.

"Hal Clooney," he said. "Are you okay, sir?"

Pete grimaced. "I think so," he said.

The deputy looked at him for a long moment, as if deciding what to do, and then said, "Are you up to telling me what happened?"

Pete stretched and felt his battered body again. "What's to tell?" he said irritably, feeling worse by the moment. "I was walking to my car and three guys jumped me in the parking lot. Someone hit me in the back of the head and then they took turns kicking me while I was on the ground."

"What did they hit you with?"

"Christ, I don't know! It was heavy and stunned me for a couple of minutes."

"Do you think you'd be able to identify the men?"

It hurt to talk, but Pete said, "Are you kidding? Did you notice how dark it is out there?"

"I'm sorry, sir." The deputy glanced at Sandoval. Then he asked, "Is there anything at all you remember that would help us identify the assailants?"

"Yeah, they had dark coats and probably stocking caps. I'm sure that sets them apart from about five thousand other men in this area."

"Anything else? Their height, were they chunky or thin?"

"When you're flat on your back and guys are kicking the crap out of you, they all look ten feet tall."

"Do your best to give me an approximate description," the deputy said.

"Medium height, I'd say, and on the burly side. Maybe they just looked burly because of the coats they had on. And big, heavy feet. Boots. My ribs can attest to that."

Pete's snide remark sailed right past Clooney. He continued to write in his notebook and then asked. "How would you describe their coats? Were they ski parkas?"

"Not ski parkas. Nondescript coats. Like mine," he said, pointing to the coat draped over a nearby chair. It was dripping water on the floor.

The deputy looked at Pete's coat and made more notes. Then he asked, "Do you know if they followed you out of the bar?"

"I have no idea where they came from. They might have been in the bar or maybe they dropped from the sky. One second it was just the cars, the next they were on me."

"They could have been hanging around the parking lot waiting for someone to come out," Sandoval volunteered.

The deputy took down what he'd said. "Did they try to grab your wallet or your watch?" he asked.

"Not that I remember. They just seemed bent on kicking the shit out of me."

"And they ran as soon as people came out of the bar."

"Yes."

"It's possible they intended to rob you," the deputy said. "Maybe they were waiting until the fight was out of you and then they planned to take your valuables. Will you be okay for a few minutes while I ask if anyone here saw three men leave the bar right after you?"

Pete waved for him to proceed.

In ten minutes, the deputy was back. "I'm going to write this up. I assume that if we come up with some suspects, you'd be willing to come in to see whether you can identify them."

He laughed derisively. "Yes, I'd be willing to come in."

"Before we let you go, Mr. Thorsen, maybe we should take you to Munson to have you checked out."

"Thanks, but I'd rather get home and sleep for twelve hours. We have a small hospital in Frankfort that's part of Munson. I'll stop there in the morning."

"Are you sure?"

"I'm sure."

"Well, I have your contact information. We'll be in touch if we have anything to report."

"Okay. Say hello to Sheriff Bond."

The deputy seemed surprised. "You know the sheriff?"

"I do."

When the deputy was gone, Pete turned to Sandoval and asked, "You don't have a pair of dry jeans that would fit me, do you?"

"I'll see what we have." He returned a few minutes later with a black garment that was part of a chef's outfit. "This is the best I can do," he said.

Pete looked at the blousy pants made of a synthetic material. It reminded him of something a character in an old Aladdin movie might wear. Harry would never stop laughing if he saw him in those pants. He went to the bathroom and stripped off his wet jeans and pulled on the blousy black garment. The pants felt three sizes too big, but the elastic waistband did an acceptable job of holding them up. When he emerged from the bathroom he ignored the looks of the bartender and patrons as they tried to stifle their titters. He might look like a clown, but at least the pants were dry.

He limped out to his Range Rover with Sandoval doing everything he could to assist him. With his battered body, he knew how eighty year-old men must feel every remaining day of their lives. Pete retrieved the blanket he kept in the back of his car for emergencies, struggled to position himself in the driver's seat, and wrapped the blanket around his shoulders and upper legs. Then he thanked Sandoval again, and pointed the Range Rover west to his bed. He shook his head. He hadn't learned anything that would shed light on Lynn Hawke's accident, he'd gotten the crap beaten out of him, and he left the scene dressed like a clown. It had been a wonderful night.

TWENTY-FOUR

The next morning, Pete knew he had to go to the hospital. Whenever he moved, pain shot through his body and he feared that one or more of his ribs might be cracked. His head hurt, too, in spite of popping aspirin like they were M&Ms. He gingerly probed the back of his neck and skull with his fingers and felt a lump the size of half a grapefruit. The good news was that the skin didn't seem to be broken.

After two hours at the local hospital and multiple x-rays and a lot of uncomfortable poking and probing by the medical staff and repetitive inquiries about what happened, he left with his rib cage wrapped in bandages and enough painkillers to sedate a platoon of wounded infantry coming back from the front lines. His ribs were only badly bruised. According to the head nurse, his storm coat had cushioned the blows and saved him from more serious injury. A rookie nurse wanted to bandage his head in addition to his ribs, but he won that battle. With the way he was hobbling, a head-bandage would make him look like the last casualty from the Iraq War.

In order to get released, he had to lie about whether he had someone to drive him home. He walked gingerly to his Range Rover, looked around to ensure that a nurse wasn't watching to see if someone met him, and spent three agonizing minutes squeezing behind the wheel and positioning himself so he could drive.

Mobile, he exited the hospital parking lot at idle speed. When he came to the stop sign, he debated for a nanosecond about which way to turn. It was no choice. He abandoned all thought of stopping at his office and turned right toward his cottage. It was going to be a day for hunkering down and licking his wounds. And, if he could stay awake for fifteen minutes, trying to figure out why a bunch of thugs had jumped him.

Getting out of his car and into his cottage left him exhausted. He built a small fire and settled down with his feet up and a blanket draped over his upper body. He soon dozed off. When he woke up, it was time for another dose of painkillers. He also knew he had to call Harry.

"I'm sorry to fink out on you at the last minute," he said when the newsman came on the line, "but I'm going to have to take a pass on the game tonight."

Harry was silent for a moment and then said, "Who's going to play off guard for me?"

"I don't know, but it won't be me. I had an accident last night. I'm in no condition to play. I'd be worse than I normally am."

"What kind of accident? You sound groggy."

"I'm at home and I've been chewing these pink pills all day." He gave Harry a capsule summary of what had happened to him.

"That's unbelievable. I told you the guys in that place were hostile to outsiders."

"Three of them were at least. They jumped me in the parking lot."

"Did you have words with them in the bar?"

"I didn't have words with them or anyone else. I don't know who the guys were or why they attacked me."

"You said that guy Sandy was friendly, huh?"

"Very. He didn't try to give me any bullshit and acknowledged that Lynn had been his accountant at one time. He seemed as puzzled as the rest of us about her accident. After I was jumped, he called the sheriff's office to report the incident and got a deputy out to the bar. He seems like a standup guy."

Harry was silent for a minute. Then he said, "You shouldn't have gone up there. At least not by yourself."

"What's that they say about hindsight being perfect? You prepared me for the hostile looks, but not for thugs in the parking lot."

"I should have scrubbed dinner with the senator and gone with you."

"Then we'd both be in sick bay."

More silence at Harry's end. "I'm going to cancel tonight's game. With you out, we're down to six players. Even with a full contingent, you over-forty guys can't run up and down the court for more than one quarter."

"Do what you have to do. I just know I can't make it."

"At 5:00 p.m., Rona and I are coming over to your place with a nice dinner. In the meantime, soak your body in a tub of hot water and try to get your health back."

"I can't soak in a tub. My ribs are bandaged, remember? I look like a mummy from the waist up."

"Oh yeah, I forgot. Well at least sit by the fire and take it easy, okay? And don't worry about cleaning up. It won't be the first time Rona and I have seen a few things lying around a house."

Pete was about to settle in for a quiet afternoon when his phone began to ring. First, Sandy Sandoval called. "How are you feeling?" he asked.

"Better." He told Sandoval about his visit to the hospital and that he was lying low for the day.

"I feel responsible in a way," Sandoval said. "The Peg is a throw-back to the last century. We've been debating for years about whether we should pave the parking lot and install lights, but a lot of people want to keep the place the way it's always been. We're grandfathered under a local ordinance. But your mugging tipped the scales for me. When the weather improves, I'm going to go forward with improvements whether the die-hards like it or not."

After thanking Sandoval for calling, he added more logs on the fire, wincing each time he tossed one, and settled back in his chair with the blanket tucked under his chin. He tried to ignore his aches and pains. Mind over battered body so to speak. He checked his watch; he wasn't due for another round of painkillers until later in the afternoon.

He had just dozed off when his telephone rang again. When he reached for it, the pain rippled through his body.

"Mr. Thorsen, this is Barbara Rodes. I guess you're sort of my boss now that Lynn is deceased," she said in her squeaky voice. "An annual report for the limited liability company of one of our clients is due in three days. Should I file it?"

His irritation bubbled near the surface, but he controlled his temper and said, "Yes, file it. It's a simple one-page document, right?"

"A page and a half. The back has signature lines."

Pete rolled his eyes. "You know how to fill it out, though, don't you?"

"I think so. Who should I charge for the filing fee? You have to pay the fee when you file the form, you know."

Pete felt like crap and Barbara's helpless questions were making him feel worse. "Charge it to the client," he snapped.

"I can't," she said timidly. "He's dead."

"Dead. Which client are we talking about?"

"Mr. Breit."

He stared at the phone. "Arne Breit was one of Lynn's clients?"

"Yes. For several years I believe."

When he got over his surprise, he said, "Charge the fee to Breit's account. If you're short on money, pay it from the funds you're depositing to the bank account for Lynn's estate and we'll reconcile things later."

Before he could get back to sleep, Sheriff Emory Bond called. Bond seemed stunned to hear of Pete's mugging in The Peg's parking lot.

"What were you doing in Maple City?" he asked.

"I had to see a client in the area," Pete fibbed, "and stopped to see Sandy Sandoval about something. Lynn Hawke used to do the accounting work for Sandoval's operation. I'm the only lawyer here with business law experience and I'm trying to work things out for her estate."

Bond seemed satisfied with that explanation. He then repeated many of the same questions that his deputy had asked and assured Pete that they'd do everything they could to find and prosecute the assailants.

Before Bond got off the phone, he said, "One of my deputies and I drove over to The Peg and looked around the area where you were mugged. I feel ninety percent certain that those guys were lurking around the parking lot waiting for someone to come out."

"What do you base that on?"

"Two things. No one saw three men leave the bar right after you. Then we found four cigarette butts on the ground under that big tree near where you were parked. I think that's where they might have been waiting."

"Can you lift fingerprints from a cigarette butt?"

"We're going to try. Even if we find just partial prints, we'll run them through the database. We might get lucky."

Pete didn't prolong the conversation by asking whether Sheriff Bond had any new information about Lynn's accident. He just wanted to get off the phone and sleep.

He was finally dozing when Harry and Rona arrived with dinner. Rona set the table for three and laid out the food. Roast chicken, oven-browned potatoes, steamed broccoli and hot rolls. No dessert, which must have disappointed Harry.

They moved to the table and Pete tried not to show how much pain he was in. They ate without a lot of conversation. Periodically, Harry and Rona would glance at each other and one of them would sneak a look at Pete. Pete knew what they were thinking, but he wasn't in the mood for another lecture. To break the awkward silence, he told them about the call from Barbara Rodes that afternoon.

"Do you think that proves something?" Harry asked.

"At first I thought it might, but then I concluded it's probably not a big deal. Lynn was a small business accountant and Arne ran a small business. Both lived in the same area. It doesn't seem unusual that she'd be his accountant."

"You've been running into a lot of coincidences."

Pete yawned and said, "Maybe, but I can't think about Lynn Hawke or Arne Breit or anyone else tonight. I need to take two more pink pills and get reacquainted with my bed."

Rona put the left-over food in the refrigerator. As Pete was showing them out, Harry said, "I know you're tired and everything, but do you think the fact you were jumped has anything to do with the case you're investigating?"

"Possibly, but I can't think about it tonight. I'm dead."

TWENTY-FIVE

For the second day in a row, Pete stayed around his cottage and nursed his wounds. His head felt better, but his ribs felt worse than the day before. He alternately played some of his more soothing oldies and dozed in his chair. When he was awake, he tried to make sense of everything that had happened the past couple of weeks. And he got mad all over again when he thought about the incident in The Peg's parking lot.

Adam Rose called late that afternoon. "I have some background information on your man Conti," he said.

"Some startling revelation, I hope."

"Not startling, but I think you'll find it interesting. I'm sending you a written report as soon as I get it typed up, but here's a snapshot of what I found. Conti was born in California in the wine country. Flunked out of Berkeley after two years and enlisted in the army. He served three years and spent a lot of that time at Fort Campbell, Kentucky. He was a Spec 4, just like you, when he mustered out.

"Here's where it gets interesting. In civilian life, he got a job in Washington, D.C. with what was then the Immigration and Naturalization Service (INS). He rose steadily up the ranks of the bureaucracy and eventually became head of the enforcement unit at INS. After twenty-four years with the agency, he left to reenter the real world. He bought what is now Conti Vineyards seven years ago. I couldn't find anything about what he did between the time he left the INS and when he bought the vineyard."

"There must be something wrong with him if he spent that much time with the government."

Rose laughed. "Here's why I found his government service interesting. You said Homeland Security is investigating a murder in your area. I think you know that the INS was rolled into Homeland Security after 9/11. Maybe their investigation has something to do with immigration violations."

"You think?" Pete said.

"I can't think of what else it would be."

"Did Conti leave before or after 9/11?"

"Before."

"Any charges against Conti that you found?"

"None. No evidence that he was ever in trouble with the law and never had any civil lawsuits against him."

"Head of enforcement is a big position, huh?"

"Very big. It was one of the top positions in his agency."

"Why did he leave the government?"

"I'm not sure. Given his age, I'd guess he retired in the ordinary course."

"No scandals or evidence that he was pushed out?"

"Not that I could find."

Pete thought for a minute and then said, "Do you have time to check out a couple of other people for me?"

"Sure, as long as I can do it in the next three days. Since we talked, I landed a case in Mobile, Alabama and I'll be down there for a couple of weeks."

"Congratulations, anything you could use a sidekick on? I could stand some warm weather for a while."

"Only if you can become proficient with a side arm before we leave. As I remember from the Brimley case, you don't even own a weapon. I'd have to spend all my time covering your ass."

"I might start carrying," Pete said mainly in jest. He told Rose about getting jumped in The Peg's parking lot two nights earlier.

"Are you okay?"

"I think so. I'm lying low for a few days."

"This happened in Maple City?"

"Yes, in the parking lot of a bar called The Peg. It's on the outskirts of town."

"Do you think the incident has anything to do with your investigation?"

"Harry asked the same thing, but I doubt it. That bar seems to attract some rough-looking characters. Maybe they remembered me from the first time I was there with Harry and were being territorial. Or maybe they were just looking for someone to roll."

"You need to be careful, friend. You seem to attract trouble."

Pete gave a little laugh. "At least I need to stay out of dark parking lots. Here are the two guys. The first is a man named Gilbert Bartholome. His birth name is Gilbert Luna. I don't know when or why he changed his name. He's lived in Seattle for at least the past five years." He gave Rose the address of his apartment there. "According to Angie DeMarco, Bartholome had forgery charges against him on two occasions, but I understand he's never been convicted. I'd like you to see what else you can find out about him. Where he's from, what jobs he's worked in, whether he's been charged with anything else, that sort of thing."

"Okay."

"The second guy is Alfred Sandoval. He goes by Sandy. He owns or at least is associated with the bar in Maple City. He also owns a string of health clubs in Traverse City, and I guess he's looking to expand."

"Why are you interested in him?"

"Just being thorough."

Rose was quiet for a moment and then said, "Do you think Sandoval had something to do with your getting jumped in the parking lot?"

"I don't. Sandoval didn't know I was coming that night and he couldn't have arranged something in the time between when I left him in the bar and when the incident occurred. It was only a matter of minutes. Plus I can't see what motive he'd have."

"Then I'll ask again. Why do you want him checked out?"

"I found his private telephone number in Bartholome's apartment in Seattle. I think there's a possibility he and Bartholome know each other."

"And you want the same kind of information about him as on Bartholome?"

"Basically. Whatever you can find."

"I'll see what I can do before I have to leave."

"What's your case in Mobile?"

"You're not going to believe this."

"But you're going to tell me, right?"

"My client is the girlfriend of one of Ma Barker's sons."

"The gun moll from the thirties? You're kidding."

"Nope. Clyde — he's named after the Clyde in the Bonnie and Clyde duo — is eighty-two now. He's in the slammer in Alabama for a bank holdup. His girlfriend, who's twenty-seven by the way, hired me to try to come up with evidence that he didn't do it."

"You better get your fee up front."

"I already have. Twenty grand by certified check."

"Now why don't I get involved in cases like that? When you get back, I think we should talk about how we could team up. Thorsen & Rose has a nice ring to it."

"Isn't there something about alphabetical order?"

Pete was still smiling about his conversation with Adam Rose when the sleep-inducing powers of the painkillers took over and sent him into la-la land again. He wasn't sure how long he'd slept, but darkness was creeping over the lake when the telephone rang again.

"Hey Pops! What's shakin', baby?"

"Julie?"

"It's your favorite daughter. You sound like you don't remember me."

Pete was wide awake now. "Not this way, I don't," he said.

"You need to get out and have more fun, Pops."

"Julie, have you been drinking?"

Silence, then, "Why do you ask?"

"Because you *sound* like you've been drinking, that's why I ask. Have you?"

Another moment of silence and then Julie said, "It sure is a downer to talk to you, Dad. You throw a wet blanket over everything."

"I asked you a question, Julie, and I'd appreciate an honest answer. Have you been drinking?"

"One of the girls had some beer in her room after exams," she said hesitantly. "I had a taste."

"How much of a taste? You're sixteen, for God's sake! You're not supposed to be drinking beer!"

"Dad, it doesn't *hurt* you."

"That's not the point! It's against the law! How much did you have?"

Silence for a third time, then she said, "I didn't count."

"Well, why don't you make a nice little educated guess for your Dad."

"Two cans," she said hesitantly. "It might have been three."

Pete shook his head, but didn't say anything.

"Dad? Are you still there?"

"I'm still here," he said.

"I'm sorry."

"Sorry isn't good enough, Julie," he said in a calmer voice.

"What am I supposed to do when all of my friends have a beer?" she asked defensively. "Just sit there?"

"We've had this conversation before. Tell them you don't drink. They'll respect that."

"Oh sure, Dad, they'll respect it and I won't have any friends."

"I doubt that will happen."

"You don't know how people are. They'll think I'm just a goody two-shoes or something."

"There's no use arguing about this, Julie. I can't be at your school and control what you do every minute. But let me make something clear. If I find out you've been drinking again, I'm going to cancel your trip to Paris."

"You can't do that!"

"I can and I will."

Silence yet another time. "Okay, Dad, I won't have any more beer until I go to Paris. When I come back, we can talk about it some more. Deal?"

"I'm always happy to talk to you, Sweetie, but I don't think it will be a very long conversation. No drinking until you're twenty one."

After they finished with their conversation, Pete thought back to a simpler time when his late wife, Doris, was still alive and Julie was a sweet, innocent girl growing up. She was still sweet, but at age sixteen, he sensed that the innocence was beginning to fade. Then, too, he remembered what he did as a teenager growing up in Wisconsin. A six-pack a person was closer to the norm when he went out with his friends for some fun. But candor and good parenting didn't always go hand-in-hand.

TWENTY-SIX

When Pete stopped at the hospital to get checked out again, they confirmed that he didn't have any signs of a concussion. He questioned his healing powers, though. When the nurse stripped off his bandages, both sides of his rib cage were ugly collages of blacks and blues and greens and yellows. Like something that had been produced by an artist with a very dark outlook on life.

The nurse gave him a sponge bath and re-bandaged him. He walked out feeling cleaner and, he thought, a trifle healthier. But maybe it wasn't his health as much as the fresh dose of painkillers.

After he got to his office, he decided he needed to give priority to his first piece for *The Fjord Herald* in view of the approaching deadline. He removed his notes from his briefcase and stared at the opening line — the hook — he'd written the night before. Not bad, he thought. He changed a couple of words and then stared at the language again.

He was tinkering with the words some more when his telephone rang. It was Keegan Harris. "Good morning, Keegan," he said. In an effort to add humor, he amplified his greeting by saying, "The temperature in Frankfort is expected to reach a high of forty-seven degrees today.

Tonight's temperature will dip into the high thirties, but should remain well above the freezing mark."

"My, my, aren't we the chipper weather boy today."

"All the facts that are fit for the public to hear," as my friend Harry McTigue likes to say.

"I'm glad to hear the weather report. Now I won't worry about wearing my ski parka when I come to your office to tell you to stay out of my case."

Her abrupt comments caught him off guard and his joking demeanor faded. He said, "I have a friend who sometimes talks in riddles, and when he does, I always tell him to speak to me in English. I'm going to ask you to do the same thing."

"Stay out of my case, counselor. You know what I mean."

"No, I don't know what you mean. I wasn't aware I was intruding on your case."

"Oh come on, Pete. Masquerading as a reporter, questioning all kinds of people. You must think I'm stupid. Did you think I wouldn't find out?"

Pete was doing a slow burn now. "No, I don't think you're stupid," he said. "For the record, I'm not either. A friend of mine died in suspicious circumstances. All I've been doing is trying to find answers to questions the police don't seem interested in pursuing."

"Unfortunately, Pete, I'm aware of your reputation for sticking your nose into things. You'll have to tell me a better story than that to convince me."

"I don't have to convince you of anything, Special Agent. Why don't you tell me what your case is about so I can stay out of your way. If I've ever been in your way."

"I told you why I couldn't tell you about the case."

"Wrong. You told me you *weren't* going to tell me. There's a difference."

"You know, Mr. Thorsen," she said, her voice even icier than when she first called, "I checked with the state and they tell me you don't have a private investigator's license." Her silence punctuated her point.

"For your information, Ms. Harris, I don't *need* a private investigator's license. If you'll check further, I'm sure the state will also tell you that

I'm admitted to practice law in Michigan. That's what I'm doing. I'm the attorney for Lynn Hawke's estate and have a duty to ask questions as part of my representation."

"I see."

Pete decided to ask about the tap on Arne Breit's telephone even though he knew it would escalate their war of words. He said, "But I'm glad you called, Ms. Harris, because I want to ask about your authority for tapping the telephone of another one of my clients."

"I don't have the faintest idea what you're talking about."

"Really? Who's being cute now?"

Harris was quiet for a moment and then said, "Does this mysterious client of yours have a name?"

"Arne Breit."

"Is my mind playing games with me, or do I remember you telling me that you no longer represent Mr. Breit?"

"I believe I told you that the one active case I had for Arne was the assault case. That doesn't mean I ceased being his lawyer when the case was over. I never resigned and he never fired me. Look it up."

"This conversation is going nowhere. You've been warned, Mr. Thorsen."

"You know, the great thing about this country is that the government works for the people, not the other way around. And I don't particularly care for threats and warnings no matter who they come from," he said. His adrenaline was pumping overtime now. "That's why I became a lawyer. Now, would you kindly answer my question?"

"What was your question? You've given so many speeches, I forgot."

"Why did you bug the telephone of my client, Arne Breit?"

"Goodbye, Mr. Thorsen."

A nanosecond after his phone went dead, Pete called Joe Tessler's office number and when he got no answer, he tried his cell.

"Joe, Pete Thorsen."

"Thanks again for brainstorming with me the other day."

"You evened things up by telling me what you discovered when you checked Arne Breit's phone. You said you were staking out his place to see if someone showed up to remove the bugs. Did they?"

Tessler didn't respond right away and Pete became suspicious. He said, "I sense Keegan Harris has been throwing her weight around with you, too."

"What makes you say that?"

"Just a guess. Five minutes ago, she called and told me to stay out of her case."

"You're right," Tessler said after another long moment. "We had a confrontation with her yesterday afternoon."

"What did she do? Tell you to stay out of your own murder case?"

"Almost. She didn't like the fact we were watching Arne's house."

"She came to pick up her bugs, right?"

"Not according to her," Tessler said. "She was with some moose of a guy, and when they came to the house, our deputy stopped them and asked what they were there for. All hell broke loose. She called me and screamed that we were impeding a federal investigation. She threatened to have the President himself call if we didn't back off. Then she refused to let our deputy go in the house with them."

"What did your deputy do?"

"He stayed outside until they left. Then I came over."

"Did you check to see if the telephone tap was gone?"

"It was. They probably also collected any other bugs that were in the house."

"Not exactly a collaborative effort between law enforcement agencies, huh?"

"Collaborative? Cell phones are wireless, but if she'd been calling on a landline, she would have squirmed through the wire and ripped my balls off. You know what I think it was, Pete? I don't think they got a warrant to put the taps on in the first place and wanted to get them out before something came to light. When I've run into this in the past, the feds have always admitted that they bugged someone's phone, but claimed they had a right to. They just wouldn't tell me why they put a tap on."

"So what do you make of it?"

"I think Harris' investigation has something to do with illegal immigration."

Pete thought back to his conversation with Adam Rose and said, "That's what I've concluded, too."

"I'm just trying to solve a murder in my county," Tessler said. "Why would she complain about that for God's sakes?"

"Maybe it's not that simple. I'm beginning to wonder if all of the trails in this mess converge in one place."

"You think?"

"I do. Homeland Security is investigating Arne Breit's death and it's clear they were interested in him before he died. The wiretaps establish that. If we're right, their investigation involves illegal immigration activities. Shortly before Arne was murdered, Lynn Hawke died in what was classified as an accident, but has a fishy smell to it. Her boyfriend took off as soon as he heard Lynn was dead. Like he was panicked. Lynn made three telephone calls to Conti Vineyards the night of her accident. Conti used to be with the old INS. It seems clear that Homeland Security is watching Conti or Keegan wouldn't have known about my interview with him. Then she calls and warns me to stay out of her case."

"I see your point," Tessler said, "but aren't you weaving a lot of facts together without proof of any connection other than your suspicion?"

"I agree it's largely conjecture at this point."

Tessler was silent for a few moments and then said, "Okay, let's stay in touch as we agreed. One more thing. I'd appreciate it if you'd keep our fracas with Keegan quiet. I've butted heads with federal agencies on other cases and believe me they can really screw you if you don't do things their way. They look down on local law enforcement as it is."

After Pete was finished with Tessler, he thought more about his conversation with Keegan Harris. It came down to a simple choice. Was he going to let her intimidate him or was he going to forge on and find the answers to his questions about Lynn Hawke's accident? He saw no reason to change his course.

TWENTY-SEVEN

"Rona, there was a Louis Vuitton bag on Lynn's bed. Did you take it when we cleaned out her stuff?"

"I have it with the rest of her things."

"Would you mind checking to see if there's a luggage tag on the bag? I'm interested in the flight she took."

"I'll look."

She came back on the line and said, "There's a tag that shows she took flight 120 from Chicago to Manistee. There's no tag showing her flight from Seattle to Chicago."

"I'm not interested in that leg anyway. Is there a flight time?"

"Sorry, only the flight number."

When he was off the phone with Rona, he called the Manistee airport and was told that the flight from Chicago arrived at 6:07 p.m. on the day of Lynn's accident. He thought for a moment and then looked at the call sheet that AT&T had faxed to him earlier. The calls to the 231 number were all made after the time Lynn's flight arrived. Then he stared at the other number she'd called that night. The one he hadn't paid much attention to before.

It was to a number in the 206 area code, which was Seattle, and was sandwiched between the calls she'd made to Conti Vineyards. He dialed the number. His call went to an answering machine and a woman's voice said, "You've reached …" Pete hung up and dialed the same number so he could hear the voice again. After listening to the greeting a second time, he had no doubt that it was Lynn's voice.

It wasn't unusual for someone to call her spouse or meaningful other to say that she'd arrived safely, but the timing of Lynn's call to Seattle made him wonder. It was made after the first two calls to Conti Vineyards and before the third call. Like the calls were business calls and Lynn had to check with Gil Bartholome before calling Conti the third time.

On a hunch, Pete pulled up Conti Vineyards' website and checked the telephone number listed. There were two — an 800 number and a number with a 231 area code. Neither matched the number Lynn had called the night of her accident. She'd called the private number that bounced to Loretta Mann if the call came in during business hours and no one answered.

The tangled mess was beginning to give him a headache and he resumed work on a draft of his article. Ten minutes later, he was totally engrossed in his work and for the moment, at least, he forgot about Lynn Hawke and the others. The words flowed as fast as his two-fingered method of attacking the keyboard allowed. The exploits of the Vikings in what is now modern-day Russia had long fascinated him and he dramatized the activities of the ancient traders as they plied the trade routes along the Volga River. He wrote using creative non-fiction techniques and described how the traders swapped furs and weapons for the fine Arabian silver coins that transformed the Norse economy back home.

Harry McTigue burst in without knocking and broke his concentration. He said, "You better get cracking if you're coming to the memorial service." His eyes lingered on Pete's jeans and tattered sweater.

It took Pete a few moments to get out of the ninth century into the present. "I'm not going. I have too much to do."

"You'll be in and out in less than an hour. Your clothes shouldn't be a problem as long as you keep your coat on."

"I just told you I'm not going."

Harry softened his voice. "I think you should go. Lynn meant something to you at one time, and it's not healthy to go around sulking about something that didn't work out."

"Harry, I'm not sulking. I'm working."

"You've made up your mind, huh?"

"I have. Thanks for stopping by."

Harry stood staring at Pete. "At lot of times, I do things for you even though I really don't want to."

"I'm sure you can give me twelve examples."

"Take the night we went to that place in Maple City. I didn't want to go, but I went anyway to keep you company."

"For which I thanked you."

"I even bought dinner."

"For which I thanked you a second time."

Harry looked at him for a long moment. "It sounds like your decision is final."

"It is."

When Harry left, he tried to get back to his article, but was out of the zone as they say. He slipped on his coat and walked down the street to Ebba's Bakery and ordered his usual breakfast sandwich. Ebba hovered over him while he ate, and taking over Harry's role as inquisitor-in-chief, quizzed him about why he wasn't at Lynn Hawke's memorial service. He could see his answers didn't entirely satisfy her, but eventually she dropped the subject and went on to tell him the latest gossip about the Arne Breit murder. He knew from his conversations with Joe Tessler that much of the gossip was just that, but he let it go.

Back at his office, he tried without success to re-engage himself in his writing. He finally abandoned it and decided to spend the afternoon hanging his artwork and certificates instead. For the next two hours, he arranged the pieces along the baseboards, stood back and studied the look, then shuffled the pieces so the order was different. He hung the law certificates over the credenza behind him. Then he centered the large framed blow-up of the photograph of Julie playing soccer on a wall where he could see it from his desk chair. After that, he repositioned four of the paintings, including two watercolors by Susan Brimley, another woman from his past, and hung them on the opposite wall. When he finished, he decided he didn't have room for the Lynn Hawke piece. He stored it on the top shelf of his closet and closed the door.

He propped his feet on his desk and looked around the office. Not bad, he thought. After seven months of staring at bare walls, it would take some time to get used to. But now his office had a more permanent look. Like he was there to stay.

On the way back to his cottage, he wondered why Harry hadn't called to tell him all about the memorial service. Maybe he was miffed at him for not attending. Tough, Harry, get over it.

He built a fire, opened the best bottle of Pinot Noir in his wine rack, and settled in for the evening. He played Julie's Straight No Chaser CD several times, always stopping when the group got into the nineties songs, and then switched to Johnny Cash and Buddy Holly. He turned up the sound and grinned again when he thought about how he'd freaked out his neighbor, Charlie Cox, the previous summer by playing music at eardrum-shattering decibels at three in the morning.

Maybe he should have gone to the memorial service. If he was determined to find out if Lynn's death was really an accident, which he was, why begrudge her his last respects? He didn't always understand his emotions, but they were what they were. He poured the last of the Pinot Noir and turned up the volume to the max as the Man in Black belted out Folsom Prison Blues to the ringing hoots and hollers and jeers and applause of the convicts.

TWENTY-EIGHT

The next morning, Pete's ribs felt better than his head as a result of over-serving himself the night before. He reminded himself of his self-imposed limit on his drinking and vowed to be more disciplined in the future. Ah well, he thought, last night was just a time to cut loose. Besides, it was only wine and not a bottle of Thor's Hammer vodka.

He'd just finished his morning routine when the phone rang. His caller ID showed that it was Adam Rose. "Ma Barker's residence," he said, using his best gangster dialect.

"I must have really made an impression on you," Rose said.

"You did. It's not every day someone gives me that kind of fodder for conversation."

"Are you sure you don't want to come with me for a few days?"

"I'll consider it if you'll promise me that Ma herself will make an appearance."

"In that case, we'll have to make a detour to Welch, Oklahoma."

"What's in Welch?" Pete asked.

"Ma's grave."

"You're a walking trivia encyclopedia. But you called me to report your findings on Gilbert Bartholome, right?"

"Before I go there, do you know what Ma's birth name was?"

"No idea."

"Arizona Donnie Clark."

"You're pulling my leg."

"Nope, look it up. Now getting to your question, I didn't find out a lot about Bartholome that you don't already know, but I did find that he once worked for the INS."

Pete was silent for a moment. "Like Alain Conti."

"Yes, like Conti. They overlapped for some period, but I can't say conclusively that they knew each other."

"It's a reasonable bet that they did, wouldn't you say?"

"Not necessarily. The INS had thousands of employees. Two people could be there at exactly the same time and never meet each other."

"Was Bartholome based in Washington, D.C.?"

"Yes."

"That increases the probabilities. It's not like Conti was in Washington and Bartholome was in Des Moines, Iowa."

"True, but the only thing I'd say is a likelihood is that Bartholome knew *of* Conti because of his position. Beyond that, we'd just be guessing."

"Okay," Pete said, "anything on Sandoval?"

"Almost nothing. No criminal record that I can find, no lawsuits against him. He must be a good man, though, because he was with the navy's SEAL Team 6."

"Not at the time you were with the SEALs I assume."

"No, he was there before I came aboard."

"Honorable discharge and all of that?"

"Very honorable. I checked with a guy who knows everything there's to know about the SEALs. He said Sandoval had a terrific reputation. I guess there was nothing the guy couldn't do. He could survive in any kind of environment, was skilled in all of the martial arts. After he mustered out of the navy, he went into the private security business for a few years and spent more time in the Middle East. Then he moved back to Traverse City where he was born and bought the bar in Maple City."

"Anything else we can do to check either of these guys out?"

"I'll think about it. But as I told you, I have to get down to Mobile to see what I can do for Ma's son."

"Okay, thanks. And be sure to send me your bill."

"It's already in the mail."

"With that fat retainer check you just got from the Barker family, I thought I'd have a few days to play the float."

"My accountant makes the rules. Get the bill out as soon as the service is rendered, he always preaches."

Pete had just hung up when Joe Tessler called. "I'm at Arne Breit's house," he said. "Someone was here before me."

"Keegan Harris again?"

"I don't think it was her. Someone trashed the place."

"You're kidding."

"I'm not. Obviously, they were looking for something."

"Is Richter with you?"

"He's on vacation for two weeks. He's in Peru hiking up to the old Incan ruins."

"It's safe for me to come over then."

"I was hoping you would."

When Pete got to Arne Breit's house and looked around, he saw what Tessler meant. Every room had been ransacked. Papers were scattered everywhere, drawers were pulled out, furniture was upended, upholstery was slashed, mattresses were off their springs.

"Jesus," Pete muttered.

Tessler handed him a pair of latex gloves and said, "Put these on."

Pete followed Tessler from room to room, eyeing the damage. "What do you think they were after?"

"It's just a guess," Tessler replied, "but it was probably the same thing that got Arne killed in the first place. This happened since I was here after Keegan Harris removed her bugs."

"Are people from your department coming over?"

"I haven't called them yet. I wanted you to see this first and didn't want you here when they arrive. If someone saw you here, word would get back to Frank and then the conversation would be about why you were at the scene rather than what happened at the house."

Pete knew Tessler was right.

"Let's sit in one of our cars and talk," Tessler said. "I don't want to do anything inside to corrupt the crime scene."

They got in Tessler's car and he started the engine and dialed up the heat. Pete tried not to think about the rancid tobacco odor.

"I'm beginning to think your convergence theory is right," Tessler said.

"Do you want to hear something else that supports convergence? I told you before that Alain Conti was with the old INS for twenty-four years. I just found out that Gil Bartholome was with the INS, too."

"You're building a great case for Keegan Harris," Tessler said. "Do you think she knows all of the stuff you've dug up?"

"She knows a lot of it I'm sure. Whether she knows everything, I can't say. I didn't find out many of the things myself until after I met with her."

"Are you planning to tell her now?"

"I don't know. She pissed me off the other day with her heavy-handed threats and made me less inclined to help her."

"Same with me," Tessler mused. "Rather than sharing information, Keegan's one of those people who wants to know everything you know, but she won't tell you squat."

"The thing I don't understand is why she shows no interest in Lynn Hawke," Pete said.

"Maybe she doesn't see the same connection to the rest of it that you do."

"Possible," Pete replied. He wondered again, as he had several times in the past, whether he was letting his former relationship with Lynn color his view of the larger picture.

Tessler flicked at some dust on his dash. "I'm thinking about my last conversation with Frank before he went on vacation. He told me in no uncertain terms that he wanted to see some progress on the Arne Breit investigation when he got back. And I don't have anything except some speculation about a case that doesn't involve us."

"What do you plan to do now?" Pete asked.

"The only thing I can do. As soon as you leave, I'm going to get our people over here to photograph the scene and dust for prints just in case the perp or perps got careless. Then I'm going to follow up on every possible lead that might help us discover a motive for Breit's murder."

"You asked me what I was going to tell Keegan Harris. I'll ask you the same question. Do you intend to tell her about what happened at Arne's house?"

Tessler's lopsided grin was back and he swiped at his forelock. "I don't think the feds would be interested in a garden variety home invasion, do you?"

TWENTY-NINE

"There were quite a few people at Lynn's memorial service," Harry said.

"That's nice."

"The minister handled the service like he'd known her for twenty years. He was parroting back what Rona told him, but he pulled it off great."

"That's what ministers are trained to do."

"I was a little worried about Ida Doell. First that guy Howard Redd last year and now Lynn. She didn't look like she was dealing with it very well."

"She's a nice lady. She's seen her share of grief."

"A couple of people asked about you."

Pete shot him a look and said nothing.

"Okay, okay," Harry said. "You told me why you couldn't go. Case closed."

Harry straightened some papers on his desk and neither of them spoke for awhile. Finally Harry said, "I don't know if you've heard, but Arne Breit's house was burglarized."

"I did hear."

"They probably thought they could go in and strip the place because Arne's dead and no one else lives there."

"Do you know what they took?" Pete asked, deciding not to tell him he was at Arne's place with Joe Tessler.

"Hard to know without Arne around to vouch for what he had."

Pete nodded and looked out the window for a while. Then he said, "I'm planning to go to Conti Vineyards to see Alain Conti again."

"You're still masquerading as one of my reporters, I assume."

"I'm not *masquerading* as one of your reporters. I *am* one of your reporters, remember?" He opened a copy of *The Northern Sentinel* to the editorial box and pushed the paper across the desk and pointed to the box.

"I was just wondering whether you plan to talk about our wine feature or some other subject."

"Both. But I'm most interested in why Conti lied to me. It's evident from Lynn's telephone records that she called him three times the night of her accident. The number she called is a private line that goes directly into Conti's house. I also called the vineyard yesterday and asked to speak to the business manager. Guess what? They don't have a business manager. The woman I talked to told me that Mr. Conti handles all of the vineyard's business affairs. Lie number two."

"It sounds like you suspect Conti of something."

"I'm not saying I suspect him of anything. I just want to know why he lied. After I hear his explanation, I'll decide if I believe him."

Harry nodded. "On another subject, I read the draft of your first article. It's damn good. I never knew the Vikings were involved in all that stuff."

"We were ahead of the rest of the world by centuries."

Harry shot him a look. "I wouldn't go that far," he said.

"Admit it, Harry. While the Scots were making cheap whiskey that rotted people's guts, the Vikings were exploring the world and civilizing it."

Harry looked at him with a disgusted expression. "You sound a lot feistier than you did a few days ago," he said. "Your ribs must be healing."

"Slowly, but they're coming around."

"Did you tell your daughter about Lynn's memorial service?" Harry asked.

"I told her there was going to be one. I didn't say when. She was a lot more reasonable when I talked to her the second time. She almost apologized for some of the things she said in our first conversation."

"What have you told her about what you're doing to investigate Lynn's accident?"

"Absolutely nothing. I have a hard enough time keeping you off the ceiling when I tell you something. I can only imagine what it would be like trying to talk rationally to a teenager."

Harry tapped on his desk with a pencil and said without looking up, "What happens after you talk to Conti?"

"I don't know. A lot depends on what he says."

"Mmm," Harry murmured.

"That was fun the other night at the ski hill," Pete said. "Watching little Jennifer reminded me of Julie when she was small. Those were good days."

The mischievous grin returned to Harry's face and he said, "You better watch out. I think Carla likes you."

"That's only because I said something nice about her kid."

"No, no, she likes you. I could see it in her eyes. Rona noticed too."

"They live in Cadillac, don't they?"

"Just outside."

"That's a long way to go for a date."

"Not that far," Harry said. "Did I ever tell you what happened to me when I first moved to Chicago? I met this girl who lived in Midlothian. Where's Midlothian? I ask. Just a short ride south on the expressway they tell me. I call the lady up and make a date for Saturday night. I'm on my way to pick her up and get the off expressway too soon and get tangled up in that industrial area on the South Side. Two hours, that's what it takes me. The girl's old man was a blue collar guy and he's standing at the door in his muscle shirt when I finally arrive. He grills me for about an hour about why I almost stood up his daughter. You know, in those days, we didn't have cell phones so I couldn't call to say I'd be late. When we finally got out of there, we had about an hour together downtown because I was scared shitless about what the old man would do if I got his little darling home one minute after midnight. That's the night I learned the meaning of geographically undesirable."

"You tell me a story like that and you're still trying to get me interested in a woman who lives in Cadillac?"

Harry waved a hand. "Getting to Cadillac's nothing compared to finding your way around the South Side of Chicago." He paused for a moment and added, "Of course, I'll have to warn Carla that the last two women you dated turned up dead."

"Oh for crissakes, Harry."

THIRTY

When Barbara Rodes called again, Pete assumed it was to ask another naïve question relating to the accounting practice she hoped to keep. Whether she should continue to bill clients who died or something. Instead, it was more interesting.

"I have this mail for Mr. Breit," she said. "What should I do with it?"

"What kind of mail?" Pete asked, thinking it might be advertising material sent to Barbara's office because her address was on the annual report forms filed with the state.

"Bills from utility companies, credit card statements, advertising materials, some other letters. There's a big pile."

"That sounds like Arne's personal mail," Pete said. "Why did all of that come to your office?"

"It *is* his personal mail. Mr. Breit had it forwarded to my office and he picked it up here."

Pete frowned. "Why? He lived right here in town."

"He was afraid someone was looking through his mail. He wanted it sent here until he got the problem straightened out."

"When did this start?"

She paused a moment, like she was thinking, and said, "About six months ago I think. I can get the exact date if you want."

"No, that's close enough." Then he said, "Are you going to be in your office this afternoon? I can stop and look through the mail. Then we can decide what to do going forward."

"A client is buying me lunch. I'll be back by 1:30 p.m. The client manual says I shouldn't take more than an hour and fifteen minutes for lunch."

"I'll see you then. Enjoy your lunch."

After he hung up, he thought about Chubs' comment that Arne had become paranoid in the period before he was killed. Maybe he should talk to Chubs again and see if he could get more details before he went to see Barbara Rodes.

Chubs' Toyota Tundra was in its usual slot at the Port City Marina when Pete pulled in. His round face broke into a grin when he saw Pete. "Pete," he said, "come in, come in. I was just sitting here filling out my application for law school. Maybe you can give me your lawyerly advice on how to answer some of these questions. I like to think strategically about these things and two heads are better than one when it comes to putting just the right slant on my answers."

Pete spent the next half-hour suggesting how Chubs might want to answer the questions on the one-page application form for admission to the A. Lincoln School of Law. Penetrating questions such as why he wanted to get a law degree, what his career goals were, and how he planned to balance the demands of the profession with family life and service to his community.

"By golly, I think that sounds real good," Chubs said, beaming at how his answers read. "It helps to have a real attorney-at-law around when you do something complicated like this. When the school looks over all of these applications, I think they'll be genuinely impressed with my answers."

"Chubs, could I ask you about something you said the last time we talked?"

"Shore. That's the least I can do after you helped me with those trick questions."

"If you remember, you said that Arne had become paranoid in recent months and suspected someone had bugged his house and telephone. Anything you can add to that?"

"Did I tell you that Arne said he couldn't hardly sleep or nothing?"

"You did."

"He said to me a lot more than once that it wasn't just them bugs, neither. He said that people were going through his mail and his garbage and everything. I'll tell you, Pete, that shouldn't happen to a man in the U.S. of A. It ain't right."

Pete talked to Chubs for another half-hour. While he repackaged his words in different wrappings, the implication was always the same. Arne Breit felt that someone was watching his every move.

■ ■ ■

The Mountain Breeze scent engulfed him when he walked into Barbara Rodes' office. Barbara bent his ear for fifteen minutes about her agreement with the late Lynn Hawke. She emphasized again how she'd not only lived up the letter and spirit of the agreement, but had gone the extra mile and alerted Pete to things she thought he should know. Like the need to file Arne Breit's annual report and that his mail was piling up. Pete adroitly deflected her questions and assured her that he'd make a decision on the agreement soon.

Barbara set the box with Arne Breit's mail in front of him and perched on the edge of her desk chair like a hungry bird while he looked through it. Besides the predictable advertising come-ons for new corporate credit cards and offers to reduce the rate on Arne's home mortgage to 1.9%, there were bills from the electric and gas and telephone companies and monthly statements from Visa and American Express. At the bottom of the pile was a plain envelope with Arne's name and Barbara's office address scrawled on it in barely legible handwriting. Pete could feel a small hard object in the envelope.

"When we talked on the phone you said Arne was concerned that someone was looking through his mail. What did he base that on?"

"I don't know," Barbara said, shaking her head, "but he said he had evidence. I felt so sorry for Mr. Breit. I was afraid someone might take something valuable from his mail."

"Like checks?"

"Like checks, or maybe somebody was even trying to steal his identity. That happens to a lot of people these days you know."

"Yes, I know. Did Arne suspect the government of looking through his mail?"

"He didn't say. Do you think it could have been the government? Mr. Breit had a tax lien against his fishing boats one time. Maybe the government thought he still owed them money."

Pete shrugged and said, "Possible, I suppose. To have the mail sent to you, I assume Arne went to the Post Office and filled out a mail forwarding form."

"Yes, there's delivery service where he lives so the mail didn't go into a box at the Post Office. Everything would have been okay if his mail had been locked up in a Post Office box."

"And you said he came in once a week to pick up his mail."

"Every Friday. That's why there's so much. That's two weeks of mail."

"Okay," Pete said. Then he remembered something else and added, "Do you have a list of Lynn's clients?"

"Not a list. We have a computer report that Lynn kept. I've updated it with changes I know about."

Pete struggled to avoid rolling his eyes. "Could I see the report?" he asked.

Barbara opened a desk drawer and handed him a dog-eared sheaf of papers. Arne Breit LLC was on the report, as was The Peg Corporation and clients like Ida Doell's limited liability company. He started going through the names again. He stopped when he came to "CV LLC." He pointed to the name and asked, "Is this Conti Vineyards?"

"It's not Conti Vineyards, but it's the company that owns it. Have you had any of their wine?"

He controlled his urge to cut loose with a primal scream. "I think so," he said. "Who do you deal with at Conti?"

"Oh, always with Mr. Conti. He's very careful with his affairs. He wants to see everything himself."

"Have you had any problems with him? Complaints about service or anything else?"

A look of alarm creased her face. "Has Mr. Conti called to complain about something?" Her voice wavered.

"No, nothing like that. I was just wondering."

Barbara expelled air in a sign of relief. "I do everything I can to keep Mr. Conti happy. I return all of his calls within three hours just like the client manual says you should and try to do everything right. He's such a wonderful client. And a *very* nice man."

"Great," Pete said. "Keep up the good work, Barbara. I'm going to take the mail with me. I'll talk to you in a few days about what we do in the future."

On the way back to his office, he thought about Barbara's comment about Conti and how he liked to see everything personally. That was consistent with what the woman had told him when he'd made the blind call.

When he got back to his office, he looked through Arne Breit's mail more carefully. He threw out the obvious advertising materials, which reduced the pile by two-thirds, and put the utility bills to one side. Then he opened the credit card statements and scanned the itemized charges. Several charges for gas and fast food near Mackinac caught his eye. The charges only went back a month, but showed Arne had been out of the area as recently as the first week of March. The plain envelope addressed in bad handwriting had "Private and Confidential. For Mr. A. Breit" in the lower left corner. He opened the envelope and found a folded sheet of paper with a small key attached to it with Scotch tape.

Pete stared at the key. There was nothing to identify it other than "A217" pressed into the brass. It looked too large to be a luggage key, and with current airport security procedures, the old custom of a traveler locking her luggage had fallen into disuse anyway. Beyond that, the possibilities were endless.

He didn't know Arne's handwriting, but he remembered the documents Arne had signed when he had the assault charges against him. He retrieved the file from his cabinet and compared the handwriting on the envelope with the signature on the out of court settlement agreement. The two looked remarkably similar.

Why would Arne mail a key to himself?

THIRTY-ONE

Pete was still thinking about the key the next morning when his cell phone burred.

"Pete, this is Sandy Sandoval. "How are you feeling?"

"Better, thanks."

"I'm in town looking at your fitness center and wondered if you had plans for lunch?"

"I was just going to grab a sandwich with my friend, Harry McTigue. He owns the local newspaper. Nothing I can't cancel."

"Bring him along."

"Are you sure?"

"Absolutely. Just warn him that I might have to go off the record with parts of our conversation. I want to talk about how you can help me if I decide to buy the center."

"Harry's been around the block. That won't be a problem."

When Pete and Harry walked into Dinghy's, Sandoval was already there. Pete introduced him to Harry and they took a table in back.

"How are your ribs?" Sandoval asked.

"Tender, but on the mend."

"No fractures?"

"No, just some very bad bruises."

"Does Harry know what happened?"

"He does."

"You have some rough characters in that bar of yours," Harry said. "When we were there the first time, I told Pete that I thought some of them looked a little hostile."

Sandoval raised his eyebrows and said, "Oh, you were there with Pete, too?"

"He was keeping me company while I made my rounds," Pete said. "I bribed him with a plate of your quesadillas." Pete noticed Harry about to say something and beat him to it with a question of his own. "What did you think of our fitness center?"

"I was impressed," Sandoval said. "A nice building and very well equipped."

"A lot of us who are regulars at the center," Harry said, "think it compares with what you find at centers in many larger cities. It has every machine you need for a good workout."

"Are you a member?"

"I am," Harry said seriously.

"I'm trying to get a handle on the usage. Is it typically busy when you're there?"

"It's busiest in the summer when the lake people are here. You can barely get in the door."

"That's one concern I have," Sandoval said. "It seems to have a lot of seasonal and other short-term memberships. That's not good from a predictable revenue stream standpoint."

"Don't all centers have that problem?" Harry asked. "The workout center I belonged to in Chicago was always running promotions to attract new members. A lot of the trial memberships were for three months or six months."

Pete asked how fitness centers were priced and Sandoval explained and told them about his plan to string together a group of centers in northern Michigan under an umbrella name. He asked Pete to summarize his experience in the M & A field.

After they were finished, Sandoval said, "I know Harry is a workout guy. How about you, Pete?"

"He doesn't have time," Harry said, grinning and answering for him. "He's too busy investigating crimes and getting beat up in parking lots."

A slight grin creased Sandoval's face. "There's not enough legal work up here to keep you busy, huh?"

Harry was about to answer for him again when Pete jumped in and said, "Harry accuses me of investigating just because I answer some of his hypothetical questions over dinner."

It was Harry's turn to grin. "Hypothetical, my ass," he said. "That's not why you went to Seattle to see what you could find out about Lynn Hawke."

Sandoval looked at Pete for a long moment before saying, "I remember the conversation about Lynn in my bar. I can understand why you'd want to investigate her accident. Driving around the Leelanau Peninsula during an ice storm makes no sense to me either."

"And why she was headed for Conti Vineyards," Harry interjected.

Pete clinched his teeth and wished he'd cancelled out on Harry and gone to lunch with Sandoval alone. Sometimes there was no graceful way to shut his friend up without calling more attention to an issue than he wanted.

"I don't know if you remember," Sandoval continued, "but you asked me whether Lynn used to do work for any of the vineyards in our area. I asked around with some people I know. I'm told she did work for Conti Vineyards for several years."

"Well, we'll probably never know for sure where she was going," Pete said. "The sheriff investigated and concluded her death was an accident. I heard he closed the case."

"Then why are you going to see Conti again?" Harry asked Pete.

"To get more information about the articles I'm writing for your news-paper on area vineyards. Or have you cancelled out my series and not told me about it?"

"I'm surprised the sheriff closed the case," Sandoval said. "If it were me, I'd look deeper because of the unusual circumstances."

"That's what you said, Pete. I think the sheriff has to take another look at that guy Conti. Particularly in light of what you told me about the calls Lynn made to his place the night of her accident."

"She made calls to Conti?" Sandoval said with raised eyebrows. "How do you know that?"

Pete was about to plunge his fork into Harry's chest. He said to Sandoval, "The sheriff found Lynn's cell phone in her car after the acci-dent. He turned it over to me along with some other stuff as the lawyer for Lynn's estate. The phone showed a couple of calls to Conti Vineyards."

"I see," Sandoval said. "So you're Lynn's lawyer and that's how you know all of this."

"She's his old girlfriend," Harry blurted out.

Sandoval just looked at Pete.

"I went out with her for two months," Pete said. "She's probably dated ten other guys since then. Now I'm the lawyer stuck with unwinding her legal affairs."

"Never pleasant," Sandoval said. "I like my business better. Sell them beer and then have them go to one of my fitness centers to work off the hangover."

THIRTY-TWO

Pete was still annoyed with Harry as he sat in his office after lunch. Maybe he should keep what he was doing to investigate Lynn's death to himself. It didn't help to have everything blabbed around town. Thankfully, he hadn't told Harry about Arne's mail or the key he'd found.

He thought some more about possible uses for the key. Three occurred to him. One was that the key fit one of Arne's boats. Another was that the key was for a Post Office box. The third was that it was for a safe deposit box Arne had at a bank. There were other possibilities, but those three struck him as the most logical.

Pete had to endure a half-hour of excited chatter from Chubs about the A. Lincoln School of Law before he got him to confirm that the key didn't fit the ignition or any of the padlocks on either of Arne Breit's boats. He also struck out at the Post Office; the key was too large and the numbering system was wrong.

That left a bank box, and there were a lot of sub-possibilities because he had no idea which bank Arne used. Or if Arne had rented a box at the same bank he used for the rest of his business. There were two banks in town and several more in surrounding communities. He decided to start with the local banks.

He walked into Betsie Bay Trust Company and asked the woman behind the counter where the safe deposit boxes were. She told him they were in the lower level. When he asked for directions, she said he had to show identification and then be escorted to the boxes by a bank representative. Hearing that, he switched gears and said all he needed to know was whether a certain individual had a box at the bank. The names of box holders was confidential, the woman said, and could be disclosed only to authorized persons. In a last-ditch effort to get what he wanted, he asked to speak to the bank manager and was told that he wouldn't be back until late that afternoon.

Pete thought about it and concluded he'd most likely encounter the same hurdles at other banks. He needed something to get past the gate-keepers. Then he thought of his new friend, Barbara Rodes.

"Barbara," he said when she answered the telephone, "do you have a power of attorney or any other authority to act for Arne Breit?"

"What do you mean?"

"Sometimes clients give their lawyer or accountant a document or a corporate title that authorizes them to act on routine matters if the client isn't available."

"I don't think I have anything like that."

"Did you sign the annual report form you called me about?"

"Yes. You can't file the report without signing it."

"You must have authority then."

"I'm only the Secretary of Mr. Breit's Limited Liability Company."

"There you go. You have authority."

"I do?"

"The corporate Secretary is one of the principal officers of a company."

"It is?"

"Sure enough. Could I draft something up and bring it over for you to sign so I can deal with some things related to Arne Breit's estate?"

"I guess so."

"I'll be there in an hour."

Pete returned to his office and drafted a document grandly entitled Authorization and Power of Attorney that permitted him to act for Arne Breit and entities owned or controlled by him for all purposes, including but not limited to marshaling Mr. Breit's assets and winding up his affairs. He smiled and hoped that the document would work. It blurred the line between Arne Breit and his legal entities, something a first-year law student would readily pick up on, but he was counting on a lay person not being as attuned to nuance.

Barbara Rodes read and reread the document and asked him seemingly endless questions about what this line or that line meant. Only when he implied in not-so-subtle terms that he was still grappling with what to do with her agreement with Lynn did she finally pick up a pen and sign multiple copies of the document.

Bolstered by his newly documented authority, with the LLC's seal prominently affixed no less, he returned to Betsie Bay Trust Company. The manager was back. Pete presented a copy of the elegant new legal document and his business card and waited for the manager to review them. When he was finished, he said, "I don't think that key fits one of our boxes, but let's take a look."

They took the stairs to the lower level. It was not exactly like visiting the morgue, but it was nearly as quiet. Apparently the safe deposit box business wasn't booming in Frankfort. The entire wall was filled with lock boxes. A small box for banking customers who didn't have much to squirrel away. A medium box for those with more. And a large box for the heavy hitters.

"Let me see the key again," the manager said. He looked at the number on the key and studied the boxes. "I'm sorry," he said. "It's not for one of our boxes."

On the way back to the first floor, the manager said, "I heard the tragic news of Mr. Breit's death. If there's anything we can do to help with his estate, I hope you'll call me. We have a full-service department devoted to trust and estate matters. I'm sure we can provide everything you'll need." He pressed one of his business cards into Pete's hand and seized his other hand in a limp-wristed, clammy grip. Pete hoped his recoil wasn't noticeable.

Pete also had no luck with the second bank in town, or with the banks in Empire or Glen Arbor. He was grateful for one thing, however. His "official" document was working like a charm.

He got to Deer Hunter's Bank & Trust in Honor just before closing time. The manager, apparently more focused on closing for the night than anything else, glanced at Pete's documentation and led him to the safe deposit boxes. "The number looks like ours," he said. Just as Pete was kicking himself for not going to Honor first, the manager added, "Yes, it's in the row of boxes on the right. I'll be right outside if you need me." The manager looked at his watch as he stepped out the door.

Pete felt his pulse quicken as the key slid in the lock. He opened the door and removed the tan canvas duffel. A number of thin letter-sized packages were inside the bag. Ten in all based on a quick count. Each package was neatly wrapped in plain brown paper and had a name on the outside. Satish Reddy. Ravi Shah. Mohan Rao. And seven others. All of the names appeared to be individuals from India.

Pete put the individual packages back in the bag and closed and locked the safe deposit box door. He walked out with the bag in hand and signaled to the manager that he was finished. He expected to be kept waiting while the manager inventoried the contents of the bag, but he needn't have worried. It was two minutes before 5:00 p.m.

A rush swept over Pete as he got in his Range Rover. He periodically glanced at the bag on the seat next to him as he drove back to Frankfort.

THIRTY-THREE

As he waited impatiently for Joe Tessler to arrive, Pete stared at the packages stacked on his desk and wondered what he'd found. And why Arne Breit had locked the packages away in a safe deposit box.

Tessler came hurrying in without a hello. "What do you have?"

Pete pointed to the packages and said, "Should we open one or should we call our friend Keegan Harris to participate in the honors?"

Tessler stared at the packages and appeared to be thinking. "We're going to get the same flak from her whether we find out what's in these packages or call her first. Besides," he continued, "the packages were within the control of a man who was murdered in my county and might contain information that's relevant to my investigation."

"I assume that means that you think we should open one."

"It does."

"That makes it unanimous," Pete said. "I'll let you do the honors." He pushed the pile to Tessler's side of the desk.

Tessler used Pete's pewter letter opener with a Viking design on the handle to carefully undo the tape that secured the ends of the top package. When the outside wrapping fell away, Pete saw a thin flat box like the kind used to hold a small quantity of fine bond paper. Tessler peeled back the tissue to expose the contents of the box. "Just a minute," he said and went out to his car and returned with two pairs of latex gloves. He handed one pair to Pete.

Pete stood so he could get a better look at what was in the box. The top item was an unmarked business-size envelope. Tessler withdrew the laminated card that was in the envelope and held it up for Pete to see. Then he withdrew several other items from the box. Among them were a driver's license and a Social Security card. All were in the name of the person on the outside of the package.

Pete picked up the laminated card and examined it. He looked up at Tessler and said, "We were right. Arne was mixed up in an illegal immigration ring."

Tessler stared at the card and then at Pete.

Pete turned the card so Tessler could see it and asked, "Do you know what this is?"

"Some kind of identification card."

"It's a 'green card'," he said.

"I've heard the term," Tessler replied.

"A green card is an immigrant visa that lets the holder live and work in the United States. Stop me if you already know this, but a foreign national can't just come to this country and live and work here. Not legally, anyway. He has to have a visa which lets him do those things. Travel is one thing, but it's far more difficult to get a visa that allows a person to work."

"Why wouldn't a person who wanted a green card just get one from the government?"

"Time and our quota system. And the red tape. A lot of people try to get a green card for years with no success. Let's try a box from the bottom of the file and see if it's the same."

Tessler slipped the bottom package from the pile and carefully unwrapped it just as he had the first one. This time the contents were different. There was no green card, only a raft of papers including one titled "H1B Approval Notice."

"Do you know what this is?" Tessler asked.

Pete nodded and flipped through the documents with his gloved hand. He saw the original petition by a company whose name he didn't recognize. Tessler continued to look at Pete and waited for an explanation.

"These are H1B visa documents," Pete said. "A lot of companies in the tech industry and other fields rely on these visas to bring people into the country to work in their businesses. Skilled people like engineers and mathematicians and the like. If you look at some of the tech firms that have made it big in the past couple of decades, you'll find that many of the people who were the driving forces behind the businesses are from India and other countries in Asia."

"I gather an H1B visa is different from a green card."

"A lot different. With an H1B visa, an American company that wants to employ, say, a software engineer from India has to file a petition with the government. If the petition is approved and the engineer successfully navigates the other hoops, he gets a visa to work for the petitioning employer for up to three years. In most cases, that can be extended for another three years. But here's the catch. There's a strict quota on the number of H1B visas that can be issued in one year. In some years, the quota for the entire fiscal year has been filled on the very first day of the fiscal year. A H1B visa is a non-immigrant visa with strings attached to it, but in the short run, it's just as valuable and highly sought after as a green card."

"I'm beginning to get the drift," Tessler said. "These are hot commodities."

"Very hot."

Tessler looked at Pete and asked, "How do you know so much about this stuff?"

Pete chuckled. "Keegan Harris asked me the same thing when she wanted to know if I'd ever advised Arne Breit on immigration matters. When I was in law practice in Chicago, a big part of my client base was European and secondarily Asian companies that were investing or otherwise doing business in this country. You couldn't practice in the area I did without knowing something about visa and immigration law."

"I see," Tessler said. "What government agency issues these visas if it's done legally?"

"It used to be the INS, but now it's Homeland Security."

"Keegan's agency."

"Yes."

"You told me Alain Conti was with the old INS."

"For twenty-four years according to my information. He was head of the enforcement division. He probably knows his way around this area backward and forward."

"Gilbert Bartholome was with the INS too, huh?"

"He was. They overlapped, but it's unclear whether Conti and Bartholome knew each other."

"Who do you think produced this stuff?"

"It would have to be someone with sophisticated equipment and an inside knowledge of the process."

"Like Bartholome?"

"Possible. I don't know."

Pete picked up the green card again and examined it more closely. "I wonder if this has a chip in it?" he mused.

Tessler looked at him with a blank expression.

"Sometime in the past few years, the government began installing RFID chips in green cards. I don't understand all of the technology, but what it comes down to is it's a security device. Without it, a card like this would be worthless if the government ever checked."

"This seems like a sophisticated operation. They wouldn't miss something as obvious as a chip would they?"

"You wouldn't think so. But a guy who's producing counterfeit green cards would have to have technical knowledge to implant the right kind of chip and do some of the other things."

"How about Arne Breit?" Tessler asked. "I didn't know him, but from everything I've heard, he wasn't a real sophisticated guy. What do you think his role was in all of this?"

"Courier probably," Pete said. "Assuming the counterfeit documents are being produced in this country, they'd have to use couriers to get them into the hands of people who paid for them. Those people would want to come here on the counterfeit documents. If they came on other types of visas and just over-stayed and then tried to justify their status by tendering the counterfeit documents, they'd risk something coming to light. Arne was probably acting as a courier on his trips to Canada. He was a natural, particularly in the summer, with his charter operations."

"You think?"

"That's what I'd guess. A lot of Asians come to Canada and then try to get into the U.S. I would think that western Canada would be more the center of that activity, but I'm no expert on immigration patterns."

Tessler looked through the rest of the packages, but didn't open them. "How much do you suppose they charge for a package like this?" he asked.

"Probably a lot. More for a green card package than an H1B package, I'd guess. But who knows? With an H1B package, the employer would have to be in on it, too, and that might affect the price. I have no idea."

"Amazing."

"I bet that's what Lynn Hawke was doing on all of her trips to the Far East."

"Acting as a courier?"

"More likely drumming up customers for the counterfeit documents."

They sat without speaking again for a long moment. "So where do we go from here?" Pete asked.

"That's what I've been thinking about. My goal is to find and arrest Breit's killer, then dump everything else in Keegan Harris' lap."

"Okay, that's your wish list. How about the real world?"

After a couple of minutes, Tessler said, "I'm going to sleep on it and decide in the morning. I might call Harris. It'd be easier if she weren't such a bitch. What are you going to do?"

"I already have an appointment to see Alain Conti a second time. My short term goal is to find out why he lied to me about Lynn Hawke."

"Be careful. It looks like he might be right at the top of this thing."

"Take away 'might' and you're probably correct. I'm going to tread lightly, believe me."

"Do you want me to stand by just in case?"

"That's out of your jurisdiction. Conti Vineyards is in Leelanau County."

"I could be out for a scenic drive on a brisk March day."

Pete understood what Tessler was saying. "I might take you up on that. Let's talk in the morning."

"What should we do with this stuff?" Tessler asked, gesturing toward the boxes on Pete's desk.

"I could lock them up in my file cabinet overnight or you could take them to the station with you."

"If I take them," Tessler said, "I'd have to log them in our evidence room and then I'd get all kinds of questions from the deputies and Frank would eventually hear about it. Why don't you store them in your file cabinet tonight? Then we can decide in the morning what to do."

As Tessler was putting his coat on, he said, "Those guys are going to be pissed if they find out we have their stuff. Remember what they did to Arne's place?"

THIRTY-FOUR

Whenever Pete woke up during the night, Tessler's words clanged in his head like a giant gong. *Those guys are going to be pissed if they find out we have their stuff.* Finally he gave up trying to go back to sleep and moved to the living room and started a fire. He sat in a chair with a blanket wrapped around his shoulders and stared at the flames. At some point, he finally dozed off and when he woke, the fire had burned down to embers and the morning light was streaming through the windows.

It was another decent day. The sky was mostly cloudless and the lake was pure blue-green with none of the angry waves that had pounded the shore only days ago. Even the birches looked more vibrant. Overnight, the bark seemed to shed the gray look of winter and replace it with the pristine white he was used to seeing in the warm weather months.

While the weather had improved, South Shore Road was as deserted as it had been in the heart of the winter. No dog walkers. No groups of women strolling along and sharing gossip. No roller boarders or bicyclists whizzing past the slow-paced walkers. No middle-aged men in garish colored Spandex lumbering along with red faces at a pace that wouldn't threaten the land speed record of most tortoises.

Across the road, where cottages of various sizes, some modest and others quite grand, looked out on the water, the same feeling of solitude reigned. Shades were pulled to shield windows from prying eyes and larger canvas coverings, almost always pale gray, protected porches from the wrath of the howling wind and blowing snow.

As Pete walked east, he reflected on how everything would begin to change again in another month. Buds would sprout on the trees and bushes and, one by one, the cottages would shed their winter coverings. South Shore would become a beehive of activity once more and people would flock to the beaches and pot lunch suppers would reign supreme in the evenings. Then it all would begin to fade again as the autumn chill returned and the season gradually morphed into winter. All part of the cycle of life.

Those guys are going to be pissed if they find out we have their stuff. Tessler had intended his comment as a joke, but there was a reality to his words that chilled Pete to the quick. He passed Walker's Trail and the sign reminded him of Cara Lane and the raw human emotions that whole affair exposed. The emotions in that case were fueled by conviction and passion and blood ties. Here it was money. And he knew that money stirred the deepest human passions of all.

■ ■ ■

When Pete walked in his office at 10:00 a.m., he was relieved to see that everything was just the way he'd left it the previous evening. His message light was flashing. He checked and found he'd just missed a call from Loretta Mann. He called her back.

"Mr. Conti asked me to tell you he has to cancel your appointment with him for this afternoon. Could you come tomorrow instead? He should be back by then."

"He's away I take it?"

"He's in the hospital," she said hesitantly. "He expected to be released last night, but the doctors extended his stay."

"Sorry to hear that. Anything serious?"

"One of his regular appointments. I don't think I should say anything more about private medical matters."

"I see. Wish him well for me and tell him I'll see him tomorrow. Same time?"

"Yes, same time. I hope this doesn't inconvenience you."

"No, that's fine. Give Mr. Conti my best."

When he was off the phone with Loretta, Pete thought about the way Conti had looked the first time he was there. He wondered about his condition and whether it was something other than advancing age.

Joe Tessler called next. "I don't know about you," he said, "but I had a sleepless night thinking about those counterfeit documents. I decided I should call Special Agent Harris and turn the stuff over."

"That's probably wise."

"I called the number I have for her and some man who wouldn't identify himself answered. He told me that the Special Agent wasn't available. I asked him to have Harris call me when she had a minute and he said he'd give her the message. That was it. Short and simple. I couldn't have been on the phone with the guy for more than fifteen seconds."

"What number did you call?" Pete asked. Tessler told him and he compared it to the number Keegan Harris had given him the day she was in his office. They were the same.

"Well, she can't blame us for holding out on her. We'll just have to wait until she gets back to me."

"What should we do with the documents in the meantime?"

Tessler was slow to answer. "From the tone of your voice, I sense you'd like to get them out of your file cabinet."

"I would."

"I don't want to hold them in our evidence vault, either, for reasons I mentioned yesterday. Why don't we rent another safe deposit box at a bank and store them there until we can turn them over to Keegan."

"Betsie Bay Trust Company is right down the street from me. I know they have boxes because I was there yesterday. I can open one and give you the keys tomorrow."

"What's tomorrow?"

"I had to switch my appointment with Alain Conti from this afternoon to tomorrow. He's been in the hospital. You were going to be driving around the area, remember?"

"Oh, yeah, right."

When Pete was off the phone with Tessler, he thought briefly about his follow-up interview with Alain Conti. Did Conti suspect he was interested in something other than wine? He decided to worry about that later. His immediate goal was to get the counterfeit documents out of his possession and into a safe deposit box as he'd just discussed with Tessler. Then he'd let Joe deal with that end of things.

He unlocked the file cabinet and removed the canvas bag and stared at it. He'd feel like a safecracker walking into a bank with the bag, and decided a cardboard box would look more innocuous. He found a box that was large enough to hold the individual packages, removed them from the bag, and put them in the box. He thought about jamming the empty bag behind the files in his cabinet, but decided he'd get rid of the bag too. He took the packages out of the box again, placed the canvas bag on the bottom and flattened it, and put the packages back in.

He then drove the two blocks to the bank and explained to the assistant manager that he wanted to open a safe deposit box that was large enough to hold the cardboard box. He filled out the application form and listed Joe Tessler as the co-holder of the box with an equal right of access and the right to remove part or all of the contents. He wasn't required to itemize what he was putting in the box, but he wrote in at the bottom of the form that he was storing documents for Mr. Tessler and identified his position with the sheriff's department.

He left the bank and walked across the street to the library where he spent fifteen minutes chatting with the staff. Then he caught up on the latest newspapers and browsed through the mystery section of the library's book collection. He read the first chapters of several new releases. The opening lines intrigued him and he marveled at how the best writers hooked a reader with their very first words.

Still feeling restless, he got in his Range Rover and drove around the area. Heat was still a problem, but with the outside temperature up and the sun warming the exterior, his car wasn't as uncomfortable as it had been the past few weeks. He followed the route Tessler had taken that day and proceeded up the hill to the overlook.

His thoughts returned to Alain Conti and he rehearsed in his mind how to handle the conversation the next day. After exhausting his made-up questions about wine, one option was to limit his probing strictly to questions that related to Lynn. That was the safest approach. The other option, which his curiosity but not his head nagged him to do, was to broaden the conversation in an effort to bring the larger picture into focus. He couldn't make up his mind which way to go and decided to let the flow of the conversation dictate his course.

Pete's cell phone burred. It was Joe Tessler again. "When I talked to you this morning," Joe said, "I completely forgot that I'm scheduled to be in Lansing tomorrow to testify in another case. Could you reschedule your meeting with Conti for a day when I'm around?"

Pete thought about that. "I'd rather not," he finally said. "I had a hard time setting up the second interview and told Loretta a few hours ago that I could come tomorrow. I'm not sure what kind of excuse I could give to postpone the interview now."

"Loretta is the woman at the vineyard?"

"Yes." Pete thought some more and added, "She let it slip that Conti has been in the hospital. I don't know if it's anything serious, but if I don't see him tomorrow, I might have a hard time getting another appointment."

"I'd feel more comfortable if I were in the area."

"So would I. But you know what the likely scenario is? Conti will come up with a cockamamie story about why he didn't admit he knew Lynn Hawke. That will end it because I can't very well sit there and accuse him of lying."

"Are you sure?"

"I'm sure." When he was off the phone, he stared at Lake Michigan for a long time and then backed away from the cable cordoning off the bluff and drove down the hill.

THIRTY-FIVE

When Pete entered Conti's house this time, he tossed his keys on the side table before passing through the invisible alarm area. A shrill buzz didn't shatter the quiet and the chef didn't magically spring from the kitchen to monitor his movements.

Alain Conti was waiting in the study. He was seated in his wheelchair with a blanket neatly tucked around his legs and looked pale and drawn. The room felt like the thermostat had been dialed up several degrees since his first visit.

"I apologize for not getting up, Mr. Thorsen. My legs aren't cooperating."

"No need to apologize," Pete said. He shook Conti's hand and took a leather side chair across from him.

"I hope you didn't mind rescheduling our appointment. I had to be away yesterday."

"Loretta explained," Pete said. He didn't ask Conti about his health or mention that he knew about his hospital stay. "It was good of you to make time for me today."

"I see you have a list of questions." Conti gestured toward the legal pad Pete had withdrawn from his leather portfolio. "I guess there must be things we didn't cover the last time." His gaze lingered on Pete and a smile tugged at the corners of his mouth.

"Just a few things I should have asked on the first go-around. It shouldn't take more than a half-hour."

Conti signaled that he was ready to begin.

"Something you said during our first interview interested me. If I took it down right, you said you match the grape varieties you plant to the soil conditions and the weather. I can understand the weather, but could you expand on the soil conditions point? I bet that's not something even a lot of wine connoisseurs are aware of."

Conti put on his professorial hat and talked about the different soils on the Leelanau Peninsula and in Napa Valley, France and the other leading wine producing regions of the world. He explained how soil affects grapes and, ultimately, the character of the wine that's produced from them. Pete asked some follow-up questions and Conti responded in his usual precise manner.

"Now, if I asked you for the top three things that distinguish Conti Vineyards from its competitors in this region, what would you say?"

Conti gazed at him for a time then said, "I'm happy to continue to answer these questions, Mr. Thorsen, but I was hoping you'd have gotten to the real point of your visit by now."

Conti's pointed comment caught Pete off guard. He frowned and said, "I'm not sure I know what you mean."

"We're both intelligent men, Mr. Thorsen. Let's not insult each other by playing games. Do you mind if we get on a first name basis by the way? Mr. Thorsen and Mr. Conti sounds so formal."

"I agree."

"What you're really interested in is why I told you I didn't remember Lynn Hawke. Isn't that right?"

Pete said, "That did make me curious."

"It's simple, really. I'm on medication and I was getting very tired. I didn't want to get into a discussion at that point that had nothing to do with the purpose of our interview."

"I can understand that," Pete said, "but I learned afterwards that you knew Lynn quite well. Why didn't you just say that?"

"Did you ever say something when you were tired and later realized you should have put it another way?"

"Probably," Pete said, "but I'll tell you why I'm interested. Lynn was a friend of mine and I had to go to the morgue to identify her body. Then when I collected her things, I noticed that she called Conti Vineyards several times the night of her accident. She was also driving this way at the time. I began to wonder why, that's all."

"You sound more like a detective than a reporter."

"Lawyers are taught to pay attention to detail. We notice things a lay person might not. I noticed the telephone calls."

"You must have been a very good lawyer, Pete. Let me tell you what I should have told you the first time. Lynn Hawke was our accountant for several years until a woman named Barbara Rodes took over. About a week before her accident, Lynn called me and said she was thinking about moving back to this area. She asked whether I'd be comfortable using her services again if she did. We made an appointment to discuss it."

"Is that what you talked about when Lynn called the night of her accident?"

"No. Lynn was seeing someone else in the area and called me several times to say she'd be late. Time kept passing and the weather got worse. Finally I got too tired to stay up any longer and went to bed."

"And you learned about her accident the next day."

"Not the next day. I tried to call her, but there was no answer. I learned of the accident in the local newspaper a few days later."

"Okay," Pete said, "that makes sense. I wish I'd known this sooner."

The little smile appeared on Conti's face again. "Then you wouldn't have needed a follow-up interview to talk about wine, would you?"

Pete let the comment go and said, "Well, I won't take up any more of your time."

"Thank you for letting me explain, Pete. And I'm very sorry about our friend."

"I'm sorry, too. I guess she got caught on the roads on a bad night."

"Very unfortunate. I tried to persuade her to postpone her visit until the weather improved, but I guess she had to get back to Seattle."

Pete nodded and stood to leave.

"Writing for a small-town newspaper must be a come-down after the career you had as a lawyer. Are you enjoying your brand new career as a contributing editor?" He smiled again.

"I am," Pete said. He sensed an opening and laughed disarmingly and said, "This is actually my third career. I started out as a Spec 4 with the U.S. Army. Were you ever in the military or other government service, Alain?"

"I had quite a long government career as a matter of fact."

"Really? Who were you with?"

"The INS before it was reorganized out of existence. I was head of the enforcement division until I left to pursue my wine passion."

"When did you leave?"

"Years ago. Before 9/11."

"That's interesting. Our firm represented a lot of foreign clients and we dealt with visa and immigration issues all the time. I don't remember bumping into you."

"I'm sure all of your clients were law abiding, Pete. The INS enforcement division probably had no interest in them."

"A lot of my lawyer friends who were with the government early in their careers can't get that experience out of their blood. Are you like that?"

"No, I've moved on. Wine is my life now."

"You're lucky. It's a whole different world out there. Low level workers pouring across our borders, skilled workers trying to get into the country and hook up with tech and other companies. I'll bet the enforcement problems are more challenging these days."

"That's what I understand. But as I said, I've moved on. Are we finished, Pete? My battery is starting to run down."

"We're finished. If I need anything else, I'll call you."

"About wine you mean?" Conti said. There was a hint of sarcasm in his voice and his thin smile didn't extend to his eyes.

As Pete passed, the nameless chef watched him from the kitchen door.

Pete walked to his Range Rover convinced that Alain Conti was a lying sonofabitch who could still be quick on his feet when he had to be.

THIRTY-SIX

The interview wasn't a disaster, but Pete knew he'd let himself get outflanked. Conti had taken control of the conversation and had an immediate answer for every question. He'd obviously thought through the story he was going to tell and left Pete with a choice of accepting it or calling him a liar. Conti probably understood human nature and banked on the probability that the latter wouldn't happen. It was difficult to call a man a liar if you only suspected something he told you was untrue.

Pete also thought about the counterfeit documents in the safe deposit box and was convinced he'd just been talking to the man who ran the ring. He was sure Bartholome was also involved, although possibly as Conti's adversary within the ring, and maybe Lynn Hawke was as well. What he didn't know was the real reason Conti lied about knowing Lynn Hawke and whether he was responsible for her death.

He turned on the county road to cut across to M-22 on the west side of the Peninsula. After a couple of miles, he glanced in his rearview mirror and noticed a dark pickup a hundred yards behind him. Two miles later, he checked again. The pickup was still there. It maintained its distance and proceeded at the same speed Pete was traveling, neither closing the gap nor dropping farther behind. Pete studied the pickup and began to wonder if he was being followed. He saw a sign ahead for another vineyard and made a quick decision to turn in. He parked next to the two vehicles in the lot and saw the pickup pass the vineyard entrance at the same slow speed it had been traveling.

He went into the tasting room and joined the two couples who were sampling the vineyard's offerings. The room was pleasant, but lacked the upscale atmosphere of Conti Vineyards. He took his time selecting two bottles of moderately-priced blended red wine and paid the lone employee who was tending the fort on a quiet day. A half-hour after he stopped, he exited the facility onto the county road again. There was still no traffic ahead of him or, this time, to his rear. He settled into his thinking mode again as he drove west. When he glanced in his mirror five miles later, the dark pickup was behind him again.

Pete accelerated to fifty miles an hour. The pickup lagged behind at first, but then picked up speed to keep pace. Pete dropped back to his former speed. The pickup slowed as well. Pete accelerated again. The pickup lost ground at first, but gradually regained it and settled into its former pattern of following Pete by about the length of a football field.

Pete clinched his jaw. He hadn't seen the pickup follow him out of Conti Vineyards and didn't understand how it could be behind him again now. It must have been parked out of sight both times waiting for him. He thought about the plan he'd originally discussed with Joe Tessler and wished he were in the area.

Twilight was setting in and Pete turned on his lights. The pickup remained dark. Pete entered Glen Arbor and decided to get off M-22 and loop around a back street and get on the highway again. If it worked, he'd be behind the pickup and might be able to get a look at its license plate. Then he could ask Tessler to run a trace. He cranked his steering wheel left and kept watching in his mirror to see if the pickup followed. He didn't see it. He turned left at the first cross street and then turned left again. When he came to M-22, he turned again and proceeded slowly through town. He watched for the dark pickup, but didn't see it.

Pete passed through the narrows between the two lakes and breathed easier as he headed out of town. Maybe the afternoon at Conti's house had spooked him. He kept watching in his rearview mirror for signs of the pickup, but saw nothing. Empire was just ahead, and when he came to the town's lone gas station, he pulled in to fill his tank. As he was finishing, he noticed a vehicle with its lights on waiting at the curb two blocks behind him. It looked like a pickup or a SUV, but he couldn't be sure.

He called Joe Tessler on his way out of Empire. The call went to voicemail and he asked him to call back. Then he called Harry and arranged to meet him at The Manitou for an early dinner. Tessler called back just before he got to the restaurant. Pete gave him the highlights of his meeting with Conti and told him about the pickup. Tessler said he was on his way back from Lansing and would join them for dinner if they could stretch things out an hour.

Pete pulled into The Manitou's lot and parked where he could observe the traffic on M-22. An occasional vehicle passed, but no dark pickup. Harry arrived his usual half-hour late, just when Pete felt frostbite begin to nibble at his toes. He gave up his chilly vigil and hurried toward the restaurant's front door.

"I haven't been here since last fall," Harry said. "I love this place. All of these animal heads on the wall and the mounted trophy fish and the black bear that's waiting to greet you."

They sat in the "pontoon plane" booth, as they called it, and the first thing Harry did was peruse the menu for something to tide him over until Tessler arrived. He settled on a double order of smoked whitefish with extra crackers.

"The meeting with Conti went okay, huh?" he asked.

"Okay, but not productive. A lot of smoke and mirrors."

"What's that supposed to mean?"

"Let's wait until Joe gets here so I don't have to tell the story twice."

"I looked at our editorial schedule. I think we can run your feature stories about Leelanau vineyards beginning the last week of June. That's when the tourists and summer people start to arrive. About June 1, we'll start running teasers to let people know the features are coming."

"Don't get ahead of yourself. You have to line up some other vineyards first."

Harry looked surprised. "I thought you were going to do that."

"I never told you that. The interview with Conti was just a ruse to get in to see him."

"Oh, great! You use my paper to help you play detective, and now you're planning to leave me in the lurch."

"I'm not leaving you in the lurch. The series might not even go forward. Conti's health isn't good."

Harry's eyes narrowed. "What's wrong with him?"

"I don't know. He's in a wheelchair and doesn't look good. His assistant said he's been in the hospital. That's why I had to switch my follow-up interview with him to today."

"Are you trying to hold me up for something?" Harry asked suspiciously.

"We can talk about compensation per word if you want."

"I knew it was something like that! You know I can't afford to pay my contributing editors. Your reward is seeing your amateurish stuff in print."

Their bickering was interrupted when Tessler walked in. "I'm glad to see that you're still breathing," he said to Pete.

"Still breathing and moderately embarrassed." He described how Conti had "outed" him and controlled the conversation from the beginning.

"He sounds slick."

"Slick and nobody's fool." Pete looked at Harry and said, "You didn't hear any of this, okay? Nothing in your paper and no pillow talk."

"Hey, I'm not going to say anything," Harry protested. He perched on the edge of his seat and seemed anxious to hear more."

"To hear Conti talk, everything I dug up meant nothing. He dismissed his earlier statement that he didn't know Lynn Hawke by saying he was tired that day and didn't want to get into it. Today he admitted he knew

Lynn, but said her calls to him that night were just to let him know she was on her way and had been held up by the bad weather. According to him, Lynn was in the area on some other business and was combining missions and wanted to talk to him about whether Conti would resume using her accounting services if she came back. He didn't flinch when I asked him about his time with the old INS. He readily acknowledged it, but said that part of his life is behind him and wine is the thing that's important to him now."

"A pat story."

"Pat and well rehearsed."

"Did he admit to knowing Arne Breit?" Tessler asked.

"I didn't ask. I couldn't find a way to work it in."

"You said you were tailed by someone after you left Conti's place."

"You didn't tell me that," Harry said, looking concerned.

Pete looked Harry's way and said, "At least I *think* I was tailed. This black or dark blue pickup kept popping up behind me."

"Did you get his plate number?"

Pete shook his head. "The pickup didn't have a license plate on the front. Plus it was too far behind me to read a plate anyway. I tried to circle around and get in back of him, but lost him."

"Mmm," Tessler murmured.

"He might have been behind me again when I stopped for gas later, but I can't be sure."

"So Glen Arbor is the last place you can definitely say you saw him."

"Yes. I waited outside for a while until Harry arrived, but didn't see a pickup go by or pull into the restaurant's lot."

"Why do you think they'd want to tail you?" Harry asked.

"*If* I was being tailed, it's probably because Conti suspects I'm onto something. I don't know what else it would be."

"It could be the feds," Tessler volunteered. "You told me Keegan knew you were talking to Conti and pretending to be a reporter. The only way she'd know that is if she has someone watching his place and he reported to her that you were there."

Pete mulled over his comment.

"Joe," Harry said, never bashful about filling the void in a conversation, "maybe you can convince Pete he should leave law enforcement matters to you professionals. All of this stuff has me worried."

Before Tessler could say anything, Pete said, "Harry and I have had this conversation before. He thinks the bad guys are going to dump my body in the middle of Main Street some night."

"You joke about it, but it's not a laughing matter," Harry said.

"Okay," Pete said, "let's not spoil a nice dinner by talking about it tonight."

When they finished eating, Harry said, "I'm sorry to be a party pooper, but I've got to get going. I'm in Rona's doghouse for some reason. I need to have a glass or two of wine with her and mend fences."

"Harry," Tessler said, "if it's alright with you, I was never at this dinner, okay? Word gets around and I don't want people to get the wrong impression."

Harry winked at him. "I understand. Sheriff Richter will never hear about it as long as one of you picks up the dinner tab."

After Harry left, Tessler said, "You should think about listening to Harry."

"He's a good friend. He's just being protective."

"You have been poking around quite a bit."

Pete gazed at the model airplane suspended above them and said, "It's something I have to do. Harry knows that."

"Still …"

"I'm not going to stop now, Joe. Unless you guys put me in a cell for interfering in an investigation."

"You're not interfering in *our* investigation. I was referring to your personal safety. You may be onto something that has some people concerned."

"I try to be careful."

"Careful? In the past week, you've been beaten silly and now you're followed by this black pickup."

"I said I *might* have been followed."

"Okay." Tessler was quiet for a minute. Then he asked, "Have you thought about having a security system installed in your house?"

Pete grinned. "Like Conti?"

"It doesn't have to be as elaborate as Conti's. But yours is the only house on the lake within a half-mile that's occupied at this time of the year."

"That's one of the things I like it about being up here during the off-season. The solitude."

"Think about it. ADT has an office in Traverse City. At this time of the year, I bet you can get a tech out on short notice to wire your place."

THIRTY-SEVEN

Pete was puttering around his office the next morning when Tessler called and said, "Keegan left a message on my voicemail."

"And?"

"She's out of the country — she didn't say where — and said she'd call me when she got back. She didn't say when that would be. Her last words were that if I needed to speak to someone in the meantime, I should call Martin Steele at the number she gave me."

"She's probably lying on a beach somewhere," Pete said.

"Either that or she hasn't heard the Cold War is over and she's meeting a mole on some dark street in Berlin."

"She's a domestic sleuth, remember? She's not CIA."

"Yeah, right."

"I guess we're going to have to hold onto the documents a while longer."

Tessler sighed. "I suppose you're right." He sounded embarrassed when he added, "I had one of our deputies camped out near your house last night. He said everything was quiet."

"You didn't tell me you were going to do that."

"I didn't want to worry you. But after we talked at dinner last night ..."

Pete wished Tessler *had* worried him. He might have slept better. Their conversation was on his mind, too. He was awake off and on throughout the night and imagined all sorts of menacing sounds outside his cottage. When he got up that morning, he felt like he hadn't slept more than two hours.

"The deputy looked like crap this morning, but he said everything was clear and it was a beautiful night."

"Does he have plans for tonight?"

"Nothing that would prevent him from hanging out on the west end of the lake and watching the moon rise over the water."

"Getting back to your message from Keegan, do you think we ought to turn the documents over to this guy Martin Steele?"

"I thought about that. I talked to him when I called for Keegan. He sounds like more of an asshole than she does."

"You seem to be saying that we should wait for Keegan to get back."

"That's my thinking."

When he was off the telephone with Tessler, he propped his feet on his desk and stared out at the bay. Maybe it was wishful thinking, but there were definite signs of spring. His thoughts shifted to Alain Conti and he wondered if Barbara Rodes could tell him anything useful. Probably not based on his past experience with her, but it was worth a try. He punched in her telephone number. No answer. He left a message for her to call him.

He stripped the brown paper off the watercolor that the art supply store had framed for him. The piece was by a local artist and showed a fly fisherman working the Little Manistee River. He admired it for a minute and then reached for the telephone again.

"I just got my fly fishing watercolor back from the framer. It looks great."

"It won't be long partner," Harry said. "It won't be long."

"I took a closer look at the painting. I could be mistaken, but I'm almost positive I'm the model for the piece. Perfect form, the line snapping out over the water, a seventeen inch trout about to go for my fly. The painting looks identical to a photograph Julie took of me last year."

Harry snorted so loud that the phone vibrated. "Ha," he said. "That can't be you or the painting would show the line snarled in a tree and you mouthing every cuss word in a truck driver's vocabulary."

After kibitzing with Harry a while longer, Pete called Barbara Rodes again. Still no answer. He left another message.

Pete took down the paintings that he'd hung a few days earlier and hung the fly fishing watercolor on one of the hooks. Then he held two of the other pieces up and studied the look as well as he could from close distance. He'd have to do some rearranging, but the watercolor had become the new centerpiece of that wall.

He called Barbara a third time and still got no answer. Apparently her call-back protocol didn't apply to him. He chafed at the lack of a response.

He laid the pieces of art on the floor and shuffled them around and tried different configurations. He found a grouping that worked, but didn't feel like hanging the pieces just then. He felt edgy and needed to get out of the office.

Pete took the roundabout route to Beulah and went past his cottage and then along the north shore of the lake. The sun was higher in the sky than it had been a month earlier and its rays glinted off the choppy water. He passed through the downtown Beulah to the side street where Barbara's office was located. The lights were off when he pulled up in front.

He shaded his eyes and peered in her office window. He was stunned by what he saw. Papers littered the floor, file drawers were open, chairs were upended, desk drawers were pulled out, the collection of ceramic animals that Barbara kept in a wall case were scattered.

He pulled out his cell phone and punched in Tessler's number. "Joe, it's Pete again. There's been another break-in, this time at the office of Arne Breit's accountant. You probably should come over if you're free. Her office is in downtown Beulah." Pete gave him the address.

"Have you been inside?" Tessler asked.

"No, I'm looking through the window."

"Don't go in. I'll be right over."

Tessler arrived ten minutes later and pulled up behind his Range Rover. He peered in the window for a good look, then used an elbow to depress the door handle and pushed the door open. He studied the damage again.

"I'm going to have our crime scene team come over," Tessler said. "We should try to reach the accountant and alert her."

"I've been trying to call her all afternoon. There's no answer on either her cell or her landline."

"Try again," Tessler said.

Pete called Barbara Rodes' numbers for the fourth time. There was still no answer on either phone.

"I bet these are the same people who trashed Arne Breit's place," Tessler said.

Pete nodded.

"I think I know what they were looking for, too."

"The counterfeit documents."

"There's no doubt in my mind."

"Do you think we should check Barbara's house?" Pete asked.

"Couldn't hurt. Where does she live?"

"Near-by, I understand. I don't have the address."

"We need an address," Tessler said.

"We can try the phone book," Pete said, stating the obvious.

"I don't want to disturb the crime scene by looking around inside for a telephone book," Tessler said.

"The rental agent for this office is Crystal Properties. Their office is right around the corner. They should have one."

Tessler started up the street at a trot without debating other alternatives. While he was waiting for Tessler, Pete stared in the window again and wondered if Barbara had received any more mail for Arne.

A few minutes later, Tessler trotted back down the street and said, "I've got the address. She lives in Benzonia. Ride with me. I'll take you back to your car later."

As Tessler cruised through the mostly vacant streets of Beulah, he turned to Pete and said, "I have a bad feeling about this."

Pete had a bad feeling, too.

They saw Barbara Rodes' house coming up on the left. It was a simple ranch with a yellow *faux* brick exterior and matching shrubs flanking the front door. Tessler parked in the driveway and they cut across the lawn to the walk. The side panels by the door were frosted, but the inside lights didn't appear to be on. Tessler pushed the doorbell and waited. After a minute, he pushed it again. Tessler looked at Pete and used his glove to turn the door knob. Like Barbara's office, it was unlocked.

Tessler nudged the door open part way and called "hello" several times. No answer. The living room draperies were pulled and the room was dark except for slivers of light that filtered in around the draperies and from the open door. Pete followed Tessler inside and his eyes slowly became accustomed to the dim interior. The living room looked undisturbed. Tessler made his way to the kitchen and clicked on a light switch with his elbow. Pete blinked at the sudden burst of light. Again, everything looked orderly and in its place.

Pete followed Tessler when he headed for the short hallway where the bedrooms were located. He looked over Tessler's shoulder at the first bedroom. The twin bed was neatly made and filled with a dozen stuffed animals that stared back at him with glassy eyes. Two small quilts with blue and white diamonds had been mounted on frames and hung on the walls.

Pete left Tessler to search the other bedrooms and doubled back to the family room in the rear of the house. He mimicked Tessler's move and used his elbow to flip a light switch. He was blown away by the sight. The ceramic collection in Barbara's office was only a teaser compared to what he saw. There were hundreds of figurines arranged on glass shelves and grouped according to theme. There was the Snow White theme and the Noah's Ark theme and the Star Wars theme and the Christmas theme and the Jurassic Park theme.

A door at the end of the room was ajar. The door opened to a stairwell that went to the lower level. It was dark. He imitated Tessler's elbow move again and clicked on the light. He walked slowly down the steps without touching the hand rail. He used the move a third time to turn on the lights at the bottom of the stairs and saw the pool table in the small rec room. *Oh Christ, no!*

THIRTY-EIGHT

A woman's body was stretched out on the table. The green felt had turned black where her blood had pooled and dried. One of her arms hung lifelessly over the edge and a cue stick lay on the floor.

Pete sagged back on one of the steps and dropped his head into his hands. He fought the tears that were welling up in his eyes.

Tessler appeared and called, "Anything down there, Pete?"

His words sounded like they came from a mile away.

"Pete?"

Tessler came down the stairs and slipped past Pete. He saw the body and muttered, *Shit!* He went to the pool table and walked slowly around it.

He turned to Pete who was still sitting on the stairs and said, "Is that Barbara Rodes?"

"I think so," Pete said softly.

"Are you okay?" Tessler asked.

"I'm going outside," Pete muttered.

Pete went up the steps and left the house. A car passed, but he didn't lift his eyes to look at it. He just stared at the cracks on the concrete walk. He breathed deeply, as if cleansing himself of what he'd just seen.

Tessler came out a short time later with his cell phone clamped to his ear. He stood with his back to Pete and spoke in an urgent tone. He ended the call and said to Pete, "Our team is coming over. They're leaving the office until later."

Pete didn't say anything. Then he looked at Tessler and said, "Who would do something like this, Joe? I didn't know Barbara Rodes very well, but I doubt if she'd harm a flea. I don't understand this."

Tessler tightened his lips and said, "My gut feeling is that these are very bad people and there's big money at stake. They're not going to let anything stand in their way."

"How was Barbara Rodes in their way?" Pete asked, pressing the issue. "She was one of the most innocuous, unthreatening people I've ever met. They could have gotten anything they wanted by just saying 'boo' to her. They didn't have to kill her, for crissakes!"

"It seems clear they were looking for the counterfeit documents we have locked away. She didn't know that. They probably thought she did and were trying to make her talk."

"The feds are responsible for this!" Pete said. "They bugged Arne's phone and snooped through his mail. They forced him to involve Barbara by having his mail forwarded to her. The feds are responsible for Barbara's death, Joe."

"They may be, but pointing a finger at them isn't going to get us anywhere. Besides, they'll never admit to doing anything wrong."

"Bullshit! They can't just play with people's lives!"

Two cruisers with lights flashing and sirens slicing through the quiet air came speeding down the street. They were followed by a boxy EMS vehicle. A civilian car arrived ten minutes later. Pete recognized the woman who got out of the car. It was the same police photographer he'd seen the previous year when they found Les Brimley's body on the golf course.

Tessler donned latex booties and gloves and led the team into the house. Pete waited outside with conflicting thoughts rattling around in his head. He remembered the last telephone conversation he'd had with

Keegan Harris and the way she'd thrown her weight around. *They really don't care*, he thought. As long as they get what they want, anyone who's hurt along the way is just collateral damage.

Tessler came out of the house after a half-hour and walked to where Pete was standing at the end of the walk. He glanced at the local residents who'd been attracted by the sirens and lights and gathered to watch.

"That body is carved up pretty bad," he said. "There's not much doubt in my mind that they were trying to make her talk."

"Yeah, to make her tell something she didn't know."

"Getting back to our conversation before I went inside," Tessler said, "someone could argue that we're as responsible as the feds. We're the ones who squirreled away those documents."

Pete looked at Tessler and asked, "What were we supposed to do? Leave the bag in the middle of Main Street with a sign saying the owner should claim it by sundown? You're just making excuses for those bastards."

Tessler didn't respond. "I keep wondering why Arne was holding the documents in the first place. He couldn't have expected to broker a deal by his lonesome and pocket all the cash."

"That's probably not what happened. Piecing together what we know, I think there's a split in the ring. Arne was aligned with one side and could have been using the documents as leverage."

"You mentioned the split before."

"Arne probably felt squeezed between the feds and the bad guys and was looking for a way to get out of the middle. Both sides wanted those documents. The feds for evidentiary purposes and the bad guys for the money."

They stood quietly for a few minutes.

"I can take you back to your car if you want," Tessler said.

"That's fine," Pete said, "I'll wait until you're finished. I'm going for a walk."

Pete walked aimlessly through the neighborhood for a half-hour, thinking. When he got back to Barbara Rodes' street, a man who had been watching the activity cut him off.

"Are you with the police?" the man asked.

"No."

"You were inside the house. You must have some official duties."

"I really don't."

The man kept walking alongside him and asked, "Could you tell me what the problem is. Is there a medical emergency or something?"

"You'll have to get your information from that guy over there," Pete said, pointing to Tessler.

The man headed in Tessler's direction until he was stopped by a deputy who was charged with keeping the crowd back.

An hour later, the EMTs came out of the house carrying a stretcher with Barbara Rodes' body covered by a blue plastic sheet and loaded her into their vehicle. The man who'd been trying to get information from Pete shifted his focus to one of the EMTs. Pete couldn't hear the EMT's response, but hoped he gave an innocuous answer so he wouldn't spook the neighborhood.

A uniformed deputy was stringing yellow crime-scene tape on the front of the house when Pete left with Tessler to pick up his Range Rover. After a few blocks, Pete turned to the detective and said, "If they suspect something about Arne's mail, which is probably what led them to Barbara Rodes, chances are good they know about me, too."

"Probably," Tessler agreed. "I'm going to have our guy watch your house again tonight. And you need to seriously rethink getting an alarm installed."

THIRTY-NINE

Pete watched while the two techs operating out of an unmarked white van wired his cottage with the most sophisticated alarm system their company offered. He nixed their proposal to put decals on the doors and windows to deter would-be burglars by warning them that the house was protected by ADT. The people he was concerned about wouldn't be deterred by the decals. Worse, it would simply alert them so they could disable the system.

After they finished the installation, the techs trained him in the use of the system. When the basic system was on, any attempt to open a door or a window triggered a loud and incessant beeping sound. If an intruder penetrated the first line of defense, he'd be detected by the invisible beams that crisscrossed rooms a foot above the floor and would set off a similar alarm signal. The system was wired so that the components could be used separately or together. Pete made sure the beams were positioned so they didn't impede his path to the bathroom, a necessary bit of foresight. In all other respects, it was a poor man's version of the sophisticated system used in art museums and, he assumed, in many banks.

Pete was reading the instruction manual for the system when Joe Tessler stopped in. He demonstrated the system for Tessler. First he had

Joe go outside while he armed the system. When Joe opened the door to come back in, the harsh beeping sound made the cottage vibrate. Then Pete had him stand just inside the door and went to his bedroom to turn on the floor beam system. He called Joe to his bedroom, and before he'd taken his second step, the beeping started again.

Tessler grinned. "What did this system cost you?"

"You know that old saying, if you have to ask the price of your life …? I didn't ask. I just told the techs to install the best system they had."

"Mmm," Tessler murmured.

"The company offered me a choice of contracts. Six months or twelve months with a ten percent discount. I took the six-month package. You don't need more than six months to catch those assholes, do you?"

"I hope not," Tessler said, sighing. He looked at Pete and added, "Do you have a weapon in the house?"

Pete looked at him blankly. "My bow," he said.

"I mean a sidearm. Most people in this area have guns of one kind or another."

"Excluding the lake people. But what's your point, Joe?"

"I'm not going to be able to have a deputy watch your house at night much longer. A couple of them are already asking me pointed questions and when Frank comes back …"

"I understand. I have my alarm system now."

"That's fine," Tessler said, "and I'm glad you had it installed. But after your alarm is triggered, how long do you think it will take someone from our office to get out here?"

"I don't know. A half-hour?"

"At least. Do you know what could happen to you in a half-hour?"

Pete was silent. He preferred not to think about it.

"An alarm system is great to alert you, but then you need to defend yourself if someone breaks in. I don't think you want to rely on a bow and arrow if someone is storming your bedroom."

"I understand what you're saying. But I haven't fired a gun since I was in the army."

"You have fired one, though."

"Of course."

"Both a pistol and a long gun?"

"Yes."

"You need to get reacquainted with firearms until this is over. For your own good."

"Don't you need to have a license?"

Tessler nodded. "If you want a handgun, at least. And there are concealed carry permits and all of that. But I have something in my trunk you can use that'll let you bypass the normal procedure."

"A pistol, I assume."

"Yes."

"Let me understand this, Joe. What if, say, I'm stopped for a traffic violation and the officer finds I'm carrying an unregistered handgun. What happens then?"

"You're not going to have the weapon with you when you're driving your car. You're just going to keep it in your house for protection in case you need it."

Pete stared at Tessler for a long time. "I'm not comfortable with this, Joe. Even with your scenario, I'm in possession of a handgun without going through the proper registration procedure. I'm not an expert on these matters, but I seem to recall that people have been prosecuted even if they used a *registered* weapon for self-defense."

"You're letting your lawyer brain overwhelm your survival brain. Which would you rather have happen: Be charged with a firearm violation or be dead?"

Tessler was right, of course. Any rigmarole he had to go through to lawfully possess a handgun could take days if not weeks. By then, it might be too late. "What kind of pistol do you have?" he asked.

"I'll get it. Turn off your alarm system so I don't get plugged with one of your arrows when I come back."

Tessler returned with a pistol and held it sideways so Pete could see it. "This is a Glock 17 semi-automatic. It's one of the most popular side arms in the world. It's the same thing I carry, although mine is a more compact version. It's chambered for 9x19mm cartridges and uses ten-round clips." He handed it to Pete.

Pete balanced the weapon in his hand and got the feel of it. He had grown up around guns and used them from a young age to hunt and target practice. But that was a long time ago. He wasn't opposed to guns the way some people were, but he didn't own one or hunt anymore. It wasn't a philosophical thing; his life had just moved in a different direction.

"There's an indoor range near Benzonia that our people use. I think we should go over there so you can get a feel for the weapon and squeeze off a few shots."

"Fine," Pete said, still not feeling completely sold on the idea.

It was a weekday afternoon and they could see through the open door that the range was deserted. The man who ran the place was in his sixties or maybe even his early seventies and wore a camouflage shirt with bright green suspenders. He scratched his gray beard when they walked in and said, "Howdy, Joe. I'm glad to see you're finally showing your face around here. Who's your partner?"

"Jake, this is Pete Thorsen. Pete's a friend of mine from over on Crystal Lake. I thought we'd practice for a while as long as we don't have to wait too long." He glanced through the door at the empty range and grinned.

"I think I can fit you in. You need some brass or did you bring your own to screw me out of a few bucks profit?"

Tessler chuckled. "We'll take two boxes of ammo for this Glock and two sets of goggles and earplugs."

Inside the range, Pete followed Tessler's lead and donned the goggles and earplugs. He watched as Tessler loaded the clip. When he was finished, he racked the slide so Pete could see what he was doing and then motioned him back. He aimed at the target and squeezed off a round. He looked at the hole in an outer ring and muttered, "Rusty." He fired again with better results. Then he fired a third time. He handed the Glock to Pete and said, "It's live. Let's see if you remember what they taught you in the army."

Pete stepped forward feeling awkward and keeping his finger off the trigger. It had been a long time. He raised the Glock with a two-handed grip, aimed, and squeezed off a round. The recoil was less than what he remembered from firing a Colt in his army days. He didn't see a new hole in the target. Maggie's drawers as they used to say. He avoided eye contact with Tessler and was determined to do better on his second attempt. This time a hole appeared in the outer ring of the target not far from where Tessler's first round had hit. He looked at Tessler and Joe nodded.

For the next twenty minutes, Pete squeezed off shot after shot with the Glock. His shot pattern was erratic, but most of his shots hit the target. When he'd gone through the first box of ammunition, Tessler said, "Okay, that's enough. You did fine. Our goal isn't to make you a world-class marksman overnight. All you have to do is make sure you can hit an intruder in the chest if one shows up."

Pete grimaced at Tessler's comment and watched as he cleaned the Glock. He handed it to Pete and said, "It's empty." He handed him the second box of ammunition. "You know how to load the clip, right?"

Pete nodded and lost himself in thought on the way back to the lake.

FORTY

"Dad, Mikki got accepted!"

It took Pete a moment to pull himself out of his thoughts. When he was focused on what Julie had just told him, he said, "That's wonderful news. I'll bet she's excited."

"Everything's falling into place just like I knew it would. Mikki has awesome talent. She just needs some help to develop it."

Pete smiled and refrained from reminding Julie that her earlier pessimism had been unfounded. "Do you know what your schedule is yet?"

Julie breathlessly told him in elaborate detail when they planned to leave for Paris, when their art classes began, and when they were scheduled to return home. "The only bummer," she said, "is that we have to live in a house with a house mother. I thought with France being so much more advanced than the rest of the world, they wouldn't treat us like a bunch of babies."

He smiled when he heard the reference to France because he knew a lot of people didn't share Julie's view. "I'm sure it won't be a problem," he said.

"I just hope we don't get some old woman who's forgotten what it's like to be young and won't let us do anything. Some people are like that, you know. Especially when they get to be fifty or sixty years old."

The age reference again. He was about to say something when Julie continued with her happy babble.

"Rona sent me a copy of the program for Lynn's memorial service."

"She told me."

"It must have been a beautiful service. I would have given anything to be there, but with our class schedule and everything ... They won't let you take time off unless it's to attend a service for a family member."

Pete was anxious to get her off the subject so he said, "I suppose the book project is back on now, huh?"

"You mean about our summer in Paris?"

"Yes."

"It's *really* on now. You're a writer, Dad. Do you think Mikki and I should keep journals to collect information for our book?"

"I do. Otherwise when you sit down to write, you might forget a lot of the interesting detail."

"That's what I thought, too."

"Have you told Wayne what you plan to do this summer?"

"Not yet."

"Don't you think you should get him on board sooner rather than later?"

"I will now that Mikki knows for sure she's going. He won't care as long as my expenses are paid by Mom's trust."

"Ah, Julie, didn't we agree that you would pay half from the money you have in your bank account and the trust would pay the other half?"

"Well, sure, Dad, we talked about that, but I thought you'd change your mind after thinking about it and realizing what a great thing this is going to be for your daughter's education. If I have to dip into my bank account, I'm afraid I won't have enough left in case I want to buy a car this fall."

Pete looked at the ceiling and said, "This sounds like *déjà vu* all over again as a famous baseball player used to say. I remember very clearly that you and your friends decided against having cars while you're in prep school."

"Dad, things change. One girl who wasn't going to get a car changed her mind and now she's going to get one. Everyone is rethinking their plans."

Pete wanted to vent and lecture Julie about a dozen things, but held his tongue and said only, "I'm too tired to talk about it tonight. In the next month or so, let's decide about Paris. Then we can talk more about the car. Don't get your hopes up, though. I'm not likely to change my mind."

"But you'll consider it?" Julie asked hopefully.

"I said we'd *talk about it*," Pete said. "Goodnight and I love you."

He stared at the cloth bag with the Glock in it for a long time. *We're not trying to make you a world-class marksman overnight,* Tessler had said. *Just aim for the chest.* Or something like that.

Pete opened a can of chicken-rice soup and heated it up along with what remained of a loaf of French bread. He finished half of it. Then he built a small fire and read some more of his Jo Nesbø book. Funny thing. He was reading more mysteries than he ever had and the protagonists always seemed to come out okay in the end. He hoped he'd be as lucky.

About 9:30 p.m., his eyes were too tired to focus on the print any longer. He'd drawn his bedroom shades when he got home. But looking at the bay window, which provided a terrific view of the lake, he wondered for the first time whether someone outside the cottage could see in. He put on his boots and a jacket and went out and peered in his bedroom window. Along the edges, where the shades didn't quite meet the walls, he could see the room fairly well when he put his face close to the outer wall. The bed and the nightstands were clearly visible. He shivered at the thought.

He went inside again and examined the window shades more closely. There was no way to close the gaps along the sides unless he used something like duct tape. The gaps had never bothered him before and in fact he'd never given them any thought. But they bothered him now.

He went outside again and looked around. Without leaves on the trees, and with the moon crawling higher over the lake, he could pretty much see the entire area. Most importantly, he saw no police cruiser. He walked out his driveway and looked both ways on M-22. Nothing. Of all the cottages, his was the only one with lights on.

He went inside again and locked the front door and dropped the deadbolt. Then he went upstairs where there were two auxiliary bedrooms. Neither was made up because he'd just moved back in the cottage a few months ago. Bedding was piled on top of the mattresses along with clothes and other objects. He began to clear one of the mattresses and put sheets on it. He topped it off with a light blanket and a comforter. Then he found a clock radio and reset the time and the alarm. He went downstairs again and got the essentials — a tooth brush, tooth paste, soap — and brought them to the second floor bathroom.

Before he turned off the downstairs lights, he stared at the master bedroom for a long time. Then he took a spare blanket from a shelf in the closet and rolled it lengthwise and placed it under the bedspread. He pulled the rolled blanket up a bit and flattened the top and rounded the corners. He turned off the lights, took his loaner Glock, and went upstairs where he set both elements of his new alarm system.

When he finished in the bathroom, he checked the Glock and racked the slide so it had a cartridge in the chamber and was ready to fire. Then he placed the weapon on the nightstand within convenient reach and covered it with a dry wash cloth. He got in bed and turned off the light. He lay there thinking about how he got himself into this mess and wondering how he was going to get out of it. Joe Tessler had a more difficult task. He had two dead bodies on his hands and only a lot of suppositions to go on. Pete was determined not to complicate things for him by becoming the third body.

FORTY-ONE

The service department at the dealership where Pete normally took his Range Rover for repairs told him they'd have his heater fixed by 4:00 p.m. That was welcome news because the temperature was forecast to dip into the high thirties again for a few days. His tolerance for feeling like he was encased in ice every time he got in his vehicle had reached its limits.

He had a late breakfast and then drove up the Old Mission Peninsula. The loaner they gave him for the day — a black Ford Escape — didn't have the same familiar feel as his Range Rover, but it was peppy and fun to drive. He enjoyed the scenery and, most of all, the light traffic.

When he reached the top of the Peninsula, he turned around and retraced his route south. He circled around the bottom of West Traverse Bay and then picked up M-22 north. He came to the place where Lynn had run off the highway and pulled over and stared at the rocks and the water beyond. He remembered one night in Chicago years earlier when he was driving on an icy suburban four-lane highway and lost control of his vehicle. He went into a skid that took him a hundred yards to pull out of. The memory still sent shivers up his spine. He wondered if Lynn had felt the same way. And again, whether she had help going into her skid.

The clock on the Escape's dash read 11:07 a.m. He got back on the highway and took the road west to Conti Vineyards. He had no particular mission in mind. Just killing time and thinking. When he came to the vineyard's entrance, he found a chain across the road with a sign that read "Closed." He thought about his second interview with Alain Conti and wondered whether Conti's health problems had anything to do with it.

The Peg was the other place that was on his mind because he'd gotten the bandages off his ribs early that morning. The nurse's gushing comments about what a great healer he was did nothing to temper the surge of anger he felt when he thought about the mugging. He plugged some addresses into the Escape's GPS system and saw a route he could take to pass through Maple City on his way back to the dealership.

He was used to coming in from the west, but found The Peg without any problem. He stopped at the edge of the parking lot and looked at the place where he'd been jumped. The area under the massive oak tree, where Sheriff Bond said they'd found the cigarette butts, looked dark and forbidding even in the middle of the day. Bond's theory that the thugs had been waiting for someone to come out of the bar made sense. He'd hadn't heard whether they'd found any prints on the butts and made a mental note to call Bond when he got back. Pete had a lot on his plate, but he'd gladly defer all of it to get at the hoodlums who mauled him that night.

When he finished surveying the spot under the tree, he rolled slowly into the parking lot. There were maybe twenty vehicles there and Pete saw Sandoval's Chevy Silverado in its usual reserved slot near the front door. He debated whether to pay Sandy a surprise visit. As he crawled along, he saw a silver Acura MDX parked next to the Silverado. It was in the second reserved slot. And it had a Washington State license plate.

Pete stared at the license plate and his mind flashed back to Seattle. Jimi had told him that Gil Bartholome had a SUV, and what were the chances he wouldn't have Washington State license plates if he'd lived there for five years? Pete's pulse beat faster. He accelerated slightly and continued past the Silverado and the MDX and exited on the county road again and stopped a hundred yards away.

He tried to make sense of what he'd just seen. The fact that the SUV was parked in the reserved slot had to mean that Sandoval and Bartholome knew each other. He also thought about the slip of paper with The Peg's phone number he'd found on the bulletin board in Bartholome's apartment. Harry believed the number had been written in a man's hand and he agreed. That was more evidence of some kind of a relationship between them.

Pete drove a block farther and pulled into an EZ Mart to use the john and get a bag of tortilla chips and a bottle of spring water. He knew he couldn't just walk into The Peg and find out what Sandoval and Bartholome were up to. He wondered if Bartholome had additional stops to make. He decided to wait a while and see if he left.

Pete turned around and parked on the side of the road about a hundred yards from The Peg's parking lot. Having a loaner was a stroke of luck. Someone — Sandoval in particular — might remember his Range Rover from his last visit and become suspicious about why he was in Maple City again. Pete watched vehicles periodically come and go from the parking lot, hoping with each departure that it was the MDX.

About mid-afternoon, the arriving vehicles far exceeded those that were departing. Pete had been there for over two hours. Just when he was about to give up and head back to the dealership, the MDX pulled out of the lot and turned left onto the county road. Pete let it get a comfortable distance ahead and then began to follow.

He knew he was taking a risk of losing the MDX, but he let a mud-splattered red pickup pass him and provide cover. He veered to the left briefly, across what would be the road's centerline if there were one, and saw the silver MDX far ahead. After a few miles, the pickup turned onto a side road and Pete was exposed again. He continued to follow the MDX and in fact closed the gap a little.

The MDX turned east onto a road with heavier traffic. Pete did the same. At one point, Pete lost sight of it, but after passing a couple of vehicles, he saw it again. It turned right onto a y-branch and pulled into a Days Inn parking lot. Pete took the same y-branch and waited by the side of the street for fifteen minutes. Then he entered the motel parking lot and cruised around until he saw the MDX. It was parked in back of the building near a unit with "17" on the door.

Pete drove to the front again and went in the office. He was positive the driver was Bartholome, but he wanted to confirm that and see what else he could find out. A young man with a blade-like body and pale skin dotted with pimples was behind the check-in counter. His yellow polyester uniform shirt did little for his complexion. He saw Pete come in and said, "Can I help you, sir?"

"Yes, I'm meeting a friend. Gilbert Bartholome. Could you tell me if he's here?"

Pimples looked at his computer screen and scrolled down. "Yes, sir," he said. "Would you like me to ring his room?"

"No thanks. I thought I recognized his car in back when I came in. He's in Room 17, right?"

Pimples looked at the computer screen again. "That's right, sir. Room 17."

"He must like this place," Pete said with a big smile. "He'd been here for a week, hasn't he?"

Pimples looked at his screen again. "Nine days, sir."

Pete nodded. "You must take good care of your guests. I'd check in myself, but I'm staying with a friend."

"Here's one of our cards, sir. We'd love to have you become a member of the Days Inn family the next time you come to Traverse City."

Pete walked out of the office and looked for his Range Rover until he remembered he had a loaner. He found the Escape and popped the "Unlock" button. The clock on the dash read 4:17 p.m. He had no idea how long he'd have to wait until Bartholome moved again. He knew where Bartholome was, and since he'd already been there nine days, it was a reasonable bet he wasn't going anywhere soon. He headed for the dealership to exchange vehicles.

FORTY-TWO

"Guess who I saw this afternoon," Pete said to Joe Tessler when he answered the phone.

Tessler paused. "Elvis Presley?"

"No, but I did see Gil Bartholome."

From his silence, Tessler seemed to be thinking. "Lynn Hawke's boyfriend, right?"

"Right. And unless I miss my guess, Alain Conti's partner in the illegal immigration ring. Bartholome had disappeared by the time I was in Seattle. And guess who he was visiting with today?"

"I feel like this is a game of twenty questions."

"Sandy Sandoval. I saw Bartholome's SUV in The Peg's parking lot this afternoon. That's the bar in Maple City Sandoval owns. I waited around for a while, and when Bartholome left, I tailed him to a Days Inn on the outskirts of Traverse City. He's been there nine days."

"What were you doing in Maple City?"

"My Range Rover was being repaired in Traverse City. I just happened to be driving around in my loaner."

"I know you well enough to know that you don't just 'happen' to do anything."

"You're too suspicious, Joe."

"Umm, hmm. But your point is that Conti, Sandoval and Bartholome all know each other."

"Or at least Bartholome knows both Conti and Sandoval. I'm not sure if Conti and Sandoval know each other."

"Plus one or more of them knew Arne Breit."

"That would be my guess."

"I told you, Keegan Harris is going to love you when she gets back. You've got her entire case mapped out."

Pete laughed with a derisive tone. "Hardly mapped out."

"And you think Conti's the head of the ring?" Tessler asked.

"Yes. Maybe Conti and Bartholome went rogue after they left the INS."

"Well, I have three suspects now because all of them seem to have motives to kill Arne Breit and Barbara Rodes."

"I'd say you have three persons of interest."

"Alright, persons of interest. It's still more than I had a week ago," Tessler said.

"If we can pin a particular individual to those counterfeit documents, you'll probably have more."

"Yeah, right. But if I get too close to that side of things, our friend Keegan would have me shipped me off to one of those 'black sites' or whatever they call those torture places and pressure me into confessing that I interfered in her case."

"Look at the bright side. They can't waterboard you anymore."

"That's right, but I'm not sure whether fingernails and toenails are covered by the torture ban."

"I'll probably be in a cell next to you. I won't let them to do anything to mess up your manicured nails."

"Ha, ha. Whatever happened to the good old days when a country detective could solve crimes with the help of a senior lady and her cat?"

"Society is changing, Joe. Getting back to the case I'm most interested in, if Lynn Hawke were trying to play peacemaker between warring partners as Barbara Rodes suggested, maybe the partner who didn't want peace was behind her 'accident.' And Conti admitted he was in telephone contact with Lynn on the night of her accident."

"You said Conti is in a wheelchair. It doesn't seem likely that he would have been the one to run Lynn off the road."

"He wouldn't have had to do it himself. Maybe he had someone do it for him. Like his bodyguard who's masquerading as a chef."

When Pete was off the telephone with Tessler, he heated up a small frozen pizza for dinner and then settled down with a glass of the wine he'd bought at the no-name vineyard the day he thought he was being followed by the pickup truck. He didn't have to worry about over-serving himself again. The wine tasted like stale camel pee.

He wondered how Sandy Sandoval fit into the picture. *If* he fit in. He seemed to be a stand-up guy. Still, the fact he obviously knew Bartholome was troubling. He had to be involved somehow. Otherwise why would Bartholome, who seemed to have ties to Conti, be hanging out in his bar?

He checked the doors to ensure they were locked and turned off the downstairs lights. Then he took the stairs to the second floor and followed the same routine he'd gone through the previous night. When he armed the security system, the small lights on the box glowed red to show that the system was on. He made sure the Glock was within easy reach again.

FORTY-THREE

The next morning, Pete opened the large manila envelope UPS had just dropped off at his office. It contained the accident report Sheriff Bond had promised to send him. The text of the report covered seven double-spaced pages and there were two attachments: A report by the automobile mechanic detailing the results of his examination of Lynn's car, and a dozen black-and-white photographs of her Volvo taken from various angles while the car was still at the crash scene.

The report contained the same information Sheriff Bond had given him over the phone only in greater detail. The mechanic's report supported the primary report. It was a thorough job, but filled with suppositions about certain details of the accident that couldn't be proven one way or the other, such as why the airbags didn't fully inflate and whether Lynn's seatbelt hadn't been on or simply came loose during the crash. He studied the photographs, but didn't see anything that would prove or disprove the basic conclusions of the report.

He dialed Joe Tessler's phone number, and when Tessler answered, said, "Joe, I've been calling you so much lately that I'm thinking of putting you on speed dial."

"Don't," Tessler replied. "Frank is due back in a few days and he'll likely launch an investigation to see who people in the office have been talking to in his absence."

Pete laughed. "I'm sitting here looking at Lynn Hawke's accident report. I don't see anything in it that I didn't already know, but I wonder if you'd look at it, too. A second pair of eyes, so to speak."

"I can't today. If you copy it and drop it off at my office, I'll look at it when I get back."

"I don't know how well the photographs will copy."

"Photographs of the crash scene?"

"Yes. A dozen nine-by-twelve glossies."

Tessler was silent for a moment, then said, "You know what you should do? You should have Amy look at them."

"Who's Amy?"

"Amy Ostrowski. She's our crime scene photographer. She knows a lot about forensics."

"Does she have a direct line?"

"She's a freelancer. We can't afford a fulltime photographer."

"What's her number?"

Tessler found it for him.

"Is Amy the woman I saw at Barbara Rodes' house?"

"Yes. Do you know what her day job is?"

"No idea."

"She's a wedding planner. Takes care of everything, does the flowers, arranges for a tent if one is used, takes the pictures. She's well known in this area. I'm surprised you haven't heard of her."

"I guess I haven't had a need for a wedding planner recently."

When Pete was off the phone with Tessler, he called Amy Ostrowski and reached her on her cell. "Amy, my name is Pete Thorsen. Joe Tessler from the sheriff's department suggested I call you. I'm unofficially working with Joe on two homicides — maybe three — and I wonder if you'd have time to look over an accident report?"

"Does this involve Arne Breit and Barbara Rodes?"

"Indirectly at least."

"Where's your office?"

He gave her his address.

"I'm meeting with a client on the north shore of Crystal Lake at the moment. I should be finished in about an hour. I could swing by your office right after that."

■ ■ ■

Shortly after noon, Pete heard the door to his outer office open and went out to greet Amy Ostrowski. He'd seen her before. Besides Barbara Rodes' house, where he couldn't observe her work, she'd been at the golf course when they found Les Brimley's body and, earlier, when Cara Lane had been found dead in the lake. In both of those cases, he'd been impressed with her professionalism.

Today, she wore her other hat and was dressed in her wedding planner finery. Pleated black wool skirt that ended at mid-thigh, black hose, medium-heel pumps. When she took off her coat, her deep red sequined top screamed for attention. Well-coiffed auburn hair ended at her shoulders. Amy obviously had two wardrobes — one for getting clients hitched and the other for photographing corpses.

She read through the accident report and then read it again. After studying each of the photographs, she looked up at Pete and said, "I spoke to Joe on the way over. He said you don't believe this woman's death was an accident."

"More precisely, I'm not *sure* if the crash was really an accident." Pete laid out the facts, skipping details that would merely complicate the story.

When he was finished, Amy asked, "Did you examine the car?"

"Not personally. I'm relying on what the sheriff's department told me."

"The reason I ask is that the damage to the victim's car looks strange. Obviously, we don't have a sequence of photographs that would tell us exactly how all of the damage occurred, but the way the back end is pushed in might tell us something. See how the left side is pushed in more than the right? Then look at some of the photographs that show damage to other parts of the vehicle. See the uneven pattern? There are huge dents and holes in the body where the car struck the rocks, which is understandable, but in back everything is pushed in evenly, although at an angle. And most important, when that Volvo hit the rocks, it must have stopped dead. Yet the rear-end is damaged."

There was something incongruous about an attractive woman in her wedding planner outfit clinically dissecting photographs of a vehicle after a crash that killed the driver. She obviously knew her stuff and had just changed hats to fit the case at hand.

"Where's the car now?" she asked.

"It's in the sheriff's department's lot somewhere in Suttons Bay."

"Would they object to us looking at it?"

"I'm sure they wouldn't. The sheriff told me they intend to keep the car for ninety days, and if no one claims it, they'll dispose of it for parts and scrap."

"I think we should look at it."

Pete stared at her for a moment. "Will you come with me?"

"I will as long as we can schedule it for a time when I don't have something with one of my wedding clients. Clients always understand if I'm called away to photograph a crime scene, but I'm not so sure they'd be as understanding if I cancelled an appointment to go look at some car wreck."

"What's your schedule look like?"

Amy put on her reading glasses and checked the calendar on her cell phone. She looked over the top rims and said, "I'm free tomorrow and then booked for the next two days."

"Let's do it tomorrow. I'll clear it with Sheriff Bond." Getting paid always raised delicate issues and he added, "What's your financial arrangement with the sheriff's department?"

"I get paid for my time on an hourly basis."

"Do you think the department would cover this as an expense of their investigation?"

"I don't know."

"Let's do it this way. If the sheriff's department won't pay for your time, I'll pay you personally."

As Pete was helping her with her coat, he asked, "How did you wind up combining police work with wedding planning?"

"When I was in college, I majored in police science and hoped to hook on with a police department doing forensics work fulltime. You know, like the CSI shows, solving high profile crimes and the like, being on television once in a while. Then I discovered that if I didn't want to live and work in a big city like Detroit or Chicago, which I didn't, there were very few full-time positions in my field. I always loved weddings and found out I was good at putting them together so, bingo, I combined careers and now I make a good living while still using my education."

"Well, I'm not planning to get married, at least not soon, but I do have a knack for getting tangled up in crimes so maybe this is just the beginning of a working relationship."

"Joe told me you're an old army CID man."

"Emphasis on old. That was a long time ago."

"You know what they say about bicycles, don't you?"

"I do. But I only drove a Jeep when I was attached to the CID."

"You drove for a top investigator, though, didn't you?"

"That part is true."

"I'll bet you learned a lot just watching."

He grinned at her. "Like how to keep my nose out of other people's business?"

FORTY-FOUR

A s they drove north along the West Bay, Pete said, "Do you want to see the accident scene first? It's a few miles ahead."

"That's always helpful," Amy Ostrowski said.

Pete slowed when he approached the spot where Lynn had skidded off the road. He pulled over on the shoulder and stopped. Amy got out and stood on the side of the road looking at the stretch of jagged rocks between M-22 and the bay. She was back in her crime scene clothes — baggy khaki pants, a lumpy hip-length brown coat, and a maroon scarf and matching hat. Gone was the flash and sass of the wedding planner from the previous day.

After standing motionless for five minutes surveying the scene, she slid into the front seat of the Range Rover again. "Any observations?" Pete asked.

"The vic must have had some help to fly off the road the way she did." She looked through the photographs with the sheriff's report again and said, "You can see from this photo where the car wound up among the rocks. Either she was driving sixty miles an hour, which seems unlikely given the conditions, or she got a boost off the road."

"When you hit a patch of ice," Pete observed, "you can really take off."

"You can," she said. She continued to study the photographs. Then she paged through the report again. As he waited, he was glad he'd finally bitten the bullet and gotten his heater fixed.

"The accident report says the police found no evidence of skid marks."

"They didn't," Pete said. "The sheriff doesn't think that proves anything, though. There wouldn't have been any if the wet roads had already turned to ice, and if it hadn't, the rain might have washed away the marks."

Pete continued on to Suttons Bay. He found the compound where the sheriff's department kept towed and badly damaged vehicles and parked outside the chain link fence. There were only three vehicles in the compound, one of which was Lynn's Volvo. Or at least, what was left of it. Up close, it looked even worse than the photographs showed.

Amy walked around the car and looked, then walked around it again and looked some more. She circled the car a third time and wound up in back where she stared at the rear end damage. Pete waited impatiently for her to venture some observations.

"It helps to see the physical damage," she finally said to him. "It shows what I thought I saw in the photographs, only you can see it more clearly now." She pointed to the trunk and rear bumper. "It looks like the rear end was hit by something flat and everything was pushed in. Now compare it with the left side. See those uneven dents and big gashes in the body? That occurred because of the rocks, but the damage in back seems to have been caused by something else. You wouldn't expect the back to suffer the same damage as the front and sides, but this still looks unusual."

"The car was on its left side when the sheriff's people arrived."

"I saw that in the accident report. When the victim hit the rocks, her wheels probably ran up on them for a few feet and flipped on its side."

"And came to a violent stop."

"A very violent stop. A vehicle wouldn't go far once it hit those rocks. It's like hitting a brick wall."

"Would this pattern of damage be consistent with the victim being driven off the road by another vehicle?"

"Possibly."

"When you say possibly, you sound like you have reservations."

"When one vehicle bumps another in the rear, you can often tell from the impact marks on the back of the first vehicle. I don't see that here. Of course, we don't know what kind of grill the second vehicle had."

"The impact would damage the front of the second vehicle, wouldn't it?"

"Almost certainly."

"Well," Pete said, sighing, "if my theory were right that a vehicle came up behind Lynn and rammed her and sent her flying into the rocks, we'd have to find a vehicle with front end damage."

"Not necessarily. You remember what I said a minute ago about the imprint on the back of the first vehicle as a result of being rammed? We had a case study in one of my forensics courses where the vehicle that did the ramming had a thick plank mounted on the front. The plank pushed in the back of the first vehicle kind of like this Volvo is pushed in. But you don't see planks on the front of vehicles anymore."

Pete stared at Amy for a moment. "Would a metal snow blade attachment create the same kind of damage?"

"It could. A snow plow blade is curved, but it could push in the back like this Volvo is pushed in. Depending on how high the blade was when it struck the other car, obviously."

"In that kind of scenario, would the snow blade have a residue of paint on it as a result of ramming the vehicle in front?"

Amy thought about his question for a moment. "Possible. It would depend on whether the blade struck the back of the other vehicle squarely or hit it with a glancing blow. Things like that."

Pete knelt at the rear of the Volvo and examined the damaged back end. He couldn't tell for sure, but it looked like it had streak marks on the paint where the rear end was pushed in.

■ ■ ■

Pete was thinking about Sandoval's snow plow blade and intimidating roof lights when Joe Tessler called him back.

"Did Amy have any useful observations?"

"She did. She agrees it's possible that Lynn was run off the road that night. She also confirmed that the damage to Lynn's car is consistent with being rammed from the rear by a vehicle with a snow blade attached."

"A snow blade doesn't narrow it down much. Half the pickups in the area have snow blades in the winter."

"True," Pete said, "but we're not talking about the full universe of pickups. We're talking about pickups whose owners have some connection to Lynn Hawke."

"Where does that leave us?"

"Sandoval has a snow blade he keeps on the side of The Peg. I'd like to look at it to see if it shows any signs of damage or has paint residue on it that might have come from Lynn's car."

"To get a search warrant to examine the blade, we'd have to have an affidavit or two attesting to the underlying facts. Otherwise, a judge wouldn't authorize one. Do you have evidence that would support an affidavit?"

"No, only a hunch."

"Then I think the Leelanau County sheriff would have a zero chance of getting a warrant."

"I'm not thinking of a warrant. I'm thinking of a more informal approach."

Tessler considered that for a moment. "You mean violating Sandoval's right to privacy."

"That's a crude way of putting it. I was just thinking about having an informal look at the blade."

"You said it's stored on the side of his bar, right?"

"Yes."

"Pete, think about it," Tessler said. "If you go there at night after the place is closed, you won't be able to see anything even if you're right about what happened. And you can't very well go there in broad daylight and snoop around with Sandoval and other people coming and going."

"What do you suggest?" Pete asked.

"I'm suggesting that you've done everything you can to prove Lynn Hawke's death wasn't an accident. When Keegan Harris gets back, we'll dump the documents we have on her and then you should get out of it."

Pete didn't say anything.

"I know you don't like to hear that," Tessler said, "but it's sound advice."

FORTY-FIVE

It was still dark when Pete left for Maple City. The Peg opened for business at 11:00 a.m. each day and he figured someone would arrive about two hours before that to begin setting up. He moved the time back an hour to provide a margin for error and targeted his arrival for 7:00 a.m. He planned to be gone no later than an hour after that and sooner if he could.

He'd been awake much of the night thinking about what he was about to do. Maybe Tessler's advice was sound, but it left too many questions that he just couldn't ignore. Besides, the way he had it planned, getting a look at Sandoval's snow blade was low risk. He had a road-cup of coffee with him, but he didn't need the caffeine. He was already on edge and rehearsed his plan again in his mind.

The night sky was beginning to morph into daylight when he entered Maple City. It was March and there were no pinks or rosy reds brightening the horizon, only a gradual illumination of the earth like millions of slow-acting CFL bulbs were clicking on. He found the road The Peg was on and drove past the bar to satisfy himself that no one was there. He tried to keep his mind on his mission and not think about the mugging.

He turned left onto the first road he came to that ran north and then turned left again a quarter mile later. He tried to judge about where The Peg was located so he could walk straight in. His map showed that the area behind the bar was mostly wooded. The map was accurate; only the occasional double-wide or old Gulfstream on cinder blocks broke the stands of maples and oaks and fir trees and underbrush.

Pete pulled off the road and crowded the ditch that bordered it. He locked his vehicle and patted his coat pocket to make sure he had his camera. Then he began to hike through the woods. The ground was wet and his boots began to feel soggy. The smell of decaying wood and leaves filled his nostrils and traces of frost covered the ground. Not far away, a dog began to bark and Pete jumped at the sound in the still morning. He hoped the dog was chained up because there were no enclosed yards in the area.

The morning continued to brighten. Pete checked his watch; he was a half-hour ahead of schedule. He continued to walk in the direction of The Peg. He held some underbrush to one side so he could avoid a wet area and a sapling broke free and snapped him in the face. The morning chill made the sting more painful. He thought of all the times as a youth he'd been snapped in the face on cold winter mornings when he ran a trap line to make spending money.

Through the trees, he saw the mottled blue back of The Peg and angled toward it. He stopped to listen and watch when he got close. No sounds, and from what he could see, no sign of any activity. He proceeded on, walking carefully and stepping around wood that might snap under foot. The dog was still howling in the distance.

Pete saw the snow blade nestled on the side of the building and stopped again. Still no sign of life. He reached the blade. It was painted red and looked relatively new. In the still morning, he heard a vehicle approaching and flattened himself against the building's wall until it passed.

He squatted down and began to examine the blade. He could see dozens of tiny dings on the surface that apparently had been caused by small rocks kicked up by the blade during plowing operations. A strip of rubber was missing from the top of the blade. Normal wear and tear as far as he could tell.

He took the camera from his pocket and began to take pictures of every place where there was a smudge or a dent or a ding. Thirty-three shots in all. Nothing major or unusual that he could see. No sign of green paint residue or other evidence that the blade had come in contact with Lynn's Volvo. He didn't know whether to be happy or disappointed.

He checked his watch again; he'd been there forty minutes. In the distance, he heard another vehicle approaching. He used the snow blade for cover and crouched down and nestled along the side of the building. The sound of the vehicle grew louder. Thirty seconds later, a black pickup with its headlights on and auxiliary lights mounted on its roofline swung into the parking lot. It made a crunching sound as it passed over the gravel.

Shit! Pete thought. He crouched lower and continued to hug the side of the building. His heart beat faster as the pickup's headlights flashed against the front of the building. Someone got out of the pickup and he heard the vehicle's door slam and gravel crunch under the man's boots. He went inside and closed the building's door behind him. Sandoval, he thought.

Pete looked over his shoulder at the woods. When he came in, he didn't notice whether The Peg had rear windows. He cursed to himself. Adam Rose would never have made that mistake.

He turned, trying to be absolutely quiet, and worked his way to the back corner of the building. He looked to his right and saw two window frames at the far corner of the building. *Yes, idiot, there are back windows!* It was lighter now and he knew he couldn't retrace the path he'd taken in.

Pete began to walk on a diagonal away from the windows. He got twenty yards away from the building. Everything was quiet. He felt his way along and tried to avoid dry branches that might snap underfoot and attract attention. Fifty yards away. A branch covered by leaves snapped and in the still morning air, sounded like he'd struck a maple with a club. *Damn!* He quickened his pace as he got farther away, periodically glancing back at the building behind him. With the foliage off the trees and bushes, there was nothing to shield him from view. He kept walking on a diagonal and looking over his shoulder as he went. He was a hundred yards away now, but in the brightening morning, he knew someone looking out the window would be able to see movement among the trees.

Pete slogged through a low-lying area with standing water and patches of snow. He looked back and saw nothing. The dog started barking again although the sound was farther away because he was walking on a diagonal. He saw the road ahead. Five minutes later he was hurrying back toward his Range Rover.

He got in his vehicle and took a final look in the direction of The Peg as he turned the ignition key. He eased back onto the road and decided not to go through town in case Sandoval happened to do the same. After a mile, he pulled to the side again and studied his map. He plotted a return that let him bypass Maple City and berated himself for not heeding Joe Tessler's advice.

FORTY-SIX

"Where are you?" Pete asked when Joe Tessler called. He could hear loud voices and other noise in the background.

"I'm back in Lansing. I'm waiting to be called for cross-examination by the defense."

"I thought that case was over with."

Tessler laughed. "I thought so, too, but now I'm told it will go another week. Then it will depend on how long the jury's out."

"It's in federal court, right?"

"It's a DEA case. We're involved in just part of it — one of the drug operations was in our county — and the defense is pursuing a scorched earth approach. They're contesting everything. I didn't expect to have to testify again, but ..."

"When's your cross?"

"Maybe today, maybe tomorrow, who knows?" Tessler said.

"If it takes you away from your two homicide investigations, the sheriff isn't going to be happy."

"Yes and no," Tessler said. "If we get a conviction, Frank will be pleased because he'll be able to take a lot of credit for it even though we were just a gnat on the Doberman's rump. If the defendants walk, then it'll be my fault and I'll have nothing to show on the murder cases to boot. People will be lining up to interview for my position."

"From what I've seen, you're tight with the sheriff. You shouldn't have anything to worry about."

Tessler laughed and said, "Yeah, right."

"When will Richter be back?"

"Three days."

"Mmm," Pete murmured.

"I was just calling to make sure you're okay and there are no problems up there."

"No problems and nothing to report." Pete debated whether to tell Tessler about his early-morning visit to The Peg, but decided there'd be no harm in doing so. He glossed over the details, including Sandoval's surprise arrival while he was still there, but told Tessler he'd examined the blade and taken a lot of pictures. There was no evidence the blade had been used to run Lynn off the road.

"You don't quit, do you?"

Pete didn't say anything.

"So it doesn't look like Sandoval is the guilty party, huh?"

"No it doesn't," Pete said. "Maybe a forensic expert would conclude something different, but I didn't see anything."

"Are you going to take my advice and give it up now?"

"I'm leaning that way. Three different people — Brenda Lyons, Barbara Rodes and Alain Conti — all said that Lynn told them she was thinking of moving back to this area. Maybe she really was here that night to check with some of her former clients about whether they'd be receptive to using her services again. Regardless of whatever else she might have been mixed up in, I'm beginning to think it's possible that her accident was just that in spite of the suspicious circumstances."

"How about the illegal immigration ring?"

"That's a separate matter. I think Lynn was involved, but Keegan Harris can deal with that."

"You know Pete, I haven't wanted to say this because you're a very smart guy, but you also bring a weakness to these things. You're too emotionally involved. That isn't good when you're trying to solve a crime."

Pete was silent again.

"Regardless, you're thinking the way I believe you should. I'll miss having the benefit of your insights, but with Frank back and everything, it'll be hard for us to work together so closely anyway."

When he was off the telephone with Tessler, he decided to bag the thought of getting any work done at the office that day and just go home and hang out. He religiously got up at 5:30 a.m. every morning when he practiced law in Chicago, but he was out of the habit. Plus, 4:00 a.m. was a bit early even for him.

He stopped to see Harry before heading home. For once, they didn't spend their time talking about Lynn Hawke and the murders that had occurred in their neighborhood. It was the best day of the spring so far, with the temperature around sixty, and they spent their time talking about the trout season just ahead. Harry resurrected his beef about the summer before when Pete had gone off to fish the Brule River without him. They made tentative plans for several fishing outings for the season and just hung out and talked the way friends do.

Pete left Harry's office in mid-afternoon and took the scenic route to his cottage. The blue-green waters lived up to the name of the lake and looked even more summer-like than the day he walked along South Shore Road just days ago. A windsurfer in a blue and orange wetsuit, the first he'd seen on the lake since last fall, skimmed over the water fifty yards from shore. An older man Pete didn't know poked around in the sand on the beach with a crooked stick.

When he got to his cottage, he changed into athletic clothes and went for a run. There was no wind and it felt good to get out. He experienced some minor discomfort in his rib cage every time his left foot hit the asphalt, but otherwise he felt good. And he felt mostly unburdened by everything he'd been trying to puzzle through in the past couple of weeks.

The pristine lake buoyed his spirits and he felt his body heat begin to rise as he loped along. He unzipped his Nike jacket part-way and enjoyed the feeling of moderate exertion again. The road was still vacant except for him. Enjoy it while it lasted, he thought.

Inside, he stripped off his clothes and took a long, hot shower. After drying himself, he put on a fleece robe and built a fire in the fireplace. Then he slipped a Stone Poneys CD into the player and tilted back in his chair and closed his eyes. Somewhere after Linda Ronstadt finished "Different Drum," he dozed off.

He woke to the burring sound of his cell phone. The sun had dipped below the bluffs lining the lake and the light was fading. A voice that had a strange muffled sound to it said, "You have something that belongs to us."

FORTY-SEVEN

S uddenly Pete was wide awake. "Who is this?" he asked.

"We've been looking for our package," the muffled voice said, "and we understand you have it. We want to know when you're going to make delivery."

An icy feeling seized him. "I don't know what you're talking about," he said.

"No games, Mr. Thorsen. I'm going to call back tomorrow morning. I'll expect you to give me delivery instructions."

The phone went silent and for five minutes Pete just stared at the floor. *God damn it!* he thought. He locked the front door and punched in Joe Tessler's cell phone number. His call went to voicemail and he left a message for Joe to call back as soon as he could. He emphasized that it was an emergency.

He had a hard time thinking coherently as he waited for Tessler to call him. His thoughts ricocheted back and forth between fear and efforts to come up with a plan. Images of Arne Breit and Barbara Rodes flashed through his mind. When Tessler returned his call forty minutes later, he said, "I just got an anonymous phone call, Joe. They think I have the documents."

Tessler was silent for a long moment. "Did a number show up on your caller ID?"

"No."

"Tell me what the caller said. Exactly as you remember it."

Pete told him.

Tessler was silent again.

"I've thought it through, Joe, and I'm going to get out of here for the night. I'm worried that the promise of a callback in the morning might be intended to throw me off guard tonight. Even with the alarm system and your Glock, I feel like a sitting duck."

"I think that's smart. Where will you go?"

"I don't know. Somewhere. I don't want to talk about it on the phone."

"I understand."

"And something else. I'm going to give them the documents if that's the only way out."

"That's the principal evidence the government has against the counterfeiting ring."

"The government doesn't have anything yet," Pete said. "I found the documents. I'm going to give them back if there's no other way out of this mess."

"The feds will nail you on some charge if you do that."

"I'll take my chances. I don't intend to wind up like Arne Breit or Barbara Rodes."

Tessler was silent again. "Why don't I talk to Keegan Harris, or if she's not back yet, that other guy at the number she gave us, and try to clear it with them?"

"What do you think will happen if you tell them what's going on? Their focus will be on getting the documents to use in their case. They won't give a shit about what happens to me. I'll just be more collateral damage."

"I'm sure they'll protect you."

"Put me in one of their witness protection programs?" Pete said. "I'm a lawyer and I know a little about those programs. I don't *want* to live the rest of my life that way. I'm going to do this my way. I'm going to do what I feel I have to do."

Another pause, then Tessler said, "Let's talk in the morning and discuss it further. Go somewhere safe for tonight."

When he was finished with Tessler, Pete called Harry on his cell phone. "Is your garage a one slot or two slot?"

"One," Harry said. "Rona parks her car in the garage and I park outside under that canopy. Why do you ask?"

"Because I have to park my car in your garage overnight."

"Why?"

"I'm staying at the hotel tonight. I need a place to park my car."

"Let's back up a minute," Harry said. "Why are you staying at the hotel? Is there some problem at your place?"

"No problem. I just have to get out of here."

No response for a moment, then, "You're not going to tell me what's going on, huh?"

"Not right now."

"At this time of the year, you can park within five feet of the hotel's front door. Why don't you just do that?"

"Because I don't want my car on the street where someone might see it. You'll have to trust me."

"Okay," Harry said, sighing, "we're good friends and sometimes one friend asks another to do something he doesn't understand. I'll tell Rona you're going to use her spot tonight."

"Thanks. Would you leave the garage unlocked in case you're not home when I arrive?"

"Sure. It's one of those old doors without an automatic opener. I …"

"I know how they work."

"Would you like to have dinner at Rona's?"

"Not tonight. I have things to do."

Pete called the private number he had for Alain Conti. Conti was the main man as far as he could tell and it made sense to go right to the top if you were trying to broker something. He listened as the phone rang and rang. He decided to try again in an hour.

He went upstairs and packed a change of clothes and his shave kit. He stared at the Glock and the extra magazine and spare ammunition and decided to add them to his carry-on. He checked his cell phone directory to ensure he had the telephone numbers he might need. It was almost dark when he finished. He set both alarm systems, locked the door from the outside, and tossed his carry-on in the back seat of the Range Rover.

When he pulled out of his driveway, he turned the opposite way, away from town, and looked for vehicles that might be parked in the area. He didn't see any. He made a U-turn on M-22 and headed toward town. He turned onto South Shore Road and a couple hundred yards down, turned into a u-shaped drive that served several cottages and parked behind a dense cluster of Lilac bushes. He turned off his lights and watched. He could see his cottage across the corner of the lake. An occasional vehicle passed on M-22, but none slowed down or stopped near his cottage. The quarter moon began to rise over the lake.

An hour later, Pete turned his lights on and proceeded toward town. Harry's garage was accessed from the alley behind his house. He looped around the block once, and seeing no cars in the area, pulled up behind the garage. He got out and manually raised the garage door. Then he eased his Range Rover into the tight space and pulled the door shut.

The hotel lobby was empty. He tapped the bell on the counter as the sign instructed and a few minutes later a woman came out of the first floor living quarters. She obviously was pleased to have a walk-in guest at that time of night. She checked him in and assigned him a second floor room as he requested.

He found his room and the first thing he did was to call Conti's number on his cell. Again there was no answer. It was almost 9:00 p.m.

Pete flopped on the bed and stared at the ceiling and counted the braided loops on the ornate crown molding. His mind alternated between depression and considering options for the next day. He recalled teaming up with Adam Rose the previous summer and remembered how meticulous he was with his preparation. He'd also learned that from Major Baumann. He felt he'd done a pretty good job after the anonymous call came in, but tomorrow would be the test. He thought about his two meetings with Alain Conti. Conti had to have some weakness. It was a matter of pushing the right button.

Shortly before 10:00 p.m., he called Conti again. For the third time, he got no answer. He went through his nightly bathroom routine and checked to make sure his door was locked and the safety chain fastened. He was about to turn off the bedside light when he stared at the door again. Better safe than sorry. He slid the tall chest of drawers against the door. Then he made sure his Glock was within easy reach and crawled under the comforter.

FORTY-EIGHT

Pete slept better than he thought he would, all things considered. He showered, shaved, and went downstairs where the desk clerk, who doubled as the daytime chef, made him a hearty breakfast. He picked at it, but wasn't particularly hungry even though he'd missed dinner the night before. Pete went back to his room and called Conti again. This time his call bounced to Loretta. He identified himself and asked to speak to Mr. Conti. "I'm sorry, Mr. Thorsen, he isn't here just now."

"Where can I reach him? It's important."

Loretta asked, "Is this about your newspaper story?"

"No, it's about something else we talked about the last time I was at your vineyard."

"I'm sorry, sir, I don't think Mr. Conti can be disturbed today."

"Trust me, Loretta, he'll want to talk to me. I wouldn't insist unless it was important."

Silence and then she said, "He's back in the hospital."

"Munson in Traverse City?"

"Yes, but …"

"Thanks, Loretta. I'm going to be over that way myself. I'll call him or stop by to see him."

"But Mr. Thorsen ..."

"Thanks Loretta." He ended the call.

Pete's cell phone burred as he was packing his carry-on. He looked at the screen. An unknown caller. He ignored it and finished packing. After checking out, he walked to his office to drop off his carry-on and then went across the street to the drug store to get the office supplies he needed. The store had only one brand of bond paper, a thin generic variety, but he decided that would do just fine. He took all of the paper on the shelf, found the other items he needed and paid for the lot.

When he got back to his office, he removed ten sheets from one of the boxes and put them in the bottom desk drawer where he kept the paper for his printer. Then he carried the office supplies next door to the realtor's office.

"Brenda, I wonder if you could do something for me. I'm not suggesting you owe me for helping get Lynn Hawke's house cleaned out, but ..."

"But I owe you, right?"

He laughed and put the bag of office supplies on her desk and told her what he wanted. "I'm going to the bank, and when I get back, I have to leave. So ..."

"I'll do my best to have everything for you when you get back. Assuming your chores at the bank take you at least a half-hour."

Pete thanked her and walked down to Betsie Bay Trust Company. When he'd opened the safe deposit box, his first inclination was to give both keys to Joe Tessler to get the documents completely out of his possession. In retrospect, he was glad he kept one key. He opened the Tessler/Thorsen box, removed the cardboard box, and copied the names that appeared on the individual packages. Then he took the canvas bag and slid the box back inside and locked up.

He looked at his watch on his way out the bank's door; it had been forty-five minutes since he left Brenda Lyons' office. Hopefully, she'd be finished when he got back. The canvas bag in his hand was an innocuous looking satchel to carry around counterfeit documents worth a million dollars. Or two million dollars or three million dollars or whatever they were worth on the market.

When he got back to the office, Brenda was finished just as she'd promised. Pete thanked her and used his list to copy the individual names a second time. He had one more stop to make before he headed for Traverse City and hoped he wouldn't have to spend too much time persuading Harry to go along with what he wanted. His cell phone burred again. It was the same unknown caller. Or at least *an* unknown caller. He ignored it again.

He thought about the Glock that was packed with his clothes. After considering the pros and cons, he decided not to take it. He'd be back before dark anyway, assuming everything went according to plan. Having an unregistered handgun in his possession might only complicate things.

He walked across the street with the tan duffel in his hand and when he entered Harry's office he said, "I have a favor to ask. I'd like to swap vehicles with you for the day."

Harry looked at the duffel and then studied Pete's face with narrowed eyes. "First you take over my garage and now you want my car. I know something's going on."

Pete's mind raced as he considered how much to tell Harry. Pete's cell phone burred again. He ignored the call a third time. "I'm meeting Alain Conti again today. I think I've figured things out. I'd prefer to drive your Explorer as a precaution because someone might recognize my vehicle."

"You're crazy, you know that? Going up to Conti's place where no one else is around? Do you realize what could happen?"

"You're right. But I'm not meeting Conti at his place. He's back in the hospital. I'm going to see him at Munson in Traverse City. That's as safe a venue as I can think of."

Harry looked at him again and shook his head. "I don't know …"

"Look," Pete said, "if you don't want me to take your Explorer, just say so. I don't have time to argue. I'll use my Range Rover and take my chances."

"No, no," Harry said as he slid his key ring across his desk. "I'll trade with you. It's right out front. You're still in my garage I take it?"

"Still in your garage." He left his own keys and headed for the door.

"Even though the meeting is at the hospital," Harry said, "I want you to promise me you'll be careful."

"I will," Pete said as he walked out the door.

Pete was heading toward Beulah to pick up U.S. 31 when his cell phone burred for the fourth time. This time it was Joe Tessler.

"Why don't you answer your phone?" he asked. "Martin Steele, who works with Keegan, said he tried to call you twice and you didn't answer."

"I thought it might be the unknown caller from last night. I didn't want to talk to him until after I meet with Alain Conti."

"Since when are you meeting with Conti?"

"Since about two hours ago."

Silence, then, "Do you think that's wise?"

"He's in the hospital, Joe. What can happen?"

"Conti's in the hospital?"

"That's what I said."

Tessler shifted gears. "Steele said to tell you that under no circumstances can you turn over the documents to Conti and his people."

Pete was stunned by Tessler's comment. After a moment, Pete asked, "How do they know about the documents?"

"Steele boxed me in with his questions. I either had to tell him about the documents or lie. I couldn't lie because everything will come out when Keegan gets back."

"Great," Pete said disgustedly.

"Steele is demanding that you not do anything to compromise the evidence."

"And I assume turning over the documents to Conti would compromise the evidence?"

"Not much doubt about that."

"Well, you know what you can tell Martin Steele the next time you talk to him? You can tell him to go fuck himself. I'm going to do what I have to do to get myself out of this mess."

Tessler was quiet for a beat or two. "I understand your predicament, Pete. You started out to investigate Lynn Hawke's accident and now you're in the middle of this other crap. Isn't there some other approach you could take? Tell Conti the documents are already in police custody or something and that you can't turn them over?"

Pete laughed derisively. "You saw firsthand what they did to Arne Breit and Barbara Rodes and you say that? What have you been smoking? If I have to give them the documents, I will. Period."

"The feds will prosecute you. I've seen it before."

"Let them try. Arrogant sonsofbitches!"

"Let's talk about it when I get back."

"It's too late for that. I expect this whole thing to come to a head today."

"Well, you be careful. You've got my number if you need to reach me."

Pete seethed with anger when he was off the phone with Tessler, but gradually settled down. He had a plan and was going to stick with it. He needed to keep his head free of distractions. The sign for the hospital loomed ahead and he followed the now familiar route to the parking lot. He parked, grabbed the tan duffel, and headed for the elevator.

When he approached the check-in desk, a pleasant middle-aged woman with an out-of-character tattoo on her upper arm that was partially visible under her short-sleeved nurse's uniform asked for the name of his physician and the time of his appointment. He told her that he was the lawyer for Alain Conti, one of their patients, and asked for his room number. She glanced at his business card and scrolled down the list of patients and gave him the number.

Pete took the elevator to the third floor. The tension ramped up inside him as he walked slowly to Room 321. The door was open and he could see a silver-haired man lying in a hospital bed that was elevated so he could sit. He was hooked up to an IV and the room was filled with an array of monitoring devices.

He took a deep breath, knocked on the door jamb, and said, "Hello, Alain."

FORTY-NINE

Conti's chef was sprawled in a chair reading a magazine and scrambled to his feet as soon as Pete walked in. Conti himself had been dozing and opened his eyes and looked at Pete. If he was surprised to see him, he masked it well.

"Sorry to bust in on you like this, Alain, but Loretta told me you were in the hospital again and I need to talk to you."

The chef scowled at him and said, "This isn't a good time."

Conti waved the chef off and said, "You must have something urgent to talk about if you tracked me down in the hospital."

"This isn't about our vineyard series, Alain. It's about something else"

Conti looked at him. "At least we're being honest this time."

"I'd like to speak in private if you don't mind," Pete said. He looked pointedly at the chef whose eyes were still riveted on him.

"You can speak candidly in front of Clarence."

"I'm sure," Pete said, "but I'd rather it was just the two of us."

Conti seemed to consider it for a moment. "As you wish. But first, I think we should attend to some formalities. Just so I'm comfortable with what you brought with you. You don't mind, do you?"

Pete thought about the metal detector in Conti's house and understood what he was getting at. "No," Pete said, "I don't mind." He looked at Clarence and said, "Have at it."

Clarence closed the door and said, "Stand over here with your hands on the wall, please." Conti watched with an amused half-smile while Clarence patted Pete down. When Clarence finished, he looked at Conti and shook his head.

Conti motioned toward Pete's duffel. Pete unzipped it and held it out for Clarence to examine. Clarence looked inside and felt around on both sides and on the bottom. He repeated the all-clear signal.

"Okay," Conti said. He nodded at Clarence who moved his chair to the hall and closed the door behind him.

Pete took the remaining chair and said, "That burglary must have really spooked you. Or is it the falling out with your business partner that has you worried?"

Conti frowned. "I'm not feeling well, Pete. I hope you didn't come here to talk nonsense."

"The telephone call I received last night wasn't nonsense. The caller said I have something that belongs to him. Or I think he said 'us,' implying he was calling on behalf of more than himself. I thought you might know what he was talking about."

Conti studied Pete's face. "I'm afraid I don't."

"Okay, to cut through the bullshit, I'm sure he was talking about what's in this bag."

"You're not making sense, Pete."

"How much clearer do you want me to be? I know everything. The immigration ring you run to bring people from Asian countries here on phony green cards or H1B visas, the couriers like Arne Breit you use to smuggle the documents out of the country, the falling out between you and your lieutenant Gil Bartholome over the future direction of the business. I could go on, but I don't think I need to bore you with things you already know."

Conti's eyes hardened. "I'm not used to having baseless charges like this made against me. I should get Clarence back in here to escort you out."

"You can do that. But understand one thing. Either we work out an agreement whereby I turn over this bag to your group in return for assurances that I'll never hear from any of you again, or I'm going directly to Homeland Security's office here in town and give them the bag. I think they'll be delighted to see me. You probably even know where their office is. They've been running their investigation of your activities from the office for the past year."

"I'm not under investigation for anything," Conti said, scoffing. "But while you're at Homeland Security, maybe someone can help you improve your poker skills. You were such an amateur when you asked me about Lynn Hawke, Pete. A blind man could see what your motives were."

Pete felt his face flush. "What I was getting at," he said, "is that I think Lynn's death wasn't an accident."

Conti shook his head. "This is so sad. I'm told the sheriff investigated thoroughly and concluded there were no signs of anything but an accident because of the icy roads. You should have continued to practice law, Pete. I understand you were good at that."

Pete ignored his barb and said, "It wasn't an accident. Somebody ran her off the highway. I had a forensics expert inspect the vehicle. She has no doubt that's what happened."

"Let's say that's true. What does it have to do with me?"

"Everything. She was coming to talk to you that night and I don't think it was about accounting services. It involved your ring's illegal activities."

Conti looked at the wall clock and poured some pills from a small paper cup into his hand. He tilted his head back and swallowed them with water.

"I'm sure you have all kinds of proof to back up your nutty charges," Conti said.

"I have enough. Lynn wanted to work out a peace accord between you and Bartholome. The two of you were warring and she felt it was affecting her relationship with Gil. You had her killed because you didn't want peace."

"This sounds like something out of a David Baldacci novel. Do you read Baldacci, Pete?"

"Occasionally."

"He's a very inventive writer. Nearly as inventive as you."

"This isn't fiction. It's fact."

A flicker of emotion clouded Conti's face. He studied Pete and his expression grew pensive and he didn't speak for a long time. Then he said so softly that Pete could barely hear his voice, "You couldn't be more wrong about Lynn. I'd have to be a monster to kill my only niece."

Conti's words stunned Pete. He stared at him for a long time and said, "Lynn Hawke was your niece?"

"My sister's child."

Pete couldn't think of anything to say. He just continued to stare at Conti. "I don't believe you," he finally said.

"It's true."

"If Lynn was your niece, why weren't you at her memorial service?"

"I was in Houston. I found out about the service after I got back."

"Do you expect me to believe that?" Pete asked.

"You can check. Why would I lie?"

"Why didn't you tell me this the second time I was at your vineyard?"

Conti shrugged. "I didn't think it was any of your business."

Pete recovered from his surprise and said, "Even if Lynn were your niece, that doesn't change anything. You used your knowledge as a former INS official to run an illegal immigration ring and make a ton of money. I know Lynn was involved, too, because I saw her passports. She was constantly making trips to India and other countries, probably to drum up business for you. It wasn't just to see the sights. You could argue that that was just a garden-variety crime, but then people started dying. You got Lynn killed even if you didn't do it yourself."

Conti seemed to lose focus. He stared out the window as though Pete weren't there and a distracted look clouded his eyes.

"What are the economics of this business, Alain? What do you charge for a phony green card or a set of false H1B documents?"

Conti remained silent.

"What I don't understand is why you killed Arne Breit," Pete continued. "Barbara Rodes I understand, even though it was a monstrous thing to do, but why Arne?"

When Pete looked at Conti again, his eyes were closed. He couldn't tell whether he'd dozed off or was just thinking. His plan was going nowhere.

Conti began to speak again. "Our immigration system is so fouled up," he said. "People come across our borders and we have sanctuary cities and the federal government refuses to prosecute obvious crimes. Yet someone who has a doctor's degree in computer science is unable to come here to work."

Conti's mutterings were bizarre and didn't relate to the conversation they were having. Pete let him talk.

"We need talented people," Conti continued. "Not the criminal element who can pay, but inventive people who can help this country prosper."

Pete thought about Conti's comment and everything began to make sense. "Is the split about money?" he asked.

"It's always about money."

Pete was trying to figure out how to get the conversation back to his main concern when Conti said, "They're sending me back to Houston for more treatment."

His stream of consciousness blathering was becoming unsettling.

"I'd like to see one more harvest," Conti said.

"What do you have, Alain?"

"Cancer. They say I have six months."

"The facility in Houston is supposed to be one of the best in the world," Pete said. "You're fortunate to be treated there."

"Six months isn't very long. I suppose we're all going to die sooner or later."

It was hard for Pete to feel sympathy for Conti, and it also wasn't going to solve his problem. "I want you to contact Bartholome and tell him I'll turn over the documents in return for his commitment to forget I ever existed."

"Why are you dragging Gilbert into this?" Conti suddenly sounded more lucid than he had the past few minutes.

"Because I know he's your partner and he wants these documents."

"Lynn and Gilbert were going to get married," Conti said, returning to his pensive mood. "I was trying to persuade them to have the wedding at Conti Vineyards."

Pete clinched his teeth at Conti's statement and said, "I'm not interested in their planned nuptials. I'm interested in getting this resolved."

Conti said nothing.

Pete stood to leave. "I can see I'm wasting my time," he said. "I came to make a deal because I know that you're the one at the top. But all I'm hearing is a lot of babble. I'll deal with Homeland Security instead."

He started for the door.

Conti said, "I have contacts, Pete. I can check around and see who might be interested in your merchandise."

Pete's pulse beat faster and he turned and stared at Conti. "Thanks," he said, playing it cool, "but I think I'll just go to the government. I thought you might have a better handle on what's going on. I was wrong."

"Give me two hours to make some calls."

"Why do you need two hours?" Pete asked. "I know Bartholome is back in this area. I'm sure you can reach him in five minutes."

"I need time, Pete." He stared straight ahead.

"Okay, two hours," Pete said. "If you don't call me by 3:30 p.m., I'm taking this bag to Homeland Security."

He handed Conti one of his business cards. "My cell phone number is on the card."

FIFTY

Pete fussed with his Cobb salad and ate little of it while he waited for Conti's call. Realistically, he didn't expect Bartholome to meet with him, but he'd have to hear what Conti proposed before he decided on his next move. His goal was to get evidence of some kind that would bolster Homeland Security's case and help them make arrests. That was the only way he saw out of his predicament.

As he sat in the restaurant and waited, he thought about Conti's claim that Lynn Hawke was his niece. He wasn't prepared for that. It made sense, though, given Lynn's apparent role as peacemaker. He also thought about Conti's insinuation that he was a hero for his role in circumventing the country's immigration laws. *The son-of-a-bitch is in it for money and now that he's dying, he tries to cloak his actions in a lot of self-righteous blather.*

Pete kept his cell phone on even though he was concerned about its charge. Two more calls from the anonymous caller had come in while he was with Conti. Conti finally called back and spoke in oblique terms. He didn't name names, but said he'd spoken to someone who was interested in the merchandise. That person was unwilling to meet with Pete personally, but if Pete dropped the merchandise off in Conti's room before

5:00 p.m., that would be the end of it. Conti said they had no interest in him personally. Both sides would have what they wanted. Conti encouraged Pete to agree.

Plan B was now in effect. Pete thought about the configuration of the hospital. Conti's room was three doors down from the elevator and the nurses' station was at the opposite end of the hall. Overall, the floor was lightly occupied from what he could tell. If Clarence were still sitting in the hall, that would add another complication. The bottom line was that there was no good place from which to watch on the third floor. His best bet was the first floor reception area where people were coming and going all the time.

He moved to the Explorer and nervously passed time. He'd made the right decision in taking Harry's vehicle. Maybe no one he was concerned about would recognize his Range Rover, but he didn't want to take the risk. Also, the more he thought about it, the more convinced he became that the chances of them forgetting about him once they had the documents were nil. They would want to tidy up, and tidying up meant doing something about him. And if they opened one of the packages, the risk rose exponentially and all bets would be off.

At 4:00 p.m., Pete paid the nominal parking charge and headed for the hospital again. He parked near the exit and took the elevator to the check-in floor. He sat in the waiting area and studied the floor for ten minutes.

He took the elevator to the third floor and felt his gut tighten as he got off. The chair Clarence had used was still outside Conti's door, but he didn't see him. At the end of the hall, two nurses hung around the station talking. Except for that, the floor was quiet. Pete walked slowly to Conti's room. The duffel in his hand felt like it weighed fifty pounds. It was 4:40 p.m. He was right on schedule.

Conti's door was cracked open a few inches. He rapped on the jamb and pushed it open. His heart skipped a beat as soon as he walked in the room. Conti was still in his hospital bed, but the man with him wasn't Clarence.

"Come in and close the door behind you," Sandoval said. He had a pistol in his hand and a thin smile on his face. "You're early," Sandoval said. "I like a man who's early. It shows discipline."

Pete's eyes flicked toward Conti. His expression gave away nothing. The bastard had led him into a trap!

Pete said, "Hello, Sandy." He tried to sound calm and relaxed, but his heart was pounding and his stomach felt like it was in a vice that was slowly tightening.

"I see you brought the merchandise," Sandy said. He shook his head sadly. "Too bad you had to make this trip, Pete. Everyone would have been better off if you'd just delivered the package like we asked."

Pete's gaze dropped from Sandoval's face to the pistol in his hand. The suppressor on the end of the barrel made the weapon look more menacing.

Sandoval smiled again. "I see you're admiring my equipment," he said. "I heard from someone that you're an old military man." He turned the pistol sideways so Pete could see it. "This is a SIG Sauer Mosquito chambered for .22 LR cartridges. With this suppressor, you can hardly hear the pistol being fired. Isn't that remarkable? People who watch police shows on television refer to these things," he said, tapping the suppressor, "as 'silencers.' This one nearly is. The nurses down the hall wouldn't hear a thing if I were to fire it in this room."

Pete could hear his heart thumping and said with all the calm he could muster, "You don't need that, Sandy. I brought what you want."

"Oh, if life were that simple, Pete. Now I'll tell you what we're going to do. We're going to say goodbye to Alain and then you and I are going to walk casually to the elevator and through the reception area and out to the parking lot. You don't mind carrying the bag, do you?"

Conti was still sitting impassively and staring straight ahead. Pete wanted to strangle the son-of-a-bitch!

Sandoval pulled a slouch hat from his pocket and clamped it on his head. He gestured toward the door with his pistol. Out of the corner of his eye, Pete saw Conti's hand twitch and all of a sudden thunderous blasts rocked the small room. *Bam! Bam! Bam!* The walls shook and the acrid odor of gunpowder filled the space. Conti's hand was free of the blanket now and his weapon was pointed at Sandoval. Sandoval clutched his chest and sagged back against the wall. He raised the SIG Sauer and pointed it at Conti with a shaky aim. *Pop! Pop! Pop! Pop! Pop!* Conti's body jerked each time a round hit him. *Bam! Bam!* Conti fired twice more and the room shook again. Sandoval slid to the floor and lost the grip on his weapon as he went. His index finger was partially looped through the trigger guard.

Pete was frozen by the speed with which it had happened. Conti's head was tilted back against the pillow and he stared at the ceiling with vacant eyes. His pistol rested on the bed with his fingers still firmly wrapped around the grip. Sandoval sat against the wall with his head slumped to one side and his legs splayed out. The blood stains were widening on his white shirt.

Pete heard excited voices in the hall. He went to the door, and after gulping air for a few moments, opened it. A hospital security guard was running down the hall toward him with his firearm held in front of him.

"On the floor!" he screamed. "On the floor! Face down!"

Pete did as he was told. The guard knelt over him and pinned him down with a knee in his back. Pete cringed as the pressure extended to his rib cage which was still tender from the beating he'd taken in The Peg's parking lot. Pete's head was turned sharply left and he could feel the coarse fibers of the hall carpet grind against his cheek. The guard on top of him looked back and forth between Pete and the door to Conti's room. He looked panicked.

"Who are you?!" the guard screamed in Pete's ear. "Who are you?!" Cold steel pressed hard against the back of Pete's neck.

"Pete Thorsen," he gasped. "I'm a lawyer. Two men in that room shot each other. Let me up and I'll explain everything."

"Stay down!" the guard screamed. His knee ground into Pete's back and the muzzle pressed against his neck even harder.

"Get back!" the guard screamed, glancing at the crowd that had congregated in the hallway. "Stay away from the door!" The crowd edged back, but continued to stare with a combination of fear and fascination.

Two policemen came running down the hall from the elevator with guns drawn. "Officer," Pete said to one of them.

"Shut up!" the officer shouted. "Keep him quiet!" he said to the hospital guard. The two officers took up positions by the door, one on each side. They stood flat against the wall with guns held in the ready position.

"Come out with your hands above your head!" one officer screamed through the open door. There was no answer. "I said come out with your hands above your head!" he screamed again. Again, no answer.

"I think they're both dead," Pete said from his prone position.

"Shut up!" one of the officers yelled at him again. The officer signaled to his companion and then leaped into the doorway with his sidearm extended in a two-handed grip. "Don't move!" the officer screamed as he edged into the room. "Don't move!"

"*Jesus Christ*," Pete heard him mutter. "Noah, come in here!"

Two minutes later the officers emerged from the room. "Get some doctors up here," one of them said to a nurse standing in the hall with her mouth open, "and tell them that we've got two men down. One's dead and the other has a pulse."

The two officers came over to where Pete was still lying prone on his stomach. "Pat him down, Noah."

After Pete was searched for the second time that afternoon, the officer told him to get to his feet and stand with his hands against the wall. Two more officers came running down the hall toward them with their guns drawn.

The guard said, "He claims he's a lawyer."

"Do you have any proof of that?" the officer asked.

"Is it okay if I take out my wallet?" Pete asked. With five drawn guns pointed in his direction, he wasn't taking any chances.

The officer who asked him for proof nodded. Pete got his wallet out and handed him one of his cards. As he was looking at it, two men in scrubs came running down the hall and went into Conti's room. They emerged minutes later pushing his bed. As they passed, Pete could see Conti's face. It had already lost much of its color and small holes dotted the blanket that covered him.

Before he told the officers what had happened, Pete gave them the names and contact numbers of Detective Joe Tessler and Leelanau County Sheriff Emory Bond and said they would vouch for him. Then he spent the next two hours answering and re-answering questions from the officers on site.

FIFTY-ONE

"Do you think this is some kind of joke, Mr. Thorsen?" Keegan Harris screamed over the telephone.

Pete pressed the button on the telephone so Harry could hear. "What do you mean, Special Agent?"

"Joe Tessler told us you had ten boxes with counterfeit immigration documents. I'm looking at them now. All I see is ten boxes of cheap bond paper made by a company I've never heard of."

"You're kidding," Pete said. "I'm sure the counterfeit documents were in those boxes."

Harry listened to the conversation with wide eyes.

"Well they aren't," Harris said. "I came back from Asia with evidence I thought would help break this ring. What I find is a bunch of stiffs we can't interrogate because as they say, dead men don't talk, and some boxes filled with worthless stationery. I should book you for obstruction."

"I'll have Joe Tessler call you. It's possible that the boxes got mixed up."

"What do you mean they got mixed up!" Harris screamed. "What …"

Pete hit the disconnect button. Harry's eyes looked like they were about to pop from his skull.

The phone rang and rang and rang, but Pete ignored it.

"Aren't you going to answer that?" Harry asked nervously. "That's probably the Homeland Security woman calling you back."

"I don't take calls from unknown sources," Pete said. "It may be someone trying to sell me something."

"I tell you, that's the Homeland Security woman."

Pete just shrugged.

"You're going to get yourself in trouble," Harry said earnestly.

Before Harry could say more, Pete dialed Tessler's number. "Joe, maybe you should call Keegan Harris. She's complaining that those packages I sent to her office contained nothing but cheap stationery."

"Stationery?"

"I might have made a mistake and gave her the wrong boxes. Check our safe deposit box at Betsie Bay Trust Company."

"You deliberately gave her the wrong boxes?"

"Not deliberately. I might have gotten confused because of everything that happened at the hospital."

Across the desk, Harry was shaking his head in disbelief. "How could you get those boxes mixed up?"

Pete shrugged. "I didn't get them mixed up," he said. "You didn't expect me to turn over the actual counterfeit documents to that ring, did you?"

Harry stared at him for a long time. "You're crazy, you know that? What if the boxes with that cheap paper had been sent to India and your trick was discovered over there? What do you think would have happened?"

"With luck, I would have bought myself a week or two of time. And if it didn't work, I would have been no worse off than if I'd turned over the actual counterfeit documents in that hospital room."

Harry shook his head and said, "I still think you're crazy."

They sat quietly for a few minutes. Then Harry said, "I think the outcome of all of this proves what I've been saying all along, which is that ..."

Pete cut him off. "I know, that Lynn wasn't such a bad person after all."

"She wasn't. Even you have to admit that."

Pete just stared out the window.

"And for Conti to turn out to be her uncle. That's amazing."

"I think that's how Lynn got involved in all of this to begin with," Pete said. "It was clear when I talked to Conti in his hospital room that he regarded himself as a 'good guy' in this whole thing. He disagreed with our immigration laws that make it so difficult to bring skilled people into this country and took it upon himself to do something about it. And to make money while he was doing it."

"Why did he shoot Sandy?"

"Because Sandy was the bad guy and I think Conti hated him. Sandy was the one who was pushing to sell counterfeit green cards to drug cartel members who'd made billions and wanted to get out of the business and live in this country."

"Did Sandy kill Lynn too?"

"We'll never know for sure, but it's a reasonable bet that he did. It fit with his plan to turn Conti and Bartholome against each other. Bartholome knew Lynn was meeting with Conti that night. Sandy probably thought that if Bartholome believed Conti was behind her death, it would enrage Bartholome, which is what he wanted."

"And he killed Arne and Barbara Rodes, too."

"Almost certainly, but for different reasons. In Arne's case, I think Sandy wanted to damage Conti's operation. And with Barbara, he thought she knew what Arne did with the counterfeit documents. Even though he wanted to start selling to the drug kingpins, he didn't want to leave several million dollars on the table. He wanted to deliver the documents to the buyers in India and collect."

"Bartholome is the last man standing, huh?"

"For the moment, but with the feds on his tail, it's only a matter of time until they catch up with him. The same with their inside guy at Homeland Security."

"Amazing," Harry said.

"As for those punks who beat me in the parking lot, I don't know who they are, but I know I'm not going back to The Peg at night without you to watch my back."

Harry smiled at his friend and seemed to suck in his gut and puff out his chest. After a minute, he said, "Are you planning to go to Richter's press conference this afternoon?"

"He's having a press conference so soon?"

"He wants to get a jump on the feds," Harry said. "He even has a theme that he conveniently let slip in an e-mail to the press this morning. Know what it is?"

"I'm afraid to ask."

"A falling out among thieves."

Pete thought about that. "That's good," he said.

Harry's eyes widened. "Do you realize that's the first time you've actually said something positive about Richter?"

Pete raised his eyebrows and said, "Really?"

ABOUT THE AUTHOR

Robert Wangard is a crime-fiction writer who splits his time between Chicago, where he practiced law for many years, and northern Michigan. *Deceit* is the third in the Pete Thorsen Mystery series. The first two, *Target* and *Malice*, were widely-acclaimed by reviewers. Wangard is also the author of *Hard Water Blues*, an anthology of short stories. He is a member of Mystery Writers of America, the Short Mystery Fiction Society, and other writers' organizations.